EVERY SHADE OF YOU

MINNESOTT BEACH BOOK TWO

GINNY KOCHIS

For the Reel sisters, Nina, Virginia, Lila Gray, and Louise. You were never too much. You were enough.

ONE

DEWITT

June, 2000

Rosie pressed the napkin in my hand as we were walking out of Daughtry's, right as Mr. Hillman stopped my father by the door. Her eyes went wide, as they dropped to the note, bursting with quiet meaning. *Don't let your Daddy see!*

I blinked twice—*Got it*—and shuffled behind a stand of Sugar Flakes. Peeled the paper off my hand; opened the napkin just enough to see *Barn tonight?* and *10* in glaze-smudged marker.

That night I stood and waited by the window, Rosie's napkin on my nightstand next to the clock glowing ten to ten. The wood floor creaked beneath my feet and nervous energy thrummed my veins, a summer after seventh grade sparkle of potential.

I wanted answers.

I wasn't waiting another night.

Static pierced the air and I jolted, knocking my head into the window glass. I rubbed the dull ache in my head and lurched across the room for the walkie-talkie I'd forgotten, dang near smashing my finger when I cut the volume off. The house stayed silent—*thank God*—but I crouched down beside my bed just to be safe. Rosie was squawking away, the handset's red LED glowing. I pressed the *talk* button down and hissed at her through the handset. "I can't hear what you're saying, so quit."

Mama had ears like an elephant—super sensitive, but a tenth of the size. One wrong move, and Dora Bell Griffin would march through my door, demanding a complete accounting. My Daddy, Luther Griffin, would be right behind her. *Deebie*, he'd say, because Dora Bell's a mouthful. *Deebie, what's going on?* Then I'd get a lecture about our good family name, and Pinecliff, our home, and how a Griffin simply can't besmirch the image of our centuries-old legacy by sneaking out the window at night.

Whatever. Pinecliff was a dumb name, anyway. Daddy's grandfather built it way back when, a behemoth of a house on a hill above the river, surrounded by Carolina pines and nowhere near a cliff. It was pretty, and I liked it, especially the wavy antique glass in the windows that creaked a little when you pushed them up. I army-crawled across the floor, shouldered my bag, and held my breath while I opened the window. Waited a second, limbs tightening, and in the quiet, scrabbled over the sill.

"Three more steps!" Rosie whisper-yelled, and I might have said "thank you," or "mmmmmpfh." Whatever it was, I meant it when my feet hit the ground and I heard Rosie's voice behind me. "Geez, Dewitt. Took you long enough."

Rosie was blunt, but I liked it. I preferred when people told me the truth. Essentially, the opposite of my dad, who hadn't outright lied when I asked about the page missing from our family Bible but was evasive enough to be suspect. Shaking my hands out from my trek down the trellis, I tugged my hair into its black ponytail. Then I turned to Ro and held out my palms, displaying my hard-won splinters.

"Shoot," she said, her auburn hair shining in the moonlight. "Didn't realize how much it hurts."

I nudged her with my shoulder. *No worries*, the gesture said. Smiling big, Rosie hooked her arm through mine and pulled us toward the forest, a stand of Carolina pine, sweetgum, and live oak thick enough to eat us alive.

"You got the book?" I asked her. We'd lifted *Highways, Byways, and Waterways* from Daddy's office a few weeks back. Books on local lore and family lines squatted the bookshelves there, detailing the Griffin family's long Minnesott history. Far as I knew, he hadn't noticed that title was gone.

Rosie hefted her book bag, the thick volume weighing it down. "It's in here. If this book rips my bag—"

"It will have died in the service of a grand adventure."

She stared at my salute, lips flattened.

I sighed. "I'll get you another one, alright?"

High on mischief and excitement, we burst through the forest's edge. Velvety darkness wrapped the field, humidity still high beneath bright stars and the moonlight. When my father was little, Pinecliff had been a tobacco farm. Daddy was a businessman now, hobby farming the fields we still owned. Remnants of the farm's old life stuck around, like the ancient tobacco barn listing ahead of us. Rosie grabbed my hand and gave a low whistle. "That thing is one gust of wind from falling down."

"You're exaggerating." It *was* a little worn, but it was still standing up, bulky and wide, its four walls tall beneath a triangular roof, a covered porch around the middle like a tutu.

Weathered wood slats hung at odd angles near the windows, scattered moonlight shining through.

"The barn has character." I tried to hide the faint tremor in my voice.

"I'm not scared," Rosie said, "In case you were wondering." She shifted. "You sure it won't collapse?"

"I'm sure."

A two-by-four chose that moment to break loose from the door frame.

Rosie whimpered. "What was he thinking, Dewitt?"

Daddy's obsession with family records meant boxes of files, and the boathouse loft was fit to burst. He'd carted several of those boxes out to the barn, putting them up in the loft inside plastic storage containers. "He was thinking he'd run out of space."

"You think the missing page is up there," she said, gaze pointing at the upper level of the barn.

"I do," I said, nodding.

Rosie shuddered. "I'm still not going in."

That earned an elbow in the side. "This was your idea, you goober. Remember?"

Freckles scrunching, she glared at me. "That was before I knew this was a death trap."

"Don't be dramatic."

"Don't act like it's not falling apart!"

The barn loomed up ahead, rough and ragged. "I'm going," I said, managing a whole six steps before Rosie scooped in beside me.

"What if the boxes are just...business records? Tax forms. Old bills."

"I don't think that's it." Not with the way Daddy unloaded the truck, like he was handling something special. "Besides, we made all this effort to come out."

We shuffled closer, staring up at the double doors and the weathered wood hanging off the hinges. Tiny ants tickled my neck. I brushed the sensation away and shoved my chin up higher. "Standing out here won't make it less scary."

"I told you. I'm not scared."

A stiff wind blew the doors open. The hinges moaned, and metal clanged. "Okay. Maybe I'm a little scared," Rosie said, and I squeezed her hand for comfort. One hesitant step across the threshold confirmed the barn was super creepy at night.

I opened my mouth to say we could do this later when movement across the barn caught my eye. A girl our age sat in the far corner, liquid moonlight reflecting off her dress. I'd never seen her before, but in my gut I *knew* her. Her dark hair twisted in a braid against the light skin of her shoulder and she held a notebook in her lap.

"Hello?" I asked.

Nothing.

"What are you doing?" I tried again. The air solidified, hot and thick, like I could cut through it with a machete, and a tight pinch gripped the muscles in my back. The girl stayed on the floor, writing, a slight smile on her lips. Whoever she was, she was trespassing. If something happened and she got hurt...

Shoulders straightened, I marched across the room. "You can't be in here," I said. My words echoed in the dark, her form wavering before it flickered and in an instant, my arms and legs went slack. This is...you can't." I squeezed my eyes shut against the dizziness. "Private property," I slurred.

My name cut through the darkness. Thick and weighty. Black. The sound rolled inside my head, loose marbles as it scattered. Splinters bit my back, my neck.

"Dewitt!"

Rosie knelt over me, white-knuckled and scarlet-cheeked.

Why am I on the floor? I tried to say, but my mouth wouldn't move, jaw frozen shut in silence.

"This isn't funny," Rosie said, and her lip quivered. She shook me. "Wake up, Dewitt. *Stop.*"

I'm awake, I tried to tell her. I peeled my tongue loose like a sticker in my mouth. "The girl.." I finally said, my words thick and halting.

Rosie collapsed in a puddle next to me. "Fine. I admit it. I *was* scared."

"I wasn't..." I wasn't trying to scare her at all. "There was a girl. She was tresh...trash..." My lungs squeezed. "She was trespassing."

"No one's here," Rosie said, her voice a tremor.

The air in the barn went cold.

I sat up. Shivered. Flailed an arm out to the side. "I was talking to her. Over there." A heavy wind buffeted the barn, and metal screeched, and the barn doors slammed shut, and the hair on my arms stood stood so far up I probably could have braided it.

Rosie shot to her feet. "We're leaving."

"The boxes—" I tried to stand.

"Forget the boxes." Rosie's arm circled my waist, and she limped us toward the door like a field medic with her patient.

"But—" I said.

"No thank you!"

Rosie kicked the door open and dragged me out.

TWO

NATHAN

I started at one ninety, counting backward to pass the time. I liked numbers more than words, and I liked words more than my substance-abusing parents, which is saying something. A six-pack of cheap beer, the last of Pop's weed, and an imaginary slight between the both of them made for a long Friday night. I was counting slow, too, and based on past observations, they should have nodded off by the time I hit the teens. But I'd been lying in the dark, wincing at their shouts for the past thirty minutes. Holding stubborn at nineteen.

Humid air licked my skin beneath my damp T-shirt. I missed my window AC. Mama sold it in the spring—she needed money to start her new *business*. Some make-up thing, selling direct to people, but she used the money to pay her dealer off. Stunts like that gave a bad name to good people, specifically our East Acres neighbors, and me. Even though I didn't smoke, drink, or steal, I carried guilt by association. Most people took one look at my Cartwright eyes and turned their noses up at the resemblance. Everything I did—my schoolwork, my odd jobs, my woodworking hobby—I did to prove myself.

It wasn't easy, not when my parents were rough-housing drunks. Flat tired of their mess that night, I snatched a clean shirt from the floor and swapped it out for the drenched one before slipping through the window into the night.

Some things were certain when you lived near the water, especially a wide, brackish river like the Neuse. Coastal heat was one. Muggy swamps, meandering creeks, and giant skeeters were another. I breathed it all in as I walked, the wind's salty brine in my mouth and the tall grass tickling my legs. Highway 306 ran up ahead, the main road through town dividing Minnesott Acres into two sides: East and West. My best friend Gil Sutton lived in West Acres, with landscaped yards and flags that read *bloom where you're planted.*

Aside from a few rusted cars and a not-so-secret grow plot, East Acres didn't bloom.

Minnesott Beach sits on a long stretch of shoreline twenty nautical miles southwest of the Pamlico Sound. It's a super small town, so small it shuts down around eight every evening and I didn't look before crossing the road. Gil lived with his parents in a bright white double-wide trailer where his mom planted red begonias out front. I spotted Gil's window through the trees, glowing like a beacon. He was still up playing *Silent Hill.*

Despite the horror game on his console, he didn't jump when I knocked. He opened the window with one hand, his reddish-brown hair askew. "They still fighting?" he asked, fanning his t-shirt at the humidity.

I pulled my lips tight.

Gil tossed his controller on the bed, shoved the window down, and disappeared into the hallway. I walked around the trailer so I could meet him out back.

What Minnesott Acres lacked in a high-class address, it

made up for in perks. Our private river beach stretched a dozen yards wide before cutting in at Acres Creek. That fed the fishing pond real nice, where we caught flounder, spot, and red drum. But neither one of us brought gear, and when we headed through the woods away from Gil's trailer we were two country boys crashing through pine trees, seeking the solace of an early summer night.

"Gummy worms," Gil said when we got to the picnic table. We'd built it and hauled it out by the pond. He pulled a bag from his shorts and sorted packages on the wooden surface. "Peanut butter crackers. Pretzels. Reese's. Red barrels if you're thirsty, too."

I sat down at the table, spinning a container of red juice on the wood. All I said was, "Cool." When I was younger, I tried to hide it—how much my living situation sucked. But Gil figured it out right quick, and in second grade, he packed extras in his lunch; by fifth grade, he brought end-of-the-day leftovers from his parents' seafood market. He'd stand in the door and look me in the eye, not at the mess of a house behind me. "They were gonna throw it out," he'd say. "You want it?"

Oh, I wanted it.

Gil pulled me from the memory, cracker crumbs flying from his mouth. "You wanna talk about your parents?" he asked.

"Nope."

Gil took it in stride, and that's why I liked him. "We need a plan for the summer," he said.

Anything to stay away from home, but I didn't outright say that. "I plan to swim and catch fish and hang out at the marina."

He screwed up his lips. "You know what I mean. I'm talking making money here. *Entrepreneurship.*"

I loved messing with him. "I don't believe in aliens, Gil."

"I'm serious." He bounced a gummy off my cheek.

I caught it and put in my mouth, then indulged him because why the heck wouldn't I? "Alright, then. What you got?"

"Landscaping." Gil scratched at his chin. He didn't have too much stubble yet, but he liked to pretend he did, and I didn't begrudge it. "We can trim hedges and spread mulch. Plant flowers, mow lawns—"

"I ain't got a lawnmower." *Or I'd be mowing my lawn.*

"I got one," he said, which was fine, but not for running a business.

"Be better if we had two."

Gil tapped his temple. "That's where I've been scheming," he said. He filled me in: by the end of June, if we mowed X lawns at Y price, we'd earn enough to buy a second mower.

I could see it.

I could see it *and* the plan's faults.

"We'll need a truck for all that equipment. And we're fourteen. Neither one of us drives."

"We'll bike," he said, like the answer was obvious.

"And drag the lawnmower behind a bicycle?"

He rubbed a palm down his face. "Are you serious? Do you, or do you not, build structures out of wood?" He muttered something to himself before looking up at me and tapping a finger on the table's surface. "Build. A trailer. For the bikes."

Man—I *was* an idiot. I built all kinds of stuff. Components swirled in my head. Three wheels. A pallet for the base, a couple two-by-fours for framing. Then we could—

Gil froze. "Incoming."

"Gator?"

"Nuh-uh. On your right."

I peered into the night toward the fishing pond. The moon shone full, its beams dancing through the trees like a strobe. Two figures moved through the half-lit dark, breaking into a run when they hit the clearing.

"Is that...?" Gil trailed off.

"That's Rosie Bennett." My stomach sank. "And Dewitt." I would have known Dewitt Griffin anywhere, thanks to that stuck-up posture she wore. She and Rosie were a year behind us in school, and Rosie was alright, but Dewitt, well. The Griffins were a Minnesott institution. More money and more pride than God.

Gil nudged me. "Why are they running?"

"Better question is, *why do you care?*"

"I talk to them," Gil said, every bit the kid who could blend in with anybody. "I don't know," he continued. "Them running like that—seems weird."

Gil stood, and before I could grab him, he'd jogged ten paces toward the girls. "What's weird is you chasing 'em down," I called, irritated. *Ridiculous.* They were probably just headed to Rosie's, a few plots down from Gil's house.

The girls must have seen Gil coming. They stopped short, the weight of their backpacks pitching them forward. I couldn't hear what Gil said, but he pointed back toward me and the picnic table. Dewitt shook her head, her long ponytail a telegram: *I'm not slumming with an East Acres kid.*

Gil shrugged and tossed an arm out before climbing up the hill. Rosie put a hand on Dewitt's arm, and I could just make out raised voices between them before Rosie dragged Dewitt in Gil's wake.

He got back to our spot, and I fussed at him. "What the heck are you doing, Gil?"

"Being hospitable, bro."

"They're girls..."

He pulled a face at me. "They ain't got cooties. Isn't that a little fourth grade?"

"We were having a conversation." I was only out there because my parents sucked.

"Something spooked those girls," Gil said, "and I intend to help them." And because he knew me so well, he leaned in a little more and whispered. "The only way we'll end up talking about your parents is if you bring them up."

Gil put up his thumb, pad outward, waiting for me to do the same. His scar shone silver like mine, the only physical sign of the blood oath we took the previous summer. My lips stretched in a grimace as I pressed my thumb to his. "I'm only doing this because you brought me food."

He grinned. "You love me." Over my shoulder, he said, "Ladies. Have a seat."

Scowling, I turned around. Dewitt stood a good six feet away, feet planted in the ground and her greyish-green eyes narrowed in skepticism. She looked me up and down. "We interrupting something?"

"'Course not." Gil motioned to the table. "Please. Sit down."

She huffed and dug at the dirt with her white Chuck Taylors. "No, thank you. We'll stand."

An apologetic smile curved Rosie's lips. "We can't stay long," she said, voice tight. A little nervous.

"You sure? We got gummy worms."

Gil dropped two green worms on the picnic table before reaching into the back pocket of his shorts. "Got this, too," he said, motioning to the sandwich bag he'd extracted. "The last of the peanut butter crackers. Might have sat on them, though."

Rosie's brown eyes lit with laughter, while Dewitt snarled

in disgust. Gil's freckled cheeks went red, his attention focused on Rosie. He was crushing on her, I could tell.

"She doesn't want your butt crackers," I said.

He glared at me, like *I will kill you in your sleep.*

Dewitt flipped her ponytail back, most of the strands falling out around her shoulders. "*Come on, Rosie,*" she said, and Gil fumbled with the crackers on the table.

"Y'all spending the night at the Bennetts?" he asked.

"Mind your business," Dewitt answered, while Rosie piped out, "Nope!"

Dewitt's eye roll turned her face to the sky. I snickered and her gaze dropped to me, the loose blue-black strands of her hair brushing the tops of her shoulders.

My brain went all fuzzy. And weird.

It looks so soft. I wanna touch it.

And right then, I choked on my spit. *What the heck was that?* I thought, because no way was I crushing on Dewitt, the only daughter of high and mighty Luther Griffin. Gil thumped me on the back as I worked out a course correction. Being ugly was the best way to go.

"Dewitt doesn't want to stay in the neighborhood. She's too rich for us."

Two pink circles warmed her cheeks, the set of her jaw like iron. "I'm at Rosie's all the time," she said.

Gil punched me, hard, on my biceps. "Ignore him," he said to Dewitt.

I shoved Gil back. "You gonna walk them home?"

Sutton was going soft. He should have crossed his arms and acted hard, but his eyes got all gooey in the dark, and I was pretty dang sure it had to do with how he looked at Rosie. "Sure am," he said, smile cheeky. "How about it? Y'all ready to go?"

I bit down on my lip. "Why were y'all running?" Being nosy might run them off. But Rosie perked up.

"You know the Griffin tobacco barn?"

"I know it," I said. That thing was old, at least ninety years, maybe older. "Were you there?"

"No!" Dewitt said at the same time Rosie let out a, "We sure were!"

I watched them both, gaze bouncing between the two of them. "That's a dumb place to go in the dark."

"We were out there tonight—" Rosie started, but Dewitt butted in right quick.

"The full moon made it creepy," she blurted out, voice edged too hard, nails piercing her fists as she clenched them.

"You're lying."

Dewitt tipped her chin up. "Am not."

I never backed down from a challenge. "Care to share the real story with the class?"

"No ghosts?" Gil wore a cheeky grin. Rosie swallowed and side-eyed Dewitt, who turned and stalked into the darkness.

"These guys are losers," she called over her shoulder. "Come on, Rosie. Let's go."

"Dewitt! Don't be rude!" Rosie's cheeks flushed red, and she turned to Gil. "We'll see y'all later."

Gil was staring at her, dumbstruck "Definitely," he said. "Y'all be careful."

His dumb grin stretched wider as he watched her disappear into the tress.

"You can't do stuff like that," I said.

"Talk to girls from our class?"

"They're a year behind," I groused. "And you know what I mean." Gil was the closest thing I had to family. If he got wrapped up in a crush...

"I don't know what you mean," he said, pulling me back to the conversation. "Care to elaborate?"

I swallowed. "What's with you and big words?"

"I pay attention in class."

"So do I."

Gil shoved the last gummy worm in his mouth and talked around it, brows wagging. "I was being neighborly. Can't help it if the neighbors are cute."

THREE

DEWITT

Folks come in to gossip at the Minnesott Beach Post Office just as often as they walk in for stamps. So when Rosie grabbed a dozen Fireball candies from the jar Miss Nora, the Post Master, kept by the entrance, and announced, "We need to talk about the *ghost*," I grabbed her by the arm and dragged her behind the postcards.

"Not so loud!" I hissed.

Nose scrunched, she blinked at me. "Nobody's listening." Rumor had it Benji Bascombe called out sick, something about his dog and a skunk and a four-foot deep hole along his fence line. Down to one employee—Miss Nora—the packed lobby had a line out the door. All eyes were at the front; all conversation on a skunkified Benji, not on a Griffin's comings and goings in town. But still...

"I can't risk it."

"They're all freaking out about stamps."

Rosie flung her arm out to the side, a la *exhibit A, for the jury*. And that's when a rogue Fireball arced outward and smacked Miss Nora in the head.

"*Ohmygosh, ohmygosh.*" Rosie babbled. Barely breathing, I slapped a hand over her mouth. We tripped out the door and around the back, laughing so hard we could hardly stay upright. We collapsed in a heap at the back of the building on a patch of sandy dirt.

"You Fireballed the Post Master." It came out with a wheezy gasp.

Rosie giggled. "I feel so bad."

"We should—" I gasped for air, lungs tight and brain fuzzy from the laughter. "We should apologize," I said.

"Gotta breathe for that to happen." Rosie leaned into my side. "Oh, that was so bad!" The giggles set back in, and when they finally petered out, we slumped loose-limbed in the dirt, happy.

Then Rosie had to go and ruin it.

"About last night..."

My blood ran cold. "Nothing happened."

Rosie snorted. "Right."

It was fine if she didn't believe me. I didn't believe me, honestly. But talking about it made it real, and if it was real, I had big problems. "Can we not talk about this right now?"

Head tilted, Rosie's eyes perused my face. "This is stressing you out," she said, and I dropped my gaze to the dirt, watched an ant wind through patchy grasses. Rosie's hand took mine. "We can talk about it another time," she said. "When you're ready. Or we can...not."

"Thank you." I breathed out in relief. What happened in the barn wasn't the first time the world went wonky. I'd been seeing things in my peripheral vision, hearing voices in the hall. I'd tried to ignore it, play it off, until the night titled on its head and dumped me on the floor of the tobacco barn.

Ro let go of my hand and smiled, a sneaky curve to her lips. "Let's talk about the boys."

I groaned. "Seriously?"

She nudged my foot a little. "You know they're cute."

"Nathan Cartwright and Gil Sutton aren't cute. They're a hazard," I said. "They put a frozen fish in Miss Brantley's desk and left it there over the weekend."

"When they were in fifth grade."

"It smelled awful, Ro."

"We live in a beach town," she said, twirling her hair around a finger. "It always smells like fish,"

"*By the docks*," I said, and I pressed my lips together. Truthfully, I didn't mind the fish prank as much as I minded the way Nathan treated me.

"They cleaned Miss Nora's yard last week," Ro said, like she could hear my thoughts.

"As punishment for *borrowing*—" I put air quotes around the word "—her riding lawnmower. They're overgrown toddlers, Ro."

She grinned. "Still adorable."

"I'm not winning this argument."

"Nope." She popped the *p*, then stood up and offered me a hand upward. "You put up a decent fight, though. Definitely proud of you."

We poked around town for the next hour, window shopping and goofing off. We were down the block from Bennett Construction when Rosie's dad, Mr. Matthew, stuck his head out and ushered my father through the door. "Your daddy building something?" Rosie asked.

We tugged open the door and Daddy's voice boomed from the interior. "There's my baby girl."

Warmth bloomed inside me. Daddy was a complicated man. High standards, deeper love, and watchful eye over his beloved Minnesott. He enveloped me in a hug.

"Heard the Post Office had a missile strike," he said.

"That was my fault." Rosie grinned, her mouth stained red from a Fireball. "Dewitt was an innocent bystander, Mr. Luther."

Daddy ruffled my hair a little. "I would expect nothing less."

I stiffened, the center of my chest running cold. Rosie took my hand, steering us toward the exit. "I'll be right back," she said, eyes focused on her father. "I'm gonna say goodbye to Dewitt."

We stood outside in the sunshine, sweat beading in places I didn't like. "I hate it when he says stuff like that," Rosie said. "You're allowed to not be perfect."

I grimaced. "Tell that to my dad."

He loved me. He loved our status in the town almost equally. I sank in on myself, glancing back through the office window, not sure if he'd noticed I left.

Rosie bumped me with her shoulder. "You're amazing just the way you are."

I hugged her, even in the heat, and we walked to the bike rack next to the Post Office. Rosie stared at her bicycle, forlorn.

"Sorry I can't ride home with you," she said.

I shrugged. "You gotta work."

"Not for pay. Daddy's files are a mess. Mama said if I don't get in there and help, his organizational skills'll send us to hell in a file cabinet."

"Isn't it *hell in a handbasket*?"

She shrugged.

I gave her one last hug. "See you," I said, and mounted my bike. I pedaled hard onto 306, toward the sign for local attractions.

One mile to Daughtry's. One and a half miles to the ferry terminal. Then my house, historic enough to earn a spot on the road sign.

Pinecliff, it read. *2 miles.*

I snorted every time I rolled past. With white columns, a double porch, and pointy dormer windows, the Minnesott Beach Historical Society deemed Pinecliff a *hallmark of Federal architecture.* I just called it my house. A house I loved, because right then, it had air conditioning.

The sun beating down on me did not.

June's humidity nearly crushed me, and the stench of hot asphalt filled my nose. East Acres lay just ahead, the oasis of trees at the entrance tempting. It wasn't a shortcut, but it would get me home in the shade. I glanced behind me for cars and angled across the highway, breathing a shady sigh of relief.

Rosie lived in Minnesott Acres, but her house was in Acres West. The trailers on this side looked sad, a little wistful. Like their inhabitants owned stock in broken dreams.

I pedaled onward, past sagging porches and overgrown cars. The pine forest thinned ahead, shade bursting into sun at the clearing.

Out of nowhere, a metallic bang shook the woods.

"Shrimp on a biscuit." I jostled the handlebars to the right. My stomach swooped as the back tire slid, and I pulled the bars back to the left, overcorrecting. I hit the ground in slow motion, gravel shredding the skin of my leg.

"Dang it." The woods were quiet, the trailers behind me empty of life. My bike tires spun lazy circles in the breeze and I lay flat on the ground, trying to figure out what happened. *What was that awful noise?*

And then—it happened. Another hollow, angry *bang.* Only this time, a voice cursed through the woods. Pain seared up my side, but when I inched up to stand, I found only minor scrapes and bruises. No longer on the ground, I could see it better: a lone trailer slumped in the clearing, surrounded by knee-high grass.

It was white, or it used to be. Time and salt air had coated it a mossy green. The screen door hung wide, swaying on its hinges. Crooked mini-blinds hung in one of the front windows, the other three depressingly bare.

I squinted, and the front door opened with a jerk. Another bang, another curse. *I know that voice*—but I couldn't place it. Curious, I brushed gravel from my legs. A pair of work boots flew through the door, followed by salt and pepper shakers pinging the railing. A toaster came next. Nathan Cartwright came next, though he didn't fly out of the door so much as he walked through it.

My jaw dropped. "Holy heck."

In a small town where everybody knew everybody, Nathan kept to himself. He only talked to Gil, so what I knew about him came from the pranks they pulled and the rumors about his parents—that they were alcoholics, maybe worse. I tried to be nice because gossip was gossip, and as a Griffin, I got the brunt of it, too. But he never responded in kind. He was ugly to me every time, and I don't think anybody would have blamed me if I left him in the clearing.

Except I'd never seen Nathan so distraught.

Light brown hair, matted. Features twisted and flushed. Bare, heaving chest and clenched, raw fists; sweat gleaming on his skin, his eyes swollen. A keening sound ripped out from his throat. His knuckles oozed red—*Is he bleeding?* Heart pounding, and leaving my bike spinning, I ran across the yard.

"Nathan!"

He nearly tumbled off the porch. But he got his bearings back quick, expression tight and shoulders straight as he stepped back inside and slammed the door closed, vibration knocking part of the porch rail into the grass. It tickled my legs as I jogged through it, and I tried not to think about snakes. The metal stairs creaked beneath my feet, and the front door swung wide when I knocked on it. No furniture, no books, no cozy space for family gatherings. Each kitchen cabinet door hung open, overwhelmingly empty of food.

Where are his parents? Is this even his house?

"Hello?" I called out. A pile of clothes lay on the floor, a leather tool bag slouched next to it. A door slammed around back.

I almost didn't go after him. Like I said, he'd never been anything but ugly to me. But I couldn't ignore the sadness I'd seen, the one that sat behind the rage and held there. Something was wrong with Nathan, and there wasn't a single soul around except for me.

My feet moved before I could think about it. Face dripping with an unholy amount of sweat, I sprinted down the stairs, into the yard, and around the side of the trailer—straight into Nathan's chest.

"*Oof.*" I wobbled. A pair of calloused hands gripped my arms. I lurched away, face flaming with embarrassment. "Get your hands off me."

Nathan let go immediately. "You slammed into me."

"I was coming to check on you."

"I don't need your help," he bit out, and my eyes dropped to his knuckles.

"You're bleeding. Where are your parents? Where's your stuff?"

A hint of shame teased the set of his face. But then it was gone, his head held high, his body leaned toward me. "My parents *left.*"

Birds chirped. Off in the distance, the ferry blew its horn. It was a normal summer day in a normal small town, and I'd walked into a not-normal situation. "Parents just don't leave," I said, a little bossy, because parents were annoying, yeah. And they had expectations and rules, but parents were *good*. They loved their children.

At least...didn't they?

Nathan rammed me with one shoulder as he pushed past me toward the front of the house. "I'll call Sheriff Kelly," I said, out of breath from chasing after him.

"He'll throw a party, Griffin. Just go."

Up the stairs I trailed him. He slammed the front door in my face. I stood rusted to the porch, frustration oozing from my pores like sweat stains.

He didn't want my help? No problem.

I'd go get someone else.

EVERY SMALL TOWN has its share of characters. Lil Rooney was Minnesott's. Older than my parents by a decade or so, she knew everything about everybody, down to the underwear brand you liked.

It wasn't that Lil was nosy. She just absorbed information. *She knew*. And when I cleared the last line of trees and saw her farmhouse straight ahead, I wasn't surprised to see her walking toward me.

"Miss Griffin. You alright?"

Though her steps were urgent, Lil's eyes were still warm and kind. Her rust-colored shift moved in the breeze, the front pocket weighed down by gardening shears. She wore her dark hair in a braid like usual, the dappled light highlighting silver strands. I met her halfway, my head pounding in time with my heartbeat.

No, I'm not alright.

"It's Nathan," I panted. "Miss Lil, his parents left."

"*Left?*" Her face twisted in concern, and I nodded.

"He's at the trailer and they're not. He said Sheriff Kelly would be glad, but he's throwing stuff, and I think he punched something because he's...he's bleeding."

"Come with me," she bit out, and I jogged to keep up with her, legs protesting with every step. She lifted the shed door with a *yank* to reveal a cherry red golf cart. Lil plucked the key off the wall.

"What are you waiting for?" she asked me, cranking the ignition to life. I climbed in, and we puttered through the woods for less than a minute. She parked the golf cart in Nathan's yard and stepped out into the grass, dodging debris like landmines. "Nathan Cartwright. You around?"

Lil's voice echoed, and even the breeze seemed to hold its breath. The ever-present sweat dripped in my eyes; movement flashed in the doorway.

The damaged screen door swung wide.

He looked the same as he did when I'd left him, only this time, he'd bandaged his right hand. Lil let out a soft, "*Oh,*" and Nathan's gaze darted to me.

He probably hated me even more.

Lil clucked under her breath and stepped forward. "Nathan, you gonna make an old woman climb those steps?"

"No, ma'am," he said, attention flying back to Lil, the careful mask on his face slipping.

"I just—" he started to say, and his voice cracked.

"Son, come here."

He did as she said, stride long and loping, and feel into his arms. Nathan didn't make a sound when he cried. But his shoulders shook, and Lil patted his back, shushing him with soft little murmurs.

I swallowed the lump in my throat—choked on it—as the clearing filled up with sobs.

FOUR

DEWITT

July, 2001

Rosie looked up from the paper. "You can say *stop* at any time."

I flashed her a toothy grin as each pass grew the spiral larger.

"Dewitt. You hate playing MASH."

I did—I hated it. With the fire of a thousand suns. MASH —an acronym for Mansion, Apartment, Shack, House—ticked me off on principle. No one's future rested on luck. But I had a hypothesis to prove, and I could suffer in the name of science. "I like watching you panic," I said.

"Panic?" She scrunched her lips up like a duck.

I looked at her, deadpan as possible. "Panic. Over the boys."

Rosie cackled, flinging a handful of M&M's at my head. I fired back a fistful of my own, then followed it up with Nerd clusters. By the time Mama peeked in my door, we were breathless with laughter, candy flung across the room.

"You're playing MASH," she said, blonde bob barely

swinging, ready for bed in a navy sleep shorts and a tee. "Anybody have better luck than a shack?"

"We haven't played yet," Rosie admitted. "There was an...incident."

Mama raised a manicured brow. "You mean the candy everywhere."

"Yes, ma'am," I said. "We'll clean it."

Her lips quirked, then flattened. "You should be asleep."

"It's barely ten," I said to her, balking like she took my favorite toy. But then Mama shot a meaningful glance at Ro, and reality hit me. "Rosie has sailing camp. I forgot."

Sailing was Rosie's thing, not mine. I'd much rather have a brush in my hand, dragging color across a canvas. And there was an art camp that started that week.

"You sure you can't get Daddy to change his mind about the art camp in town?" Mama could work magic most days, but I wasn't sure about this one. Daddy didn't like my art habit. He called it a *dabbling pursuit.*

Mama shook her head. "He's got plans for you this summer." She turned to Rosie. "You need to get some sleep. Camp starts at eight, and your mama will have my hide if you show up dragging."

Rosie flopped back on the floor. "My mother is so dramatic."

I side-eyed her. "Like you're not."

"Alright," Mama said, voice warm with affection. "Clean the candy up. And for Pete's sake, go to bed."

My mother's footsteps faded down the hall, and when they finally stopped, I turned to Rosie. "One round?"

Rosie tallied our numbers while I swept the candy into piles. "Ready," she announced, bouncing a little. "House category first."

We ticked through our choices, and I snorted when my pen stopped on *shack*. Rosie whooped. "Mansion," she said.

"Ha. I'll come visit you."

Next, we counted out jobs.

Rosie landed on veterinarian. "You better get *artist,* Dewitt." I felt my face get hot as I looked at my paper. I'd stopped on studio art.

Painting had crept up on me. We had a new art teacher, Ms. Schulz, for eighth grade. I'd dabbled in art before, but not with good quality paints and a focused purpose. Watercolor rainbows at five were one thing. Ms. Schulz's oil paints, canvases, and infectious energy brought a completely different vibe.

"Even MASH knows you're destined for it," said Rosie, and cautious optimism swept through my chest. MASH relied on random chance, but what if—*what if*—I could run the house and the farm and keep alive our Griffin legacy while making a living as an artist?

Rosie peered at me. "You look constipated."

"I'm fine."

I tapped my finger through my choice of cars. "Scored a ten-speed bike," I said, and Rosie paused, watching.

"You're changing the subject."

Yes, I was. But it was too hard to explain my family ties and expectations. Rosie knew about some of it, but the rest, I didn't think she'd understand. It was a foreign world to her, one where freedom of choice existed within limits. *Time for a distraction*, I thought, ready to move forward. "You gonna go through that list of boys?"

Rosie took the bait, straightening her spine and counting through while I gnawed the inside of my cheek. "Eighteen, nineteen, twenty," Rosie whispered. Her pen landed on Gil Sutton. She squealed.

"You like him," I said. "I knew it."

She tossed her pen at me. "I do not."

Then why are you blushing right now?"

"Fine." She huffed. "Maybe I do. A little."

"Rosie..."

"Okay. I like him a lot."

Her face got all warm. Dreamy. She kept going. "He has such pretty eyes. And his hair...it's, like, red, but...*darker*."

"You're a goober," I said. I meant it.

"Like you don't have a thing for Nathan," she shot back.

My lip curled, but my insides did a little twist. My opinion of him had changed, but that didn't mean I liked him. I mean, I kind of liked him. But not like *that*.

Rosie kept going. "My gosh. That year-round tan. The light brown, scruffy surfer thing he has going on, especially right now, in the summer? I'm into Gil, obviously, but you can't tell me Nathan's not cute."

I swallowed. "He is. Objectively."

"Objectively." She arched a brow. "Did you even write him down?"

My eyes dropped to the blank white space I'd left on my paper. "I didn't write anybody down."

Rosie's hands went flying. "That's the most important one! You could have put someone famous down at least, if you didn't want to risk catching Nathan."

I shrugged. "I'm focusing on art."

Even as I said them, the words didn't feel like what I meant. I'd put Nathan aside. The way he made me feel lately—that light flutter in my gut—it was just...unnecessary. Unsettling. Drawing a brush through paint made me feel powerful. I pointed my attention to that.

Rosie shook her head. "Choosing artwork. Choosing artwork over cute boys!"

I was, in a way. I thought about painting a lot—at home, at school, while washing dishes after dinner, lost in ideas that wouldn't let go. I'd lie awake at night and stare into the dark, let my hands drift with each brushstroke I imagined. "I'm...a little obsessed with art, Rosie."

My cheeks went warm.

"You don't have to be ashamed of that," she said. You're a natural with a brush. Maybe you're obsessed, but if art is your thing, why does it matter? I love sailing, but it doesn't speak to me the way art does to you. Nothing does, unless I count pelting you with candy." Rosie picked up a pink Starburst and tossed at me. "I could lose myself in that."

———

I WOKE WITH A START. "ROSIE?"

We had fallen asleep on the floor. We'd turned off the lights. Made a pallet of quilts by flashlight. We had Bobert and Grint, her stuffed rabbit and my plush hedgehog. We'd drifted off about a quarter to one.

Why, then, was Rosie missing? And where did our quilt pallet go? I shivered on the hardwood floor, uncovered and alone in the spot we had chosen. I stood up and looked around.

This was my room, but not really. My bookshelves and my reading chair were gone. A writing desk stood against the far wall, the mahogany surface of it shining in the silver light from the window. A single lamp—antique, with a stained-glass lampshade—cast its reflection against the glass.

The girl was here. I faltered. A year had passed since that strange night in the barn. Long enough to think the whole thing was a fluke, to forget that part of my life until this moment, her solid figure sitting, real, at the desk.

She wore her hair pulled back from her face in a headband,

her long-sleeved pajamas cut with sharp with lapels. She hummed as she reached inside the desk, pulled out a book, and settled it on the surface.

That's an old-fashioned composition book.

Daddy had a ton of them in his office and in those bins out in the barn. The books he had were at least fifty years old, but this one looked new, the brown cover on it shiny. The spine cracked when she opened it up.

"Hello?" I eked out, heart pounding. "I don't know you and you're...you're in my room."

Her eyes floated up, not to me, but to the ink-black sky outside the window. She tapped her pencil against the desk and murmured something before moving it across the paper, content.

The girl was young, that much was obvious. Barely older than me. Was I dreaming? I pinched my forearm, hard. "Yeowch!" I'd felt that, the tight burn signaling I was awake. I heard Rosie mumble, too, and I spun around, expecting to see her. But the pallet was still gone, and I was still alone without a single sign of Rosie Bennett.

This was my room—my life—and whoever this girl was, she wasn't welcome. I closed the distance between us and slammed my hands down on the desk.

She didn't flinch.

I had one second, maybe two, to glimpse the name she'd written on the top of the paper.

Effa Griffin, in looping script.

"Dewitt? What are you doing?"

I pushed back from the desk. Put my hands down by my side and felt the soft give of quilts and blankets. The desk disappeared. The girl, too.

"Dewitt?" Ro said again, voice shaky.

I jammed my fists against my eyes. I breathed in and out, in and out, until my heart slowed.

"I'm here," I said. I wasn't. "I think I had a bad dream."

FIVE

NATHAN

If you wanted good fishing on the river, your best bet wasn't late afternoon. Fish were biting then, but the winds kicked up most days around three, maybe four in the evening. I looked at my watch—four-thirty. With calm water still on the river, we'd lucked out.

"Mama Lil?" I stuck my head inside the screen door. In the summer, she didn't have many rules. Tell her when I headed out. Be in for the night with the streetlights. Considering everything she'd given me since my parents left—food, clothes, a house to live in—it was the least I could do.

"You leaving?" She came from the kitchen with a dish towel in her hands.

"Going fishing," I said, and she nodded.

"I made extra biscuits on accident. Come get some. You can feed 'em to Gil."

The biscuits weren't for Gil and we both knew it. *She* knew I hated charity. The farmhouse was my home and Lil my legal guardian, but most days I still felt like a burden.

Some habits were hard to break.

"Nathan," Lil said. "You coming?" She held a floured hand against the door. I nodded and shuffled through, ignoring the warmth in my ribs when she patted my shoulder. "Here." She motioned to the butcher block counter. "Take six of them. Heck. Take all twelve."

I watched as Lil pulled a container from the pantry and loaded the biscuits inside. "Butter, too," she hummed. "And a little knife, 'cause I know y'all will try to use some sort of fishing implement to spread it..." She stopped and turned, tapping her fingertips against her chin as she surveyed the kitchen. "Oh!" She made for the refrigerator and returned with a pot of jam. "Can't have biscuits without jam, now, can we? And Gil likes strawberry, right?"

Strawberry jam was *my* favorite. I made a face at her and she laughed. "Guess I'm not as sneaky as I thought," she said. "Well. Long as you take them. That's all I care."

She sealed the container and held it out to me. "You got your gear?"

"Yes, Ma'am." I'd left it in the shed the last time Gil and I went creek fishing.

"Better take the golf cart, sugar. That's a lot to carry on your own."

"The golf cart?" I cringed at the crack in my voice. It wasn't an actual car, but it was driving. "Mama Lil, you sure?"

"As a pickle in a pot of pine needles. Plus, why ever not?"

"I'm fifteen," I said. "And I don't have a license."

"I taught you how to drive it, didn't I?"

"I mean, yes, ma'am. But—" My parents weren't trustworthy people and everyone knew I was their son. They weren't around anymore—last I'd heard, Sheriff Kelly heard tell of an arrest warrant out of Wilmington. But the people you come from are *your people*, and this town wouldn't let go of that.

Lil put a hand on my shoulder, squeezing once before she leaned in. "Don't go there," she said. "You're not like them."

I nodded once. I appreciated what Lil said, and I knew, of course, that she meant it. Applying it, though, was hard.

Gil rolled his bike to a stop as I walked out through the screen door, his brand-new Shimano reel strapped to the front. He bought it with his share of the money we'd earned from landscaping. Mama Lil *suggested* I put my share in a savings account.

"Sweet," Gil said. "We're taking the golf cart."

"I'm driving." I set the biscuits on the seat.

"Fine with me," Gil said, unhooking his pole and dropping it down into the PVC pipe I'd attached to the fender. He spotted the biscuits and rubbed his hands together. "Gives me time to eat."

He'd finished his second biscuit by the time I got behind the wheel. "You better leave some for me."

"Then you better drive fast, sucker."

I turned the key in the ignition and floored it, grinning as Gil let out a shriek. I had to hand it to him—he held onto the container something fierce, even managing to eat a few more biscuits. But I was relieved to find it half-full by the time I parked in front of the river, next to the Minnesott Acres pier.

Gil was the first to exit the golf cart. I pulled the key out and set the parking brake. "Think they'll show up?" Gil asked.

"Who?" I played it off like I was clueless. Probably, he was talking about the girls.

We'd been spending more time with Dewitt and Rosie, which was fine, I guess. But I missed hanging out with Gil, the old one I'd grown up with. The new Gil was such a dweeb.

New Gil used words like *please* and *thank you*. He went downwind to fart. He collected junk for the girls, dumb stuff like rocks and fossils and sea glass. When Rosie was around, the new Gil stared at her, nearly drooling.

I'd been shoving him a lot.

"I told Mrs. Sarah we'd be here." Gil tugged on his Sutton Seafood cap.

"You told Rosie's mom our plans." I set my lips in a grim line and unloaded our tackle.

"Are you mad?" he asked, and he laughed a little, like he couldn't believe it if I was. I snapped a fishing line in half, the taut cut of the string stinging my fingers.

"Why would I be mad?"

Gil's eyes went a little wide. "That fishing line offend you?"

"You invite the girls to everything, Gil."

"So what?"

"So they get in the way."

"Of?"

I waved my hand in the air. "Of...I don't know. Everything."

Gil set his fishing pole down. "Nathan. We've been best friends since first grade. We hang out all the time. And I'm cool with that, I am, but it's...good to expand our circle. Get to know more people. Like me and Rosie—we have the same taste in books."

And there it was: the great divide between Gil Sutton and me. He loved to read, and I hated it. The letters moved across the page. They flipped around and looked the same and it was awful and hard and pointless and I preferred to work with my hands, anyway. Fix stuff. Build. Whittle something out of scrap wood.

Gil's brows lifted. "You don't think Rosie's cute?"

"Why are you asking me that?" Rosie *was* cute, but no way in heck was I admitting that to Gil. If I did, he might ask about Dewitt, and something about *her* made my stomach funny, like

I'd chased four packets of Pop Rocks with a Coke. Even thinking about her set the fizzing off, and I had to settle that out. "You gonna stand there dreaming about long hair and freckles? Or are you gonna help me carry this stuff?"

Thirty minutes, two decent-sized spot, and about a half dozen blue crabs later, raised voices floated down from the hill. Rosie and Dewitt crested the top and my grip on the crab bucket tightened. I nodded my head up the hill, not smiling. "Looks like you got your wish."

Gil glanced up, eyes wide in horror. "I smell like fish guts. Help."

"You been cleaning fish."

"You got deodorant in your bag?"

"Yes, because I'm so concerned about smelling like a daisy."

"Cartwright."

Whatever. "Center console of the golf cart, dude."

Gil's shoulders sank with relief as he took three steps backward, his heavy steps shaking the wood of the pier. "You got Axe Body Spray?"

"Nope. Mama Lil left something in there. Strawberry Cream. Maybe Lilacs."

He retraced his steps and shoved me in the shoulder. I elbowed him. He pinched me on the pec muscle and I yelped.

"I didn't know we had tickets to Fisherman's Fight Club." Dewitt peered up at us, brow raised, from the sand.

Mama Lil had this thing about eye contact. "It's a sign of respect, son," she said. But standing there in the afternoon light, the long skirt of her dress scraping the ground and those thin, barely-there straps crossing her shoulders, Dewitt looked...well, she *looked*, and my eyes dropped to the ground as my heart rate shot upward. I forced them back up to her face and the paint smeared on her cheekbone, a shade the green of sunlight on grass. Her dark hair fell in waves, and while there wasn't a lick of wind I could have sworn the breeze was moving it. I swallowed quick and said the first thing I could think of. "Who goes fishing in a dress?"

Stupid, stupid, stupid.

Gil nudged me. "Would it kill you to be nice?"

My face flamed hot. I turned on my heel and headed for the end of the pier, away from Gil and the girls and the stupid words I put out there.

"Where are you going?" Gill called.

Away from the mess you created, you idiot. "Checking the crab pots for Lil."

SIX

DEWITT

I pulled my arms across my chest and glared at Gil Sutton. "What is Nathan's problem, Gil?" I'd saved that boy from a lifetime of abandonment. Not being ugly was the least he could do.

Gil's hands went to his hair, and he grimaced. "Well, Nathan...He, uh...I'm...I mean..."

Rosie shifted next to me on the pier, the warmth of her hand comforting. "Gil, you got something to say?"

He barked out a tight laugh. "I'm sorry. About him. He's... cranky. Today."

"Try every day?" muttered Ro, and I bit back a smile.

"I *like* wearing dresses on the beach," I said.

"I do, too. I mean...*dang it.*" The tips of Gil's ears glowed pink. "*I* don't wear them, but I can see why girls — why you — why people might *want* to wear them. Dresses are...nice." He waved a hand. "Maneuverable. Breezy."

Rosie sighed. "Just stop, Gilly."

Gilly? I shot her a glance. The side of her mouth quirked in response—*It fits,* she was telling me.

Gil's gaze bounced back and forth between us. "Y'all are doing that thing."

Rosie snapped toward Gil. "What thing?"

"Where you talk to each other but don't use words."

I lifted my chin a little. "You got a problem with that?"

"No, Ma'am," Gil said, face scarlet as my mother's tomatoes. He looked down at the tackle box by his feet. "I, uh, I brought some extra lures. You attach them to the hook and they attract the fish 'cause they're, like, shiny."

Rosie's dad, Mr. Matthew, had been taking us fishing since we were preschoolers. "You got a bucktail jig in there?" I asked.

The flush on Gil's cheeks eventually faded as we dangled our legs over the pier. We talked about summer and books—Gil was the first boy we'd ever met who liked to read, or maybe just the first boy who liked to read that we'd ever talked to. He was halfway through *The Call of the Wild* by Jack London. "Y'all ever read it?"

"No." I tossed my line into the water, watching the ripples move outward from my lure. "It sounds kind of intense."

"That's what makes it so good," Gil said, sneaking a glance at Ro. She kicked her feet over the edge of the pier, eyes forward.

"I can't read books with death in them," she said. "I'm too sensitive."

Gil's voice cracked. "You're not too sensitive."

I bit the inside of my cheek.

Our sleepover from three weeks ago had birthed two constant ghosts. Rosie came away with a Gil Sutton obsession, all "Gil said this," or "Gil said that." My personal favorite was "Gil walked by Daughtry's the other day and waved at me through the window."

It was getting tiresome.

My ghost, though, was disconcerting, a secret I carried

inside. Shadows made me flinch, and every flip of the genealog-
ical page turned up absolutely nothing. I'd come to accept I was
out of my mind *or* I had an Olympic medal-worthy
imagination.

I didn't know which was worse.

"Woah, hey. I think I got something." Rosie's voice cut
through my thoughts. "Something big," she eked out, and I
helped her to her feet, bracing her back with my arms so she
wouldn't go flying. Her line pulled *very* taut.

"Reel it in! Reel it in!" Gil shouted, reaching to help her
with the reel.

"She can do this by herself," I snapped as sweat glistened
beneath her hair and she tugged hard, attention focused.

"This is a tough one, y'all!" she said.

I held her tighter, bracing against the dock. We lurched
forward once, then back, and then *ping!*—the catch broke free,
and we toppled, the freed hook jangling from Rosie's line.

"Dang it!" Rosie yanked the pole back toward her. It raked
the hook right through my hand, catching the skin beneath my
knuckles.

"Rosie," I said, my voice even.

"What the heck kind of fish was that?"

"Rosie." The hook's barbs jutted through my soft flesh.

"I'm still gonna catch him," Rosie said. "That thing's mine,
and he better watch out. I'm coming."

"Rosie!"

This time, I yelled it, pain intensifying as she stood. "It's
stuck in my hand! The hook got me!"

"Sorry?" She turned around, and her eyes dropped to the
red river running down my fingers. "Oh no," she said and
whimpered before crumpling, unconscious, to the pier.

Gil stood there, mouth open, his eyes moving back and
forth between me and Ro.

"A little help here?" I asked.

Gil shook his head and regained his capacity for language. "Shiiiii—Shoot. Rosie. Let me..." He stopped, hands tugging at his hair as he turned in my direction. "You're bleeding."

Boys were absolutely useless, for Pete's sake.

"She'll be fine, Gil. She always faints at the sight of blood. Just..." I winced. My hand throbbed, a hot, sharp pulse that radiated outward. "Just help her when she wakes up."

Gil spared a long look at Rosie before asking, "What about your hand?"

"It's got a fishhook in it, Gil," I said, hoping my glare telegraphed my opinions. "Get me a rag and I'll tug it out."

He nodded and took off toward the golf cart. I was glad — I needed Gil gone. There was no way in heck I was crying in front of these two goons, not that Nathan was paying attention, anyway. He was at the end of the dock, putting crabs in a bucket.

But still.

The pier shook underfoot as Gil jogged toward me with a clean towel in his hand. "Miss Lil had this in the cart," he said, and I nodded, grateful he didn't pull one from the fish bucket. "I got some water for Rosie. You said she's afraid of blood?"

I pressed the towel to my hand and winced at the pressure. "Not afraid. Just not a fan."

"But...you said earlier that y'all clean your own fish."

I did, and we did, but was any of this necessary? "Human blood, Gil. Human blood." Rosie mumbled something to my right and I tipped my chin toward her. "Go help her. She's waking up."

Rosie would be fine, mostly. Embarrassed, but unhurt aside from that. I'd be fine, too, long as I could get this fishhook out of my hand and stop the dang thing from bleeding. I held the towel in my teeth and tugged at the line to snap it, a sharp pain shooting tears into my eyes. I needed privacy *right then*, but I was stuck with Gil and Rosie, the two of them blocking my path. My only choice — and the least appealing option — was to move farther up the pier.

With Gil and Rosie behind me, I stopped about three-quarters of the way to the end. Nathan still looked oblivious to the scene, so I gritted my teeth and wiggled the fishhook. Stars swam in my vision. *Criminy.* It hurt real bad.

Ears roaring, I wavered, trying to figure the best way to get it out. The hook got me good: through two sections of skin, stuck tight with a barb on one end and a circular curve on the other. I'd have to cut the hook.

"Dewitt?"

Nathan. He sounded cautious. Slightly annoyed. I turned my head and blinked back tears, squinting at him in the sunlight. "I'm busy," I bit out.

His eyes flicked to the towel, more crimson now than white. "You busy with all that blood?"

"None of your business." My voice broke, and I coughed. His standard scowl melted into concern, and he thunked the bucket down on the pier, the scrabbling of a dozen crabs inside filling the quiet.

"Let me see your hand."

I balked. "No, thank you."

The dumb boy took it anyway. "You get hooked?"

My plan was to tear right into him, but that fell apart when I turned around. Nathan's eyes — that brownish-green — they were so darn pretty I had a hard time catching my breath. My legs shook, and my head swam, and I cursed as I toppled to the side. Nathan caught me before I went down, holding onto me by the elbows.

So much for adrenaline.

"Hey, woah," he said. "Hang on a second. You need to...can

you sit?" He pointed at a spot by our feet and I wanted to run, but even I knew that wasn't happening. I lowered myself down and dangled my legs off the side, the plank edges digging into my legs.

Nathan stood over me. "Don't go anywhere," he said. The only *where* I was going was *out,* and I let out a little giggle. Rosie called my name, I thought, but it was hard to tell through the constant whooshing in my ears. I pulled my knees to my chest and propped my forehead against them, breathing in through my mouth.

Minutes passed, or maybe days. But then the pier began to bounce, vibration churning the water. "You don't look good," Nathan said. He was back, it seemed, and he brought reinforcements. "Rosie, can you help Dewitt lie down?"

"I can do it." I shifted to lie back, my head floaty and light and lolling. Rosie placed a palm beneath my neck, my only tether to consciousness. Nathan slid onto his knees at my side.

"Hook got her good," he murmured. I breathed in sawdust and pine. Something—a calloused finger?—touched my hand. *Get up,* I thought. *Get away from him.* I tried to roll to my side. But my insides rolled and swooped, and my tongue sat useless in my mouth, fused to the roof like sticky cotton. Rosie tightened her grip on my neck.

"You alright, Rosie?" Nathan's voice rolled through a tunnel in the air.

"Is it the blood?" Gil asked, the note of panic in his voice endearing. *She's fine,* I wanted to tell him, but I knew Rosie didn't need my help.

"I'm not looking at the blood, you dipwad," said Rosie. "I'm looking at her face. She's gone white."

Gil's low whistle pierced my foggy head. "Look at the barbs, man," he said.

Nathan's fingers left my skin for a fraction of a second. Rosie screeched. "You're going to *cut her hand?*"

"No." He drew out the word. "This is a multi-tool. I won't cut her." I heard a click, then the smooth *shush* of metal against metal. "I'll use the pliers to clip the hook."

Pressure eased below my knuckles in the space of two sharp snaps. Cool moisture passed over my hand; I must have flinched, because Nathan's voice breathed a *sorry* at my earlobe. A light tingle climbed the back of my neck.

Rosie *tsked* in disapproval. "You're gonna do more than just rinse it, right? I mean, that hook was in a fish. Who knows what kind of flesh-eating amoeba it might have carried?"

My lips curved. *Rosie drama at its best.*

Nathan didn't take the bait, he just acted. "Gil, hand me an alcohol swab?" A plastic case snapped to my right, and I heard the rip of a waterproof package. "This might sting," Nathan said, and it did, but his presence made it tolerable. "Sorry," he breathed again, then addressed Gil and Rosie. "There's antibiotic ointment in the first aid kit, right?"

"Yep," Gil said. "And a bandage."

Rosie shifted and propped my head in her lap. "You wanna see it?" she asked, and I nodded, still shaky. She held my hand in front of my face.

I'd been bandaged, an oblong band-aid stretched across my hand. My skin was free of blood, save the dried brown bits around my fingernails. Nathan moved beside me, and I turned to look at him head-on.

"She should drink something," he said, eyes averted, darting everywhere but at me. He cracked a bottle open and gave it to me. Blinking in relief, I croaked out a tiny, "Thank you."

Nathan turned away, his ball cap crooked, the only sign he'd heard me a shrug.

SEVEN

NATHAN

October, 2001

Gil bumped me in the arm. "You're staring."

"Shut up," I whispered, cheeks warm. I fumbled with the wrench in my hand and winced at the sound of metal hitting tile. Dewitt glanced up in the room across the hall, her eyes leaving her canvas for a fraction of a second. Even with the distance between the art room and my shop class, I saw the corner of her mouth tilt up.

Eight weeks into tenth grade, and I still grappled with Dewitt's freshman presence in the halls. I'd managed the summer alright, learned to live with the carbonated sensation that took up residence in my gut. In the summer, I could get away from her—fish by myself or keep busy with chores. But the yellow and black corridors of Pamlico County High School were different.

Crowded with paint splotches on a pair of weathered overalls.

I was all fizzy again, watching her, but it faltered as soon as

Gil handed me the wrench. I scowled, pretty sure I was about to get an earful. "One word, Gil," I murmured, "and I punch you in the face."

"You're allowed to like her," he whispered, voice barely audible over the drone of a saw.

"Do you enjoy living dangerously?" I asked him.

"Don't tempt me." He smirked.

I leaned over our workbench and fiddled with the C-clamp. "Fine," I grumbled. "You were right."

Gil's grin dang near knocked me over. "So you *were* staring at her."

"I meant you were right, like, in general." I waved my hand in the air.

He snickered. I turned the collar on the C-clamp—hard.

"You were right about the girls," I emphasized, resolving to keep the conversation away from Dewitt. "You said they were cool, and you were right. Rosie figured out why I hate to read in, like, one conversation."

Gil stepped back, affronted. "You never told me the words moved."

"You never asked." Rosie had. She studied me when I told her why, said *that sounds like dyslexia. It's a reading challenge my cousin has.*

"True," Gil continued, his hip against the workbench. "You got the dyslexia diagnosis after that. But you weren't staring at Rosie..." He trailed off, the pause pregnant with meaning.

My jaw ached from all the clenching. "I should have done this project by myself."

"But you didn't. And you know what that proves."

"That I've lost my mind?"

"That you love me, bro, I'm your perma-partner."

"You're perma-irritating."

Gil beamed.

"The audacity," I murmured, fighting the C-clamp one more time.

"Wood's cracking," he said, and sure enough, I'd over-tightened it.

I let out a long, low curse.

Gil retrieved a new block and we started over, this time with a lot less torque. Neither one of us spoke for a solid twenty minutes, probably 'cause Gil was waiting on me. I had nothing to say that wasn't incriminating. I *had* been staring at Dewitt, at the messy bun on her head and the blue paint along her jawline. Bubbly feeling or not — I wasn't *interested*. I was...curious. Confused by her, I guess.

Because Dewitt might have been a high and mighty Griffin, but she didn't act like one. She fished and climbed trees. She hated cotillion and white gloves and fancy parties. She drew all over her hand, using the two dots from her scar to make eyes or feet or whatever the heck else she saw there, waiting. She was creative, and I liked it a lot. And while Rosie led the charge with my dyslexia, Dewitt pushed me toward a hobby I loved. We went to the library once, and while Gil and Rosie huddled in fiction, drooling over some book about wizards, Dewitt and I pulled books on art, architecture, and construction—marine construction, specifically. "You could build that," she said, pointing at a simple boat plan.

I put the thing together in four weeks.

So yeah, I liked Rosie. And yeah, I liked Dewitt. But Gil was gaga over Ro, and as far as Dewitt was concerned, I didn't *like her*, like her.

Definitely not like that.

Gil took a deep breath beside me. "I think I'm gonna ask Rosie out."

My mouth opened before my brain. "You don't have a

license or a car. I could take you on the bike — the both of y'all'd probably fit in the trailer."

Gil's shoulders stiffened as he tightened a carriage bolt. "You don't have to be ugly. That landscaping gig worked out for you."

Guilt crawled up my spine, and I muttered a quiet, "Sorry." I flexed the grease pencil in my hand and dragged the tip across the workbench. "But I'm still not interested in Dewitt."

OCTOBER WAS KIND TO MINNESOTT. The leaves changed but the sun and the air were warm. When the bell rang to end class, Gil and I walked upstairs for lunch in the courtyard. It was less crowded than the cafeteria proper and less likely to fill up with punks. But there was a flaw in that plan, unfortunately, which was that bullies had working legs. I watched the courtyard door open up and groaned down at my sandwich. "Brent Summers. Three o'clock."

"*Cartwheel,*" he called across the courtyard, and Gil snickered, because Brent's nickname game was week. As far as bullies were concerned, he was probably one of the least creative, making up for lack of wit with his size.

Gait lumbering, Brent closed the distance across the quad. His letter jacket stretched across his frame, and Gil shook his head beside me. "Why's he wearing that? It ain't even cold."

I nudged Gil under the table. *Don't engage,* it said. I had one class with Brent. A supervised study hall for kids with learning challenges. And for a minute or two, five years ago, Brent's dad had been my dad's boss.

"Cartwheel, Cartwheel, Cartwheel. I'm having a hard time reading this book." He set his tray down on the table and flashed a paperback copy of our assigned English novel.

"Ignore him," Gil said, jaw tensing. "He'll go away when he gets bored."

Brent turned to Gil. "You're friends with a loser."

"Go away, Summers," I muttered, but he didn't move. Greasy red hair tipped over his forehead as he leaned in over our table.

"What parents don't want their own kid?"

A flash stirred in my peripheral vision—denim overalls and dark hair. Streaks of purple and blue and green and *bam*—Brent sprawled out in the grass, holding his jaw and gaping. Nobody breathed for a second.

Two seconds.

"You just hit him," I said.

Dewitt grinned back at me, her smile brighter than the surface of the sun. "I hit him," she said. Well, she squealed it.

"You aren't supposed to hit people, Dewitt!" Brent scrabbled on the ground in front of us, face red and eyes bulging from his head. And dang it if Dewitt didn't just bounce on her toes like a prizefighter.

"You aren't supposed to bully people, yet here we are."

I laughed into my fist. She was brilliant. Rosie pushed through the crowd. "I am so stinking proud of you," Ro said, tackling Dewitt like she'd won the lottery.

"That was..." Mouth gaping, Gil was at a loss for words.

"That was one hell of a right hook," I said.

"I learned from the best," Dewitt said, aiming an adoring look at Rosie.

Gil choked on his tongue and sputtered. "*Rosie. You taught Dewitt to throw a punch?*"

She shrugged. "It's a life skill, right?" A hazy glaze covered Gil's eyes, and I swear on my life that was the moment he fell in love with her.

And when Dewitt smiled again, all teeth and bright cheeks

and eyes that danced like starlight, I couldn't say with any certainty that my heart wasn't next.

I DIDN'T SEE Dewitt for the rest of the school day. Usually, I glimpsed her in the hall. But she'd disappeared after lunch and that fizzy feeling tinged with something heavier, like foreboding. Not that I'd admit any of that to Gil.

"You think she got in trouble?" Gil's hands were in his pockets as we crossed the field toward his house. I thought probably she had, and it made me twitchy. She'd punched out Brent *for me.*

"I don't know why you care," I said, squinting into the sun.

"Because I *like* Dewitt. I'm not in love with her like you are —ow!"

My hand stung from smacking him. Gil rubbed the back of his head. "Would you quit it?" he asked. "She's our friend and I care, and if you'd just admit to yourself that you're sweet on her, you'd have the potential to be, like, *happy.* Instead of moping around like you don't deserve good things."

The ground reached up and grabbed me, and I stood there, field grass tickling my legs. I *was* happy, right? Maybe not crazy happy, like, *delirious.* But things were mostly good.

Rosie's voice interrupted my thought train with a far-off call from across the field. She sprinted toward us through the grass, her arms and legs a blur of movement. Gil put his nose to his armpit and sniffed.

"Cut it out," I said. "You smell like sawdust."

He breathed easier. "Definitely better than gym."

Rosie stumbled to a stop, hands planted on her knees as she caught her breath, wheezing. "Y'all could've met me halfway."

"You're right," Gil said. "I'm sorry. I've got water in my

bag." Gil was an idiot for this girl, and I couldn't help it—I snickered. He shot me a dirty look. But then a smile stretched his face and he handed the water to Rosie. Her cheeks were all pink, maybe from running.

Probably from talking to Gil.

"Thanks," she said and twisted the cap off before draining it in one long sip. "Talked to Dewitt," Rosie breathed. "She's grounded, until, like, February."

"*February?*" Gil and I said.

"I'm exaggerating. She's grounded until next week."

Pulse thrumming in my ears, I asked Ro, "Where is she right now?"

"She's...up at the house," Rosie said, slowly. Gil's eyebrows shot my way. Rosie looked at me a little sideways, too. But she carried on: "Suspended from school until Monday."

That word—suspended—scraped sharp needles up the back of my throat. *She'd* stuck up for *me*, and now Dewitt was paying the consequences. I tried to wipe my voice clean of any emotion. "Is Dewitt upset?"

Ro laughed. "Are you kidding? She gets to paint."

And that was Dewitt Griffin right there: punch out a guy's lights and be happy with the punishment. Nothing she did made sense. I hated how attractive that was, but I also couldn't wait to figure her out, tease apart all her pieces. Rosie spoke again, and I startled, her words yanking me out of my thoughts.

"We can't talk to her, not for a couple days, at least. But she's gonna sneak out Friday night," she said, taking a few big steps backward. She kept her eyes on Gil.

"Meet you at the pond?" she asked him. "Probably like, nine fifteen?"

"Yeah—" Gil's voice gave a squeak; he flushed red and pushed his next words an octave lower. "Sounds good," he said, all baritone and growly.

I coughed to cover my laugh.

If Rosie noticed Gil's embarrassment, she was nice enough not to say. She just gave a sharp nod of her head. Then she pointed at me. "Pebbles at the window. Nine thirty?"

I'd be ready by nine, at least.

EIGHT

NATHAN

Mama Lil hovered over me, eyes shifting from glitter to gloom.

"No fever," she said, the soft palm of her hand pressed against my forehead. She scanned my features. "You got other symptoms, son?"

"No, ma'am."

I choked on the guilt, coughed a little.

Lil screwed up her eyebrows and hummed. "You've got chest congestion," she said, and the guilt pressed even harder.

"Cookie went down the wrong pipe."

The snickerdoodle plate sat on the kitchen table, plain accusation in its eyes. I squirmed and tried again, excitement over the night's plans warring with shame over my behavior. "I promise, Mama Lil. It's nothing. I'm just tired. I've been having trouble sleeping. That's all."

Lil studied me, her attention sending shockwaves up my spine. I almost confessed right there, but then she turned to the stove and lit the burner under the teapot. "I got the perfect tea for that."

My stomach soured. I was going straight to a group home—

or hell. But Dewitt was *in my head*. I'd dreamt about that mean right hook, those freckled, paint-streaked cheeks, those waves of dark, wild hair, and the overalls. But I hadn't *seen* her since the day she knocked Brent flat. It had been a long couple of days, my gratitude and admiration mixed with a butt load of awkward cold sweats. I was going through shirts like a minnow in a fish pond.

Basically, I thought about her a lot.

Lil set a giant mug in front of me, empty save for the tea ball thing she used. "The infuser's got my bedtime blend. Chamomile, cardamom, and lavender." Steam lifted from the mug as she tipped in the hot water. "Two minutes, then you can drink."

She sat across from me, her ministrations stoking the panic in my gut. I didn't *want* to lie to Lil, and a big part of me squirmed at my desperation. These were Gil Sutton-level shenanigans, letting my decisions get ruled by a crush.

"Son," Lil said slowly. "Is there anything you want to tell me?"

I coughed again. "No."

Lil's lips fluttered with amusement so quickly I thought I'd imagined it. But her eyes glimmered when she patted my arm. "Drink your tea and get some rest. I need your help around the house tomorrow."

"Yes, ma'am." I wanted to crawl under the table and hide there forever, especially when she gave me one last, long look. But when I didn't speak, she hummed and left the kitchen, her "Goodnight" hanging in the air. I drained the tea, hands jittery, and washed the mug out in the sink. Equal parts anticipation and remorse, I padded up the stairs to my room.

When Lil first brought me to stay with her, I camped out in the guest room down the hall. It didn't feel right to settle in; she wasn't my mom. She wasn't even a distant relative. Lil was the crazy neighbor lady who zoomed past our broken trailer on her golf cart, waving to me as she bumped along the road. If he was home, Pop gave her the stink eye. Mama used to warn me about that "crazy old witch lady up the way." I'd catch sight of Lil sometimes on my walk home after school, the back of her golf cart disappearing into the trees as I stepped into the clearing. I'd find a bag of fresh groceries at the door.

So before my parents left, I knew her. And we'd talked in town a couple times. But I was still this derelict kid from the wrong side of the road with parents who were worthless. I didn't know why Lil wanted to keep me, and the guest room seemed more appropriate, somehow. Until six months had passed, and Sheriff Kelly came to the door with paperwork and a summons. The State Police found Mike and Sue, drugged out of their minds at a motel in Fayetteville.

My parents went to prison. They also surrendered their parental rights.

I moved into my bedroom a week later—the *Blue Room,* Lil called it, at the top of the stairs. The craftsman-style bed was dark wood, the mahogany desk along the wall a rugged companion. She'd gone into town and bought sailboat schematics, framing them to hang on the wall. The guilty lump in my throat swelled larger when I spotted the folded laundry on my bed. I choked it down, closing the bedroom door tight and cutting the lamp on my bedside table before peering through the window into the dark.

Two silhouettes stood at the tree line. Not willing to risk the ping of pebbles, I shoved up the window and waved. One leg over the sill, then two, and I was dangling from the roofline before dropping, quiet, to the ground.

Gil held out his thumb, and I met it. "Told you he had ninja skills," he said to Ro.

Rosie balked, her dark hair inky in the shadows. "I never said I didn't believe you, Gilly."

I choked on my laugh. *"Gilly?"*

He shoved me in the shoulder with a scowl.

Gil held Rosie's hand as we ran through the darkness. I couldn't wait to give him crap for that. At least until we reached Pinecliff, anyway, when my stomach flipped about a million Dewitt-sized somersaults. My body keeping me humble, I guess.

"Does Dewitt know we're coming?" We huddled under a magnolia in the yard. It was huge, its blooms were heavy and white, their fragrance fresh and spicy.

"She does," Rosie said, and held up a two-way radio. "And in a second, she'll know we're here."

"Dewitt," Rosie whispered into the mouthpiece. "Dewitt, do you copy? Look outside."

Static crackled first, then a whispered, "Rosamunde. I copy."

A strangled laugh escaped Gil's throat. Rosie whipped around, gaze pinning him to the tree like two daggers. "Yes, Gil? What was that?"

He moved back like he could shrink into the shadows. "Nothing." He scratched his nose. "It sounded like she called you Rosamunde."

"Bad idea..." I murmured.

Rosie's nostrils flared in the dark.

"I'm named after my great-grandmother," Rosie said to him, "and if you—"

A window squeaked up above. It saved Gil from a deeper hole, but I fell right into mine as a single leg crossed over the sill, bare from mid-thigh to a pair of low-top Chuck Taylors.

Good gravy, there was so much skin.

So much...*danger,* considering she was either gonna fall and break her neck, or I was gonna hyperventilate from her appearance.

I opened my mouth like a dummy. "She's climbing out the window? In shorts?"

Rosie's hands went to her hips. "What's your problem? You did the exact same thing."

"I have on jeans," I said. "And I knew what I was doing."

Her dark stare went straight to my soul. Then her mouth tipped up, and I knew I'd been busted. She said sweetly, "Nathan, I appreciate your concern. But Dewitt is fine. She's been climbing out that window forever. That's how she met me the night we ran into y'all at the pond."

I remembered that night—my parents fighting; the way sweat pooled between the mattress and my skin. The way I left and went to Gil's; the way they skipped town a day later. What I remembered the most, though, was the best moment of my life from that point forward: Dewitt refusing to let my stubborn heartache win.

Dewitt's feet hit the ground, and I exhaled. "Dude," Gil whispered. "You're so gone."

"Quit it." I flicked his ear, right as the air shifted with a new presence.

"Are you two ever *not* fighting?" Dewitt's mouth tilted in a playful smirk. "What are we waiting for?" she asked, and I honestly didn't know—she was standing there with those legs and that hair and a smile that made my heart hurt. Looking back, I was waiting for her. But maybe neither of us knew it, or we were too young, or she didn't feel it yet. Whatever the case, she took off running, dragging my heart through the night.

From Pinecliff, Minnesott Marina was a ten-minute walk. We ran it in five, skidding out through the trees tight-limbed and breathing heavy in front of the Dock Master's hut. Dewitt dropped her hands to her knees and looked up at me, mischief alight in her eyes. I stood rooted to the spot, heart pounding in my chest, until Gil knocked me in the head with a bag of candy. "Alright, everybody. Time for snacks."

Dewitt leaned over my shoulder and plucked a package of Skittles from the stash. "Wanna split these with me?" My eyes went from her hand to her face and then back to the candy. Skittles were crap. But this package was an excuse to sit and talk, to get tugged into her orbit. The dang bubbles in my gut went nuts.

We spread out across the porch, the four of us, Gil and Rosie against the building's front wall. Dewitt and I sat on the steps, Skittles between us and our bodies tilted inward, our backs against the railing's slats. Conversation drifted, the tide flowing from books to movies to school. When Rosie and Gil shifted into an argument about some science-fiction series, I stretched my legs out and gazed up at the sky.

"Hey, so, about Wednesday."

I jolted. While I wasn't looking, Dewitt had moved. She sat a few steps up, facing the yard, her feet inches from my knee.

"Wednesday?"

"Yeah. During lunch, when I punched Brent Summers." Dewitt's teeth caught her bottom lip. I watched, entranced, as she tucked a strand of wavy hair behind her ear before looking at me, wincing. "I, uh. Owe you an apology."

An apology? "What for?"

"Brent was out of line, but I got involved, and I probably shouldn't have. You were handling it. And that was nosy of me, so yeah. I'm sorry. I'm done. Not with talking, with...punching people. For the foreseeable future." She winced again. "Yeah."

A little soft, a long strong—she wore her vulnerability like armor. Gosh, she was so darn cute. "I sure hope you aren't done."

Her eyes danced in the dark. "With punching people?"

No, I thought. *With me.*

But I nodded. "You've got one hell of a right hook," I said. My cheeks burned red, my voice raspy. "I'm serious. You've defended me twice."

"Twice?"

I didn't say anything. I just kept my gaze on hers, waiting for her to get it, hoping she remembered like I did.

"Oh," she said, and I breathed easier. Relieved the moment meant something to her, too. "So, you're not mad?"

"No."

"Good. Because you're brave and you're smart and you're super capable, and I worried I'd made you doubt that, somehow." Her eyes dropped to the ground and she tugged a loose thread on her hoodie. A heathered gray, it looked soft and worn. "Because I really like those things," she said. "About you, Nathan Cartwright."

All the air left my lungs in one giant exhale. I couldn't feel my hands. I mean, I could, but all the blood in my body had rushed to my cheeks, burning.

"I told you," Gil said, his voice in a tunnel. "Totally gone, that dude."

———

LIL SWEPT into the kitchen the next morning and plopped down in the chair across from me. Smug look on her face, she folded her hands on her lap and addressed me. "You didn't have to climb in through the window, sugar. I left the back door open last night."

Cereal lodged in my throat. "Window?" I inhaled and about near hacked up a lung. "I don't—" I said, tears from the coughing in my eyes and sandpaper coating my windpipe.

She waved a hand, dismissive. "You absolutely do."

I swallowed, the sensation like knives in my throat. When Lil took me in as a foster, I agreed to a certain set of rules. Since I'd broken a few by sneaking out, she had every right to end my placement. I dropped my spoon in my bowl and stared at it, tracking the motion of the flakes in the milk.

"I was trying to sneak back in," I said, the room's silence echoing off the walls. I stood, my chair scraping the linoleum. "I'll go pack my stuff, Miss Lil."

"Nathan Fitzgerald Cartwright," Lil said. "You sit down this instant, you hear?"

I sat. Milk sloshed from my bowl and splattered across the table. I kept my eyes focused on that—not Lil. But gentle fingers tilted my chin up until I had no choice but to look at her. "Now you listen," she said, her wizened gaze holding mine. "I'm Mama Lil to you, not Miss, and we're not going on vacation. You have no reason to pack your bags."

I inhaled, sucking air through a straw. "I broke a pretty big rule. I went out without telling you."

"I knew where you were."

Lil's arms slid to the table, and I blinked about a million times. "I'm old," she said, "not blind, and I had my own misadventures when I was your age. When you didn't admit what you were planning to do, I made a strong cup of herbal tea for myself and waited, here in the kitchen, watching the three of y'all run off into the trees. Figured you were marina bound, so I called Luther, who called the Bennetts. The Bennetts called the Suttons, and, well..."

"You all knew."

A sharp nod.

"And nobody got mad?" *This is crazy.*

Lil chuckled. "You forget we grew up in this town. How much trouble could you get up to at nine o'clock at night?"

"It was nine-thirty." I shifted.

"So I was half an hour off. The marina's security cameras work, and the liquor cabinet had nothing missing. Gil's mama did say she couldn't find her five-pound bag of Halloween candy, but we figured y'all'd be alright."

My sharp burst of laughter filled the room with disbelief. "But...I signed a contract. It was binding. About my behavior for foster care."

"I signed one, too," she said, "but you are not a job to me, and your presence here is more than a contract. Am I hurt you didn't tell me what you were doing? Certainly, but I'm not *mad*. You went out for Dewitt, Nathan. Your little group is thick as thieves. You've been that way since the end of the summer, I reckon. Warms my heart to see the way you look out for each other. Reminds me of my childhood, actually."

For a moment, we sat in silence, the only sound the refrigerator's hum. I surveyed the room, studied the photos on the wall and on the sideboard. Searched Lil's face for the girl she used to be.

"Miss Lil—"

"Mama Lil."

"Mama Lil, I don't..." *Adults don't love me like this.*

Lil took my hand across the table and held my eyes with a steady gaze. "You're worth fighting for," she said.

I slumped back in my chair. "Not really."

"Nathan, your parents were fools."

Maybe. "But—"

"They were selfish and sick. They were fools to let you go, and I'd be a fool not to love you. You are loved *unconditionally* in this house."

My chest expanded, my heart a beautiful balloon. "Did you —did you say *loved?*"

She gave a nod, hand trembling a bit as she smoothed her

shirt down. "I'm your guardian right now, but I'd like to adopt you. If that's what you'd like, of course."

A home. A mom. A family. "I'd like that," I said, "when I'm ready. I think I'd like that a lot."

Lil's shoulders went slack, deflating. "Well, that's settled, then." She stood and ruffled my hair, smiling as she walked past me. "Next time, though, Nathan, tell me when you're sneaking out."

NINE

DEWITT

Dawn woke me after our late-night adventure, its silver fingers spreading unrest on my skin. I grabbed my wetsuit from my drawer and slipped outside, across the yard and down the hill to where the beach lay empty. Unlike most mornings on the river, a brisk wind pushed heavy breakers into the sand. The river mirrored my mood—not angry. Definitely unsettled and choppy, though. My mixed emotions churned, my brain trying to catch up with my gut as I sorted last night's events into boxes, shoving my weird, electric feelings down beneath the raging surf.

Shoes abandoned in the sand and wetsuit zipped and buckled, I sucked in a deep breath and dove beneath the first wave. My hands carved the brine, cold water whooshing past my ears and stealing my oxygen until the pressure was too much to bear. I let my body go limp and floated to the surface, blinking hard at the morning sun. October's breath nipped at the air as my toes brushed the bottom. I'd swum out to the end of the pier.

Content with my surroundings, I leaned back and let the

current set my course. Colors swirled inside my head. Cobalt violet for Rosie, the deep bruise of secrets I'd kept from her. For Gilbert, a pop of sunshine—cadmium orange. And then Nathan, of course, his hand brushing mine in scarlet sienna. I dragged the pigments through my mind; washed them in the river. The water didn't care what I felt or why I felt it. The tide took me as I was.

Icy fingers grabbed my ankles and yanked me forward in the surf. Brackish water ripped up my nose and I flailed, realizing as my feet hit the sand that I'd floated to the shallows. I stood, nasal passages burning, river water streaming from my face. Rosie was right there, arms crossed in the knee-deep water, a bright blue one-piece beneath a threadbare shirt and sailing pants.

"Thanks for the brain-eating amoeba." I closed one nostril with my finger and breathed out—sharp—through my nose.

"I've been calling you from the shore for the last ten minutes. Wasn't sure if you were deaf or dead."

"It's *windy*." I held my hands out, presenting the wind on a plate. "Plus, my ears were underwater." I sulked. "You're annoying. You know that, right?"

Rosie grinned at me. "I'm persistent. And you love me for it, don't lie." She took my hand and led me upward, through the shallows. "I brought a blanket. Come on."

Short of breath from my nose full of water, I collapsed onto the yellow blanket Rosie brought. She plopped down at my side, a tease tugging at her voice when she nudged me. "You and Nathan looked cozy last night."

If my skin could have unzipped like my wetsuit, I would have peeled it off right there. I could still feel his hand on mine, his fingers calloused and cool and just as *right* as they were out of the ordinary. It was an awkward sensation I wasn't used to, one I'd come to the river to wash away.

"You like him," Rosie said.

I lifted a shoulder. "Sure."

"You know what I mean."

I did, but that sure as heck didn't mean I would actually admit it. "I'm not the one who got kissed."

Rosie's giggle floated from behind a curtain of dark curls. "It wasn't a *big* kiss," she said. "It was, like, five seconds."

"Y'all were behind the dock master hut a lot longer than that."

"To *talk*," she said. "Privately."

"You still kissed him. And you held his hand all the way back to my house."

Rosie's knees came to her chest, and she propped her chin on them. "I'm smitten."

My lips curved. "Pretty sure Gil is, too."

"You're not distracting me from you and Nathan," she said, jumping back to her favored topic at hand.

I plucked a trio of pine needles from the ground and weaved them together. "I just told him I was sorry for punching Brent."

"Well, that's stupid. Why did you do that?"

"Because he can handle himself."

Rosie's legs dropped flat on the blanket. "Of course, he can handle himself. He doesn't have to, though. That's why people have friends. To help them."

"Maybe *you* should have stood up for him, then."

It was a snotty thing to say. It was a snotty way to say it, too, straight vinegar and teeth. Rosie reared back and popped up from the blanket like I'd leaned over and bitten her flesh.

"I'm sorry," I called, scrambling after her. "That's not—I shouldn't have said that, okay?"

I caught up to her at the hillside, and she whirled around,

feet kicking up loose sand. "You're being snippy, and I'm not loving it. What's going on with you?"

Everything.

When I was younger, probably around sixth grade, my father decided it was high time I learned about *cognitive bias,* a psychological phenomenon. You see something once, he said, and then, out of the blue, you start seeing that one thing *every-where,* assuming it's more common than it is. I'd discovered that the opposite was also true. You experience an event more than once, and then it stops for so long you start to believe it never happened.. That's kind of how things were with Effa. She'd disappeared for a while—a long while. And then she came back.

Effa appeared more frequently when school started, so often, I called the moments *trips. Haunting* wasn't right. *Hallu-cination* was too scary. *Trip* encapsulated how I felt, like I'd been picked up by my hair and deposited into an alternate reality where the changes were just notable enough. The trees on the shore still there, but smaller. A piece of furniture swapped out. Same, same, *different*, and same, like my surroundings recreated for a movie. Effa would appear and then go, and then my blood would run hot with this...surge of energy, intense and electric in my bones. It lived inside me for days. I'd churn out like a machine, staying up all night, completely vibrant. Like deep down, I could do anything and everything all at once. It happened the day I punched Brent; I crossed the courtyard *convinced* I'd been the only person capable of intervening.

A lump sat in my throat, frog-sized. "I've been lying to you, Ro."

The wind tousled her hair. "What?"

"I saw someone that night. In the barn."

Cogs turned inside her brain. "The summer after seventh

grade," she said. "You promised...are you kidding me right now?"

"I'm sorry, Ro." I twisted my fingers.

"You could have told me the truth. You could have admitted, just once—"

I winced, and Rosie stopped, eyes narrowing. "It hasn't been just once."

Shrinking inward, I admitted, "It...doesn't happen all the time."

"Neither do earthquakes, Dewitt! That's what makes them newsworthy."

"It's not newsworthy if it's just me!"

I was fuming. Not with Rosie—with myself. For having to deal with this stuff, for not telling the truth, for letting any of this happen in the first place. "I'm sorry," I said. "I shouldn't have yelled. It's just—" How could I explain this to her? Admitting it felt like defeat, like I wasn't perfect enough, or right, or a a good example of the Griffin family.

Rosie took my hand. Squeezed it. "You don't have to go through this alone."

Relief, warm and comforting, rushed over me like a late summer wave. "Thank you." I wiped my cheeks with the back of my free hand and inhaled. "I was worried you'd think I was weird."

Rosie laughed. "You are weird. So am I. I support you, no matter what. You could start a grocery store for squirrels and I'd be out on the street, passing flyers."

My answering giggle was wet.

"Look," Rosie said, pulling me closer. "You don't *have* to tell me anything. I just want you to know that you can."

It was the permission I didn't know I needed. "It's the same girl every time. I think her name is Effa Griffin."

"Wait. She's related to you?"

"I don't know. Every time I ask, it's like that Bible page all over again. Clams up tighter than a rotten whelk."

Rosie's nose wrinkled. "That's an image."

I almost smiled. "I did a little digging in the barn." My fingers itched, the brittle paper I'd found a sense memory. "The page wasn't there, but I found an acceptance letter from a writing school in Asheville. Addressed to a Griffin. Effa Marie."

Brow furrowed, Rosie's eyes looked deep in thought. "Lil's lived here a long time. I feel like she kind of...*knows things*." She waved her fingers. "Knows things...like....*woooooo*...."

I laughed for the first time in a while, the feeling foreign and awkward in my throat. "I don't want Lil to think I'm nuts," I said, the heavy weight of my fears crashing back on me.

"She's not gonna think that. She'll know what's going on, I'm sure. Like if it's a land thing—"

"*What?*"

"I was at the library with Gil—"

"Surprise, surprise." I snorted.

"Shut up," she said, but grinned at me. "*I was at the library*, and Gil pulled a book off the shelf. He knows I love ghost stories and stuff, so when he saw the title, he grabbed it. It's called *Residual Hauntings*. About how the land kind of remembers things."

My sigh was deep and heavy. "Rosie."

"I'm serious," she said. "The scientist who wrote the book, she argued that when something awful happens like a murder or a...a house fire, the energy imprints on the ground and there are—what did she call them again?—*after images*. Like when you look at something for too long and then close your eyes, you know how the outline's still there?" Rosie looked out over the water, thoughtful. "What if it's something like that?"

I didn't buy it. "So something awful happened to Effa, and it left a recording behind?"

Rosie was quiet for a minute. Then, "I think you should talk to Lil."

"Maybe." The after image thing didn't sound right. Every appearance felt real, like being inside a snow globe instead of watching it from the outside. And then the after-effect—the surge. Could you get energy from hauntings? "I hate all of this. So much."

Rosie's arm slipped around my waistline. She smelled like strawberries and fresh cut grass. She smelled like our old plushies, Bobert and Grint, like love and trust and belonging. Maybe Rosie was right. But it didn't matter *right* now. I could let the water have it all, at least for a little while I clung to Rosie, warm and stable in the shifting sand.

TEN

DEWITT

May, 2002

I learned a hard truth about stability that winter: the bottom will always fall out.

"This art thing," Daddy said one November night at dinner. "You can't do it full-time."

I stalled with my fork halfway to my mouth, not surprised by what he said, but bothered. We'd been talking about career choices and I mentioned I'd been thinking about art.

Mama's face pinched over her mashed potatoes. "Luther. She's fifteen."

"She also has a legacy to uphold."

"You act like you've got one foot in the grave," Mama said, eyes tensing as she resisted an eye roll. "You're too stubborn to die, and Dewitt has plenty of time before this house and this land get passed down to her." She looked at me, expression softening. "I think it's great that you want to pursue art."

Daddy's gaze bent in my direction. "I'm not suggesting we ignore your talent, but we need to be practical. That means a serviceable degree, like business or political science." He pressed his palms against the table, flat. "This summer, we visit State. The head of the business school is a colleague. Once you talk to him, Dewitt, see the school, learn more about the programs, I'm confident you'll-"

"No."

It echoed across the ceiling and bounced around the room. My parents stared, open-mouthed, at their rebel of a daughter, Mama looking more amused than mad. But Daddy's teeth clenched, and I watched the pulse in his neck beat. I pushed it, though, because this was my future, my life, and I wasn't about to be railroaded. "I want to see the art school at VCU this summer. I'm not interested in State."

The grandfather clock chimed out in the hallway, its rich tones hanging fitfully in the air. Daddy's voice held zero emotion—it was creepy—when he finally said, "Virginia Commonwealth."

I gave a sharp nod. "In Richmond. Ms. Schulz went there." She'd been my art teacher in eighth grade, as supportive and kind as she was talented and exacting, and I'd hung on every lesson she gave. Color theory, design, perspective—she opened my eyes to a world as bright as vivid lake green tugged across a canvas. She believed in me and my art, and it was life-changing. An interest became a calling because of her.

"Let me get this straight," Daddy said, and Mama's lips pressed together, tight. "Your choice of a degree and desired institution hinge on your middle school art teacher and where she went to school."

"Is it that hard to imagine? Teachers inspire their kids all the time."

A muscle jumped in Daddy's neck, and Mama's hand went to his arm. "Luther..."

Surprisingly, he seemed to pull back, closing his eyes for

the space of two inhales. "It is not," Daddy said, "that hard to imagine. *Children* have heroes of all sorts. But how many of those children grow up to be movie stars or...pro athletes? Hardly none, Dewitt, because children grow up, and they learn that life isn't just about what we love or what inspires us. It's about what we do with the responsibilities we've been given. And you have a rather large one coming your way."

I blinked at him. "So we should all just give up what we love. Force ourselves into boxes that don't fit because someone else's expectations require it. Is that what you're saying, Daddy? That dreams are worthless if they aren't practical? Because as far as I can tell, you've never dreamt beyond living in this house and being a Griffin. I want something better than that."

"*Dewitt*," Mama said, features falling. Daddy's fist banged the table and rattled the plates. "*Luther*...." Mama's face went red, and she grabbed my father's hand before he could do anything else with it. "Both of you—stop it. Dewitt, clear the table, please."

My face flushed. "Look. I'm sorry, but-"

"No," Mama said. "Not now."

It was the steel magnolia voice, the one that dripped with grace while sealed in iron. A *do not argue with me.*

"Fine." My chair squeaked as it scraped across the kitchen floor. I cleared the dishes in a huff, then strained to hear their muffled voices over running water as they hissed about *changes* and *a long time ago.* By the time I climbed the steps up to my room, I'd determined they were, indeed, talking about me. My fingers itched to paint; I pulled out my supplies and poured my anger on the canvas. And when the first light of dawn crested my window, it didn't bother me that I hadn't slept.

Body buzzing, I walked in the school building ready to conquer the world. The less I slept, the more productive I

became; the more creative and alive the canvas. It was like...
someone had plugged me in and set my on switch to the high-
est, most exhilarating setting. For a whirlwind week, I was on
fire.

And then the darkness snuffed it out.

You know that feeling when someone wakes you from a
deep, cathartic sleep? That sort of disorienting spin, the heavy
legs, the arms that won't move no matter how hard you flex
them? That's what it was like, only bleaker, with my brain
fumbling around in pitch black. I cancelled plans. Stayed home
from school. Let my grades slip into the toilet. Mama took me
to the doctor; it wasn't mono, leukemia, or the flu. The last guy
we saw knit his brow over the desk at my parents and
suggested, "We might be looking at mental, not physical,
health."

I'd wondered. Because what sane person had a life like
mine? Sane people slept, and when they got enough rest they
got out of bed and went to school or work or just did simple
things like take showers. But my parents disagreed. Daddy
muttered something about *dangerous half-baked quacks* while
Mama pulled me out of my chair and declared I needed a
distraction. "You can help me with my Shrimp Fest committee.
You just need a purpose, sugar. Something to do."

It wasn't the worst thing, planning a small town summer
festival. For all I knew, Mama was right: *something to do* would
pull me out of the funk. I dove into spreadsheets and assigned
vendor booths, feeling better with routine but wishing my art
would stop eluding me. Trying to paint felt oversized and
stabby, like eating soup with a very large fork.

By the time May rolled around in all its springtime glory,
I'd shaken off some of the blues. The Saturday of the Shrimp
Fest Committee's monthly meeting, I rolled out of bed *alive*.
The sun was brighter. Colors held deep, vibrant hues. My

fingers remembered how to move, and when I picked up a brush, it didn't bite me. Giddy, I bolted for the shore, desperate to let the salt cover my skin, I stripped down to my suit and dove headfirst into the water. When I surfaced, I had company. A woman on the shore, wading in the shallows. Dark hair, ivory skin. Long white dress trailing the water.

Effa flickered and wavered out.

I swallowed, trapped somewhere between elation and fear. The desire to create won out, my wet swimsuit soaking my clothes as I scrambled up the hill. My hands sang and I slid through the sunroom door. Brown oxide; indigo. Cerulean blue and Naples yellow. With morning's golden hour in her hair, Effa dallied in the water, a bright white foam of sea salt circling her feet.

Finished with the first piece I'd done in ages, I leaned back and surveyed my work. It was so darn good. The liquid drape of morning light maybe the best thing I'd done, *ever*. *A series*, I thought. *Yes*.

With piece one set to dry by the window, I stretched a new canvas across a frame. My palette bled with blended paint, an image already forming. I heard the front door slam, then my father.

"*Dewitt!*"

It nearly cracked my skull.

Daddy appeared in the doorway, sweat soaking the front of his shirt. His face wore the red reserved for political debate and parental fury.

It wasn't an election year.

"Do you have any idea what time it is, young lady?" That vein throbbed in Daddy's neck.

"Eleven?" The sunroom didn't have a clock. But it couldn't be that late—did he think I'd missed Mama's meeting? "The Shrimp Fest committee meets at two."

A strangled sound bled from my father as he stalked across the floor. "You're late," he said, looming over my stool and shoving his arm out. His watch read two fifteen.

Bitter cold swept out from my center. "How—"

I'd lost six hours' worth of time. The floor rolled, and I swayed to my feet. Only the swaying didn't stop—something slick adorned the floor, and I slid to the right, desperate for purchase. Bright color puddled beneath me, splashed the walls, and streaked the furniture. I clutched my stomach and gagged —*what have I done? How did this happen?* "I didn't...I didn't know. I'll clean it."

I spun around, arms flailing, until Daddy's hands held them tight. He ground out his next words, rough and raspy. "I'm not doing this again, you hear me? Losing *her* was enough."

Pain shot through my arms from his fingers. "Stop it," I begged. "You're hurting me." Faint red lines marred the whites of his eyes, a mosaic I could trace as they widened. Daddy's face went slack and let me go, rubbing at the center of his chest. His gaze darted to the painting of Effa and he let out a strangled cry, a broken wail from a man I'd never seen falter.

Losing her was enough.

"You meant Effa." My teeth chattered as I tried to speak. Color drained from Daddy's face, his features wracked with pain. Whoever Effa was to him, he'd loved her. "Daddy...what happened to her?"

He paced, his movements jerky and his hands tugging at his hair. "I warned your mother," he said. "Told her this was dangerous."

"Daddy—"

He spun toward me, face contorted in rage. "*Don't Daddy me,*" he roared. "You are done—*done*—with this God-forsaken hobby. No more painting, Dewitt."

Damp heat pooled behind my eyes. My stomach rolled, and

for a moment, I thought I might vomit. I couldn't let him take my art away—I'd just clawed my way out of the cellar. I blinked away the tears—if he was anything at all, Luther Griffin was a man of business. Steel straightening my spine, I ripped a page from his playbook.

His motto: *Negotiate, don't quit.*

"Pamlico Arts." I whispered. Cleared my throat and tried it louder: "Pamlico Arts." It had opened last month, a display and workshop space for local artists. "I can rent space at Pamlico Arts."

My father laughed, devoid of humor, but I wasn't giving up. "I'll have structure there. A space made for creating. I'll have a schedule, and I won't mess up the house."

"I don't care about the house," he yelled at me. "I'm *protecting* you from—" He stopped, and I leaned forward, waiting.

"From what? I'm good at what I do. I don't understand why you can't see that."

"It's not about talent," he said, liquid grief floating around us. "There are factors you can't control. And by God, if I let this go...If there's one more loss—"

"*I'm* losing!"

The wind dropped from his sails. "More than you know," he said. "Clean up this mess and call your mother."

Then he turned on his heel and walked out.

ELEVEN

DEWITT

The Neuse River starts as a trickle west of Raleigh, pushing wider as she moves across the state. At Minnesott, she's three miles across, mud banks replaced by sand and white caps both powerful and unpredictable—especially around Wilkinson Point. The wide sandbar hooked out from the shore, carving a curved spit of sand two hundred yards into the water. I'd walk the length down to the end, a six-inch bit of sand the only barrier between me and the water. It was foolish, yeah. A little dangerous.

My favorite kind of therapy.

After Daddy left the sunroom, I cleaned up as best as I could. I called Mama too, her *I'm not mad, just disappointed* chasing me toward the point. Since I didn't have a boat—you could access it by water—I'd have to cut across the edge of Lil's yard. I'd just reached the edge where web-like centipede grass gave way to the sandy hill above the river when Lil's voice—a "Dewitt Griffin!"—bit the back of my neck.

The sun beat down on my shoulders and I squinted, spotting Lil near her azaleas along the front porch. The sharp claws of southern manners dragged me toward the house where Lil clipped at dead blooms as I approached her. "Well, now," she said, turning toward me. "I reckon I haven't seen you in months."

My mouth went bitter, a lie on the edge of my tongue. "I've been sick," I said, and wise blue eyes peered my way from underneath her sunhat.

"Nathan said you'd been poorly, but you don't look all that sick. What you do look is madder than a wet hen, and I'm willing to bet I know exactly what's caused it."

Rosie's voice popped into my head. *Lil knows things.* She did, but not in the way Rosie meant. She'd know about Effa and my dad, and if I wanted the truth, all I had to do was ask her.

While I would have jumped at the chance an hour earlier, standing in front of her, I wasn't so sure.

I inhaled. "Did you need something?"

Her lips pursed. "Do you?"

My enamel squeaked as I ground my jaw, and Lil must have heard, because she changed direction. "You can prune that rose. The Virginia." She motioned to a leafy bush with full blooms. "It's an heirloom, though. So don't be too aggressive."

White knuckled, I trimmed the leaves beneath the dogwood-looking blooms. Sweat pooled inside my bra and a sand spur invaded my flip-flop. I dropped my shears and toed it off, a move Lil took as an opening.

"You're wearing *the Luther.*"

"The what?" I quit shaking my foot out, staring up at her, confused.

"The look on your face," she said. "I call it *The Luther.* Worn by the many women he's irritated over space and time."

I bit down on my cheek and scowled a little, determined not to be amused. "Daddy and I are fine," I said, and Lil hummed, thoughtful.

"You've got paint on your arm."

My eyes jolted at the mess of blue. It streaked the outside of my arm, stretching from wrist to elbow. "I was painting," I said. "Earlier."

She watched me. "I see."

Lil Rooney excelled at the literal and figurative. In this case, I assumed she meant both. My perception was right, a sinking feeling coating my gut when she said, "You argued."

"Who did?" I asked, knowing the answer.

"You and your father. Over art."

"I don't want to talk about it." See also: *Yes, I fought with my dad.*

"Alright, she said. I'll drop it. But I know you love to paint. If this is something you plan to keep up, y'all need to talk about his sister."

My painting. The way he flipped out when he saw. "*Effa,*" I breathed, and Lil beamed, like she was proud of me.

"She was my best friend in the world."

When I was little, maybe seven, Daddy brought home a kaleidoscope. It wasn't fancy: two paper tubes, one nestled inside the other, capped with flimsy plastic and colored beads. I loved that thing immediately, and I'd stare into it for what felt like hours at a time. The way the colors coalesced, dropping here, then there as I turned it. I didn't know that, years later, I'd have a mental picture of my father and his sister falling into place like that.

"Effa's dead, isn't she?" *The missing Bible page.*

Lil nodded, a sympathetic dip of the head. "Your father was barely ten. Effa and I were twenty, and mercy, did she dote on that boy. Did a number on your father when he lost her. Grief's gnawed at him ever since."

Pain flared behind my ribcage as we faced each other, steeped in loss. While Effa's death was long ago, I could feel

Lil's grief, still palpable. A hidden current underneath a quiet lake.

I thought about my father, about his anger and frustration with me. "Was she an artist?" I asked, the kaleidoscope shifting.

"Close," Lil said. "A writer."

"The notebooks."

I slapped a hand over my mouth as the world stopped moving, even the wind ceasing to blow. *Please don't notice,* I prayed. *Please, don't let her have heard me.*

Lil's mouth curved.

It didn't work.

"*Finally,*" Lil breathed, a look of wonder and satisfaction on her face. The stillness shattered with a shot, the pop of Nathan's truck tires on gravel. I found my voice beneath the whooshing in my ears.

"Finally what?" I asked, and Lil shifted.

"Nathan's home."

The woman was lying, straight up through her teeth. She didn't have any tells, but I knew Lil hadn't meant the boy in the truck, the one climbing from the cab with his ball cap pulled low and his stupid forearms strained against two bags of groceries.

Lil's *finally* was all about me.

"I haven't seen Effa. Not in...not in real life. Just in pictures, Miss Lil, and my father, he—"

Her hand touched my arm, maternal. "I need a minute. Let me get him settled and we'll talk."

Lil left me in a swirl of worry to meet Nathan at the edge of the drive. She took a Daughtry's box from one of the bags he held. I dug my feet into the ground, the sandy earth not all that comforting.

I never should have opened my mouth.

"You should be ashamed of yourself, Nathan Cartwright."

Lil's teasing earned a rare Nathan grin.

"Took you so long to get home," she carried on, "Dewitt had to help me in the garden."

"I got pecan rolls," he said, dipping his chin at the goodies. "Does that mean I'm excused?"

He sounded normal, like I hadn't just ghosted him for months. But then his gaze slid my way, lips hardening into something wary. I pulled my eyes from his mouth—it was oddly appealing—and begged the ground to swallow me whole.

Lil peered into the box of pastries. "Just how many'd you get?"

"Half a dozen. Only that's not why I'm late." He shot a furtive glance my way, and Lil leaned in, suspicious.

"For all I care, you could have been caught up in a parade of possums and potatoes." She looked at his ears, the flush growing deeper. "Nathan, what's going on?"

"I saw Mr. Luther. On my way home. He, uh, kind of offered me a job?"

Lil's eyes narrowed. "Kind of."

I blurted out a stupid, "*What?*"

If my father offered him a job, that meant he'd be at my house. *Daily.*

Nathan's response was knife-sharp. "That so hard to believe?"

"It's not that." It was everything else, where my mental health had been; where it seemed to be heading...

Dried paint itched on my skin, and I floundered.

"Dewitt's had a rough day, son."

The tension in my arms evaporated and I wished Lil a silent *thanks.* "You've had a rough couple months," Nathan said, and I fought the flutter in my soul.

Don't look at him.

"Tell me about this *kind of* job, son," Lil said, and when I looked up, Nathan's eyes were on me, hesitant.

"I should put the groceries away," he said.

"The job, Nathan," Lil said. "Food can wait."

A short burst of air pushing from his lungs. "I left Daughtry's, and I promise, I was gonna be home on time. But I got up to that field off 306—" he glanced at me—"the ryegrass Mr. Luther grows for bailing. He was out there with his tractor, trying to mow. Only the hood was up, and he was sweating up a storm leaning over the engine." Nathan stopped, took a breath, and seemed to make up his mind before continuing. "He looked like he was having trouble, so I figured I'd be neighborly and stop."

Dang it. That tractor always gave Daddy fits. And now I had, too, probably right before he went out there. My face flushed hot with guilt.

"Anyway," Nathan said, "I fixed it. Just needed to adjust the choke. He tried to pay me twenty bucks but I wouldn't take it. And that's when he offered me the job."

Lil crossed her arms. "Doing what?"

"Mechanic stuff," he said. "General maintenance."

"But you do landscaping with Gil," I said. "And then...you know. The boat building."

The flint melted in Nathan's eyes, and his lips quirked. "You worried about my time management?"

"No." Nathan working for my dad meant me, up close and personal. *That's* what I was worried about.

Lil had more questions. "So instead of twenty bucks, you took the job?"

"Yes, ma'am." Nathan said, and they squared off for a minute.

Surprisingly, Lil broke first.

"Alright, then. Dewitt, go fetch Rosie, please. Nathan, you

call Gil. I'll fix a mess of drumsticks and y'all can celebrate with a bonfire."

Celebrating was the last thing on my mind. "I need to go," I said, and I'm pretty sure Lil hid the truth all over it.

"Nathan," she said, eyes on me, "take the groceries into the house, please. Right now."

Nathan's eyes bounced back and forth between us. "Mama Lil—"

"Ice cream's gonna melt."

He nodded in assent, climbed the steps with the bags, and let the screen door slam behind him. Lil ambled back to me.

"You've seen Effa," she said, and a giant fist wrapped itself around my lungs.

"I don't—"

"You don't have to tell me now. But when you are ready to talk, there's something I want you to know ahead of time. You have a *gift*. You are not wrong, or weird, or, for heaven's sake, *crazy*." Lil's hand reached out and held my cheek. "I'll be here, Dewitt, when you need me. Family secrets always out."

TWELVE
NATHAN

June

Mr. Luther's job offer just about knocked me flat. He had to ask me twice, standing on the side of the road while tall grass tickled my shins and I stared at him. "You want me to what?"

"Work for me." He'd smiled. "High past time I had an extra set of hands."

"All I did was fix the choke."

"And all I did was cuss at the thing for half an hour, Mr. Cartwright. Word around town says you're handy. I've seen the boats you build. I got a business to run on top of a hundred-year-old house and half as many acres. Now, do you want the job or not?"

I wanted it, especially as an East Acres kid. My big question was Dewitt—we went from talking every day and flirting in the fall to hardly speaking come winter, and I didn't have the slightest clue why. Rosie said she wasn't feeling well, but I wasn't so sure that was true. The last thing I wanted was to push Dewitt's boundaries, especially if she was done with me.

Luther, though, was convincing. Well, it was mostly the pay. And I figured the grounds were big enough—if Dewitt didn't want me around, she'd figure out how to avoid me.

I really hoped she didn't.

Day one on the job had me out in the boathouse digging through gallons of paint. The upstairs hall needed a fresh coat, and Luther was as frugal as he was wealthy. He had about twelve cans on hand—I'd opened three and was prepping a fourth one when two bare, sandy feet caught my eye.

The nails were painted, a delicate chain wrapped her ankle down to one toe. My hand slipped on my heart; the dang church key slid out, and it skittered across the floor making seven kinds of racket.

Dewitt bent to pick it up. Brow raised, she peered down at me. "Need some help with that?"

As far as grins go, the one I gave her dang near split my face. "You offering?"

She cocked a hip, and the deep red fabric of her skirt clung to her thighs and swished around her ankles. "Thought I made that clear."

Dewitt looked good. *Happy.* The winter doldrums had sloughed right off. Her sleeveless top flowed as she moved, the loose hem brushing her ribs and exposing an inch of wonder. I stood, then fought a head rush unrelated to the change in altitude.

"You can help," I said, more casual than I felt it. Her hair shone like fireworks backlit by the sun. "You brought an easel, though." I'd just noticed it leaning up against the boathouse wall, a supply caddy on the floor next to it.

Her soft smile immediately hardened. "You got a problem with that?"

I backed up an inch, hands raised. "No," I said. "Just, if you want to paint, you should do that. Don't *not* paint on my account."

Her shoulders relaxed and she smirked at me. "That's a double negative, sir."

"You sure it's not a double truth?" Those fizzy bubbles in my chest went wild.

"Might could be a dare," she said.

The teasing heat in her voice was so heady my voice grated when I answered her. "Stay," I said. "I'd love your company."

And for at least a dozen days, she did.

Dewitt appeared like sunshine every morning, rainbow paint colors in her wake. If I worked out on the grounds, I made excuses to see her, claiming I was looking for a tool. She'd lean back from her work, ask me what I thought, and then smile real big when I told her I liked it.

And then one day, she quit showing up.

If I hadn't been so young and stupid, I probably would have just asked. But I was both, so I'd stare at her across the counter at Daughtry's or watch the bonfire throw shadows across her face. And then I'd wonder where she'd gone, or if maybe I'd misread things.

Mostly, I sat and wondered if she missed me like I missed her.

The answer came one humid July morning when Mr. Luther ambled down to the boathouse. "Nathan." He leaned against the frame of the door, voice raised above the hum of the sander I was using. I cut off the machine.

"Morning." I propped my goggles on my head. "Almost done," I said, running my thumb over a rough spot on the kitchen door I was treating, touching it up after a century of peeling paint.

Luther gave a satisfied grunt. "Hiring you was an excellent decision. Looks better than it has in years."

Face flushed with embarrassment, I gave Luther a quick nod of thanks. I wasn't used to praise, especially not from a man like Luther Griffin. But he waved off what I said and ambled closer, all loose-limbs and confidence. "Can you refinish wood floors, too?"

"Yes, sir," I said.

"We had an...*incident*...back in May. Dewitt spilled some paint; used turpentine to remove it. Stripped the varnish straight off. Deebie's been after me to get it fixed, and I wondered if you could do it."

An incident back in May. That was when I got the job, about when Dewitt hauled the easel outside and set up shop before she quit coming. "Does Dewitt paint in the sunroom, sir?"

"Not anymore," Luther said, mouth pinched and a vein pulsing in his forehead. He tossed me the keys to his truck, the big dually that ran on diesel. "Hillman's Hardware has my order up."

———

DEEBIE CAUGHT me as I was climbing into the truck.

"You're headed into Oriental, right?" she asked, looking a little frazzled. I couldn't fault her—Shrimp Fest was less than a month away.

"I am," I told her. "Going to Hillman's to pick up supplies. Need me to grab something while I'm there?"

"I need you to drop something off for me, actually." Her manicured hand held out an envelope, letter-sized and sealed. I caught her scrawl across the front as I took it. *Dewitt Griffin-July rent.*

"I'm up to my eyeballs in Shrimp Fest and I know I could drop it in the mail, but Pamlico Arts is right there. Do you mind taking it over?"

"No problem," I said, happy to do it.

Dewitt had moved to Pamlico Arts.

Distracted by this new development, I made the mistake of calling Gil. He had the day off from work at his parents' shop, and in my addled state, I figured extra hands would be helpful —a decision I was starting to regret.

"Even Deebie thinks y'all are fated," Gil said as I pulled onto 306. He'd seen the envelope on the dash, and like an idiot, I told him.

"Dewitt and I are not *fated*." We weren't fated. *Right?*

"You're magnets." Gil's hands flew in demonstration around the cab. "Identical poles. You circle around, getting closer and closer until *bam—*" he shot his hands out wide. "You bounce off each other, back to your respective corners."

I took my turn a little faster than normal. "You speak in metaphors now?"

"I speak the truth, brother."

I talked to Gil about most things. But, "My business with Dewitt is just that—my business."

"And you're the smartest, most mechanically inclined *idiot* I know. She's a great girl, man. You're fumbling."

I sped over a bump, bouncing Gil's head against the ceiling. "You were saying?"

Gil glared at me. "Never mind."

Guilt pricked at me a little as I drove into downtown. Gil did have a point. My relationship with Dewitt was a perpetually moving target. Were we friends or something more? There'd been moments with her—like the work visits—where I felt things between us shift. Holding eye contact a beat too long; watching her cheeks pink up if we were down at the shore and I helped her from the water. Things were good, and I thought we were moving towards more-than-friendly territory until she quit coming down while I worked.

Pamlico Arts and Hillman's Hardware faced each other on Main Street, Hillman's red brick against the Arts Center's bright blue. I backed into Hillman's loading dock and pulled the purchase order from the center console. Gil got out and slammed his door.

"Hillman knows I'm coming. Hopefully, this won't take long." Gil didn't respond—he stood at the back of the truck, staring across the street at the Arts Building.

"Actually..." He lifted his chin toward a shiny black Honda. "That right there is Rosie's car."

I grimaced. I had the rent check, so I'd be going over there, anyway. But if Rosie was there, Dewitt was probably inside, painting.

A funny feeling settled in my gut.

"You good?" Gil asked, and I nodded. Old Man Hillman had the order up front. Twenty minutes was all it took to fill the flatbed full of stain and my stomach full of windmills.

Cross the street. Get Gil. Drive back. Unload the work stuff.
This is not a big deal.

It sure felt like one, oddly, like seeing Dewitt here was... intimate. Each step across the street took more effort than I had and less time than I needed for prep work. Gil's profile shone through the plate-glass window as he leaned across the front desk. Rosie was tucked into his side, and—*shoot, I forgot* —Mama Lil was behind the desk. Today was her volunteer shift at the Arts Center.

I was entering a perfect storm.

Cowbells knocked the door glass, paint and sawdust filling my nose. "There's my boy," Lil said, the standard twinkle in her eye mischievous.

"Hey, Nathan," Rosie said, and Gil smirked.

"Might wanna check out what's going on back there."

Rosie smacked him in the arm so I didn't have to, but my gaze moved involuntarily to the right. Dewitt sat at the far end of the room in front of an easel, hair piled like usual on her head. A blue halter tied at her neck, the open back exposing muscle and skin. I scraped my palms against my jeans and smacked myself mentally.

Nathan. Get a grip.

"Son, have you eaten?" Lil's voice rolled through a fog.

"That's an excellent idea," Rosie said, her smile plastic. "Gil, you hungry?"

"Not really—" She punched him. "*Oof.*"

Gil rubbed at his biceps. "Now that you mention it, yeah."

"I already ate," I said, even though I hadn't. "Gotta get back to work."

"Let's hit Deli Dock," Gil said, the smarmy look on his face punchable. Because ladies were present, I declined. But I gave him an especially dark look: *I know where you live, Bozo.*

"Totally worth it," he mouthed.

Rosie grabbed her purse from behind the counter. "Dewitt, you want anything?"

She didn't even look up, just gave a half-hearted "Eh." Lil stood and pushed in her chair.

"Your usual? Coastal Club on rye?"

I grabbed her wrist, a little frantic. "You're going, too?"

"It's my lunch break." She shrugged. "Normally, I'd close, but Dewitt's in the zone and you can man the front desk for me."

All three of them looked exceptionally springy as they swept through the front door.

Perfect. Trapped in the Arts Building with Dewitt. Who was now straddling her stool, the hem of her skirt hiked to mid-thigh like Tori Amos straddling the bench of a piano. Throat suddenly dry, I grabbed Lil's water bottle and sucked down roughly half.

Desperate for a distraction, I looked *elsewhere* around the room. It wore an industrial vibe thanks to the open ceiling's exposed ductwork and caged light fixtures looped around rebar. The concrete floors were smooth, and local artists adorned the walls with brightly colored murals. Dewitt's signature brushstrokes spelled out the front of Sutton Seafood; in the window, she'd put a glimmer of Gil's auburn hair.

Still itchy, I pushed myself toward the back. Rows of drafting tables filled the room, flanked by a line of easels, and a large workbench sat against the back wall. My boots scraped the floor, one foot in front of the other, until I stood in front of cubbies filled with wood. My parents took a lot of things—my childhood, my stuff. But they hadn't taken this—my love for woodworking. I selected a block of birch and moved a knife against the surface, cutting off the rest of the world.

"*Ohmygosh.*"

"What the—"

I recoiled, drenched from head to toe. Dewitt stood at the nearby sink, water dripping from her skirt, hair stuck to her cheeks, her thin halter glued to curves I really shouldn't have been watching. I stood up and averted my eyes. Words rushed from Dewitt like rainwater while I busied myself with a towel. "I'm so sorry. It's not sealed. Did I wreck the wood? I was rinsing out my brush. I forgot. I always forget. I forgot about the faucet. They need to fix it because it sprays and clearly it goes everywhere. I bet I could fix it, honestly. Maybe there's a wrench around somewhere. I mean...gosh. I'm so sorry. So, so sorry. Are you okay? I'm sorry. Let me help."

Dewitt sputtered in fast forward like a sped up VHS tape. Loose brushes clattered into the sink, her jerky movements the culprit. "There's got to be a towel or a rag or..." She spotted the one in my hands. "Let me dry that!"

Dewitt lunged at me, pushing me backwards, the carving blade still in my hand. I dropped the knife just in time, falling into the chair like a rag doll.

"I'm screwing everything up," Dewitt cried. "I made you drop the knife. I ruined your carving—"

"Dewey." I held her wrist. "You didn't ruin anything, okay? I had the knife in my hand and I didn't want to cut you. I didn't want you to get hurt."

Deflating, Dewitt dropped to her knees. We were at eye level now, her hand on my thigh and gaze fixed on my mouth. Sparks fired where our skin touched, and I loosened my grip on her wrist. She twined her fingers with mine; I prayed she couldn't feel the tremble. Water droplets licked at her skin.

I looked away. *Moses.* "You, uh, hungry?" I coughed. "Wanna go grab lunch?"

Dewitt shook her head in my peripheral vision and then her breath was on my cheek. "So beautiful," she said, and my eyes dropped to the carving—*that's what she's talking about, right?* "I've, uh, barely started it," I said. "But that's kind of you. Thanks."

Dewitt seated herself in my lap. She slid her arms around my neck and whispered, "You're welcome," our lips barely a breath apart. Something twisted in my gut—an awareness. A warning.

Dewitt wasn't acting like herself.

I put distance between us. Rasped out, "You okay?" Dewitt pushed out of my lap, foot knocking the carving across the floor and hands flush against her face, neck heating. Her whole body her demeanor—had changed.

"Oh my gosh," she said, a little watery. "I'm so embarrassed. Oh, my gosh. I soaked you and your stuff! Then I knocked your carving on the floor and..." She twisted her hands, and while I wasn't completely sure, it seemed clear she regretted the lap-sitting.

I had *really* mixed feelings about that.

"Dewey." I stood and wiped her tears with my thumbs. I wasn't sure about it at all; we were friends. We flirted. Touching her like this, offering comfort, was a boundary we hadn't crossed. But I could feel it in my soul, the ache of her embarrassment. I cared about her too much to let that stand. "That carving doesn't matter. *People* matter to me. People like Rosie and Lil, and that idiot, Gil Sutton. And you—you matter to me."

She sniffed. "You called me Dewey. No one's ever called me that before."

"Sorry." I flushed.

"I like it." Her smooth arms circled my waist. Her touch was different here, less hungry. More like she was desperate for relief. She rested her cheek against my chest, and I couldn't help but think how perfectly we fit together.

Two magnets, finally aligned.

THIRTEEN
DEWITT

August 2002

Life in rural North Carolina involves a certain level of
disrepair. Houses get old, the people who live in them die, and
if Aunt Betsy's kin live up in Raleigh, sometimes the property is
left to rot. Buildings often cost more to tear down than they're
worth, and growing up, I figured the tobacco barn would be the
same. But Minnesott Beach had been vying for an event space.
That long ago meeting between Rosie's dad, Mr. Matthew, and
my father set the stage for Griffin Barn (in fancy font with capi-
talization) to be renovated and reborn.

"This is beautiful," I murmured, eyes trailing the new rafter
beams. Gone were the gaping holes and rotten floors, replaced
by smooth, dark wood and antique glass set in wrought-iron
fixtures. Two full bars capped each end, the outer area dotted
with velvet-covered lounge chairs. Tables and bench seating
hugged the walls, and a dance floor filled the center. I *oohed*

while Rosie stood beside me, unimpressed and studying her nails.

"I liked the original better. Less magnolia, more *Southern Decay*." She looked up at me and winked, smoothing the skirt of her pink A-line dress. She copied her mother's twang, teasing: "Though there's nothing wrong with a little *Rustic Farmhouse Chic*."

"*Rosie*," I said, laughing. "Your parents did an amazing job."

She beamed. "Mama's dreamed about rebuilding this space for years. I just miss the old barn. It was our space, even if it was creepy."

I gave her a *look*. I could still see the spot where Effa first appeared, now adorned with a magnolia arch for photos. *Seventeen's a big deal*, Mama said. *And the new Barn's the perfect place for your party.*

Rosie leaned into my side, perceptive. "I'm sorry they pushed this on you."

"It's fine," I said, shoulders lifting. "What I get for not doing cotillion, I guess. Daddy wanted the first event to mean something."

"Doesn't matter. You're old enough to decide what kind of party you're having, or if you even want one at all."

"I know." I was irritated with my parents. But I couldn't say I was mad. The more I gazed around the Barn, the more my irritation faded. "The barn's perfect," I said, taking Rosie's hand and squeezing. "The light fixtures along the roof beams alone..."

"Stop mooning over light fixtures, you weirdo." She nudged me. "And take a look at *that*."

Rosie motioned at the broad, double door where my father stood, welcoming guests as they arrived.

"Are you talking about Brent?" He'd just arrived and I was

thoroughly confused. Brent had mellowed over time and made up for his bullying ways after he started dating Katie Cleghorn. That girl deserved a medal. Or a new car. But Rosie was still sweet on Gil, so pointing Brent out was kind of ridiculous.

"Not Brent," she said and cupped my cheeks, turning my face to the lounge chairs by the doorway.

Nathan Cartwright...and Gil.

"They could model," she said. "For, like, *Abernathy.*"

"I don't need them half-dressed in black and white on my wall." She was right, though, I had to admit: the broad shoulders, cut jaws, and intentional bedhead were really working for them. They'd even rolled up the sleeves on their shirts.

"Act normal." Rosie nudged me. "Or at least try to. They're coming over here."

I could handle him from across the room, but hot shame crept up my neck as he got closer, an unreadable expression on his face. The last time I saw him, I'd climbed into his lap. In the middle of a surge, I'd hyper-focused on the pine scent of his skin, the feel of his breath on my cheek, and the strength of his legs beneath me. The frantic urge I reserved for hours of painting transferring (horrifically) onto him.

"Water," I croaked, and booked it, dodging well-wishers as I slalomed toward the bar. My stomach lurched at how forward I'd been. I almost painted his body right there, a human canvas, deep reds and dark blues lining the contours of his arms. I fell apart much later, that night, in my room. I poured my shame into five twisted self-portraits, each one of them finished in tears.

Fingers lassoed my wrist as I stood there, jerking me out of my thoughts. "Are you *kidding me?*" Rosie asked.

I drained the water bottle in one gulp, dragging my forearm across my mouth before speaking. "No. I'm overwhelmed."

The freckles on her nose folded. "All you had to do was let me know."

"Well, I'm saying something now."

She looked like she wanted to volley back, but her hackles stood down and she softened. "If you need space," Rosie said, "I got you. Next time, tell me before you hightail it. Not after."

I hugged her. "I owe you. Thanks."

"Anytime." She shooed me on my way, and I'd nearly made it to the courtyard when Brent's firm hand took mine. He pulled me into a side hug, a mischievous little smirk on his face.

"Still got that mean right hook?"

Eyebrows pushed up in jest, I volleyed. "Nonconsensual hugging's a good way to find out."

Brent laughed, head tipped back and hearty. I caught a hint of smokiness—bourbon?—on his breath. "Sorry," he said. "You're right. Let me try that again, Miss Griffin. May I have this dance with the birthday girl?"

I studied him. The last thing I needed was a sloppy romp across the floor. "Have you been drinking?" I asked, and his cheeks flushed before he held his thumb and forefinger together.

"Did a little pre-gaming," he admitted. "Just a tiny bit."

I rolled my eyes. *What a goober.* "I'll dance with you. Keep your hands where I can see them, please."

"You have my word," he said, extending his right hand. "Katie will kill me if I don't."

I laughed as he swept me out on the floor, his confident stride guiding us in triplet. "You're good at this," I said.

"I joined Cotillion to meet girls. But Katie barged into my life, and all I've done is learn to waltz and use table manners."

"So, life skills."

"Sounds like you've been talking to my mom."

"Excuse me." Nathan's voice alerted right in my ear. I

jumped, begging the floor to split apart and drop me into oblivion.

"We're dancing," I said, tone shaky. "What do you—" I inhaled. "What?"

Brent's smile dimmed as he looked between us. "Cartwright. Good to see you, man."

"Mind if I cut in?" Nathan leaned into Brent's ear and whispered something, and I watched Brent's face light up.

"Sweet," he said, started toward the door without his cotillion manners. But then he turned and skidded to a stop. "Happy Birthday," he called. "I hope it's a great one. And thank you." He bowed. "For the dance."

"What did you tell him?"

Nathan's sandy brown hair fell over his eyes. "I mentioned the keg."

"There's no keg. My parents are hosting."

"Give him thirty seconds and he'll figure it out."

"You are terrible," I said. It didn't mean much coming from me, considering I'd been the one to throw myself at him.

I took a deep breath. "Nathan—"

"Will you take a walk with me? Please?"

Nathan looked so earnest, like I was all that mattered in the world. I gave a small, sharp nod, and Nathan's hand found the small of my back in a gentle, innocent touch. He guided me out through the Barn's back doors, into the light of the patio. He held up one hand, forefinger extended, and grabbed a small wrapped parcel from the table to our left.

"A present?"

His shoulders hitched. "It's your birthday, isn't it?"

"You didn't have to get me anything," I said, scanning his face for signs of awkwardness.

The only thing I saw was hope.

I pulled the tape from the seams and removed the paper,

then lifted the small lid on the box. A carving stared back at me, blond wood. A sailboat.

It was his project from the other night.

"There's a mast," he said, a little rapidly. "It's removable. And a sail. I tucked them underneath..." Nathan reached forward to pull them out, accidentally brushing my hand in the process. Warmth spread up my arm to my ribs and settled there, nestling against my ribs.

"This is the boat."

"I finished it."

"Nathan. Oh, my gosh."

The blush deepened on his cheeks, a deep rose in the soft half-light. He took the boat from my hands and turned it. "I put something on the aft."

There were letters. Six of them, engraved. I traced the marks with my thumb. "*Dewitt.*"

"She needed a name, obviously."

I stood there speechless, my heart turning inside out. One heartbeat, then two, then three, and Nathan shifted.

"I mean, all boats have names. It's not a *real* boat, I know, but I thought...crap. This is stupid. I should have just left it blank or something because now I—"

"Nathan. Stop."

Lips parted, he watched me, more wary hope in his eyes. "It's perfect," I said, and his face melted into a smile, slowly tugging at the corner of his lips.

"You really like it?"

I nodded. "I really do."

His soft laugh pierced the dark, and his calloused fingers caressed my cheekbone. This time, my whole body flushed hot. I swayed forward into his space, the pull of him immediate. A magnet dragging me in.

"Dewey," he whispered. I let my eyes flutter closed. Felt the ground beneath my feet; breathed the charged and salty air in the tiny space between us. Felt him shift forward by an inch.

Pulse thrumming, I pushed up on my toes. Wrapped my arms around his neck and leaned in, my stomach lurching as the whole of me took flight.

But not into Nathan, not into his embrace or the soft press of his mouth. I fell into the air, weightless, without an anchor, like I'd slipped straight from his arms. Sharp spikes of grass bit my knees and my fingers and the sharp tang of copper filled my mouth. The stench of fertilizer stung my nose, the heavy scent of it precursor to a dry heave.

My hands dug into the soft, loamy earth.

I'm hallucinating.

This is a trip.

None of this, I knew, was real, and when I forced open my eyes, I wasn't surprised to see the barn gone. "Get it together," I told myself.

I stood, a little wobbly, took in the field in front of me and the tall corn. A highway ran to my left. The squeal of tires rent the dark; a blaze of headlights caught my eyes and the crash of metal and glass rent through me. The car rolled and came to rest on its roof. Tires spinning in the air; steam rising from the mangled engine.

The nausea won when I saw her in the wreckage.

Effa Griffin, pale with lifeless eyes.

FOURTEEN

DEWITT

Voices whispered in the hallway. I pulled the sheet around my head.

".... five days..."

"I'm aware..."

The words faded out. Or maybe I did.

"We've tried everything," Daddy said.

Mama challenged him. "Luther, we haven't tried this."

Whatever *this* was, I didn't want it. All I wanted was oblivion.

The door to my bedroom opened, Rosie's footsteps giving her away. Two hands yanked me down the bed until I flopped, dead weight, onto the hardwood. "You're like my neighbor's dog," she said, "but more difficult. At least I can motivate him with food."

I felt her crouch beside me. "Wake up, Dewitt."

I'd been trying. Or maybe I hadn't at all. I didn't remember much—just flashes of paint and aching limbs and the sting of raw skin under turpentine. The act of stumbling into my bed.

"Go away, Rosie." I buried my face in my knees.

"Candy first." She shoved a Fireball in my mouth. "You look scrawny," she said, cursing, apparently, at my appearance. "Dewitt, you need to eat."

"Not hungry." Instinctively, my arms folded around my waist. I couldn't remember the last time I ate, not surprising given the ridges where my ribs were.

"I don't care," Rosie said. "I stopped at Daughtry's. You can eat when I get you to the car."

My head spun at the thought of exertion. "Not going anywhere."

Rosie moved across the room. She dug through my drawers, talking at me more than to me. "You wouldn't answer my calls. Your parents had to let me in—I guess five days in bed is their limit. And honestly, you've been creeping everybody out. I'm here to extract you from this room," she said, pulling my blue two-piece from my wardrobe.

My legs dropped to the floor. "I saw Effa."

A drawer closed. "That's happened before."

"Not this," I said, gaze drifting to my closet. A walk-in, technically. Rosie followed my line of sight, and her hands stilled on the knobs as she held the French doors open.

"Holy mackerel. *Dewitt.*"

"There was an accident." I didn't sound like myself. More like a robot, I guess, if robots were hallucinating artists.

Rosie's strangled laugh landed between horror and amazement. "You painted a car crash on the back closet wall. *There's a dead woman in it, Dewitt.*"

This trip—the accident—was so different from the ones I'd had before. The others, I came out aware, if not a little unsteady, fully cognizant of what had occurred. This time, though, I'd startled to consciousness to find the clothes in my closet scattered across the floor. I'd gasped at the mural along the back wall, the wrecked car and the broken glass in Effa's hair, glittering like starlight. Whimpered at the crimson flower blooming on her chest.

"*Moses*." Rosie shut the closet doors. "Deebie said—I thought—*we* thought—"

"Nice to know you were thinking."

Rosie padded across the room and slipped down beside me. "It's beautiful, don't get me wrong—"

I stopped her. "I'm not *crazy*."

Lil promised. She said.

"Give me a little credit, Dewitt." Rosie stood, her hands yanking me to my feet and out of the dress I'd worn since Friday. "Go put on your swimsuit. I'm getting you out of here."

STEERING wheel in one hand and a pecan roll in the other, Rosie pulled onto 306. "Eat." She shoved the thing in my face and my stomach lurched in answer.

I leaned against the window. "No, thanks."

Tires squealed and my seatbelt tightened a split second before we lurched to a stop. We sat motionless on the road while Rosie's stare rained hellfire. "Take a bite of that thing. *Or else*."

I nibbled. Vanilla sugar surged through my veins. One bite became two, then three, then more, until the only sign I'd gorged was the glaze shards stuck to my fingers.

Rosie's face split in a vindicated grin.

"All I did was eat," I told her, the words sharp and foreign-sounding to my ears.

"You're also *dressed* and *in my car*."

I wiped my hands over the skirt of my maxi dress, the one Rosie pulled on me before we left. "This isn't voluntary," I said.

She scoffed. "Your parents gave permission. They think I'm a miracle worker now."

"Congratulations. Doesn't mean I want to go." Not to Alligator Gut, anyway. An oddly named creek winding its way through the forest, its biggest draw an old trestle above a swimming hole.

"I'm not jumping."

Rosie shrugged. "You can watch me and the boys."

"You did *not*." I wheezed. Dread surfaced from the deep, a sea serpent. A kraken. "I'm revoking your best friend card!"

Rosie switched on the radio, unbothered. "Best friend cards are irrevocable. And Nathan—"

She took a pause, and I waited until I couldn't take it. "Rosie. Nathan what?"

Her whole body sighed, weary. "Nathan's been a total mess since Friday night. He thinks the whole thing was his fault."

"That's...that's stupid." I said it, but the words weren't quite right. I was the stupid one this time, the thought of hurting him searing my chest. "It wasn't his fault," I said. "It wasn't."

"Well, you kept all three of us in the dark."

It wrapped around me, an accusation I didn't expect. "I told you, Ro. I saw Effa—"

"You told *me*, and not until *today*. Not until I stormed into your room and retrieved you. All Nathan knows is he gave you a gift. You *oohed* and *ahhed*, and then he *thought* y'all were about to kiss, but then you freaked out and ran and—"

"Ran?" I didn't remember.

"Verb. Past tense. Means to move, with a quickness."

"I *know* what the word means, thanks."

A stabbing ache jabbed my eyelids. "I don't remember running, Ro. I remember waking up in my room, covered in paint and with a freaking mural in my closet." I let my head fall against the seat back, weary. "I don't think you're being fair."

Without warning, Rosie swung a hard left onto a gravel road. Dust kicked up in our wake, and we jostled in our seats as the tires bumped along the surface. "This is about being honest. This is not about being fair. Trust is a hard thing to earn. Nathan's life before Lil—he put up with Mike and Sue's abuse for years and then the losers just...up and left him." She tapped a beat on the wheel, thinking. "If Nathan loves you, that's a major feat."

If Nathan loves you? "What are you saying right now?"

"That Nathan cares about you, dummy. I'm talking head-over-heels. And I know you don't mean it, honest, but the way you've been acting lately...it looks like you're leading him on."

The ache slid to my ribs. "I haven't."

"You nearly gave a lap dance to the boy."

My insides swooped so hard I thought we were falling. "He *told you?*"

"I had to hear it from Gil."

Thick and heavy, a lump lodged in my throat. "I can't believe he told Gil."

"Nathan doesn't kiss and tell. Gil's persuasive."

"I don't care!" I yelled. "It was none of Gil's business!"

She tapped the brake. "So it happened?"

"No, it—not like that."

Ro's hands flexed the wheel. "Then what was it like, Dewitt Griffin?"

The answer burst out of me, rough and harsh and raw. "It was like wanting to die. You don't have a *clue* what it's like, the way my brain takes off, the way everything moves so fast and I feel like, like I can conquer literally anything. Like seducing Nathan or...painting a dead girl on my closet wall. And then when I wake up and it's all over, I'm freaking pressed under this...wall of *shame*. I'm not human. I can't breathe. I'm so freaking tired, Ro, but I can't sleep because my body's bruised and hurting. All I want to do is drift away into some dark oblivion and I *hate it*. I hate it so freaking much. Because I'm alone, and there's not a single thing any one of you can do to fix it. I'm not normal, and I'm completely alone."

The car went deathly silent, tension thick as Rosie parked next to Nathan's truck. "If you think—I can't—" She took a deep breath, jaw flexing. "I need to get out of this car."

"Rosie..."

The door slammed. She took two steps, then stopped. I heard her curse through the glass, watched her spin around fast and throw the door back open, wild hair in her wilder eyes. "I'm sorry you hurt and you're worried. I'm sorry you feel alone. But you've got to meet us halfway. If you think no one can help, then none of this," she waved a hand between us, "none of *us*, matters." Stone-faced, she grabbed her bag out of the back.

"Rosie," I said again, throat closing.

"I can't. Not right now."

She shut the door in my face and I watched her walk away, the silent tears on my cheeks hot and sticky.

What am I going to do?

FIFTEEN

DEWITT

I didn't get out of the car.

Eyes shut, I leaned my head back and let the heat push into my skin. It wasn't safe, I knew, but getting out of the car was pointless. Rosie was ticked off, and I'd ruined things with Nathan. I hadn't even wanted to come.

I liked it in the car. It was quiet. Like a mausoleum. A tomb.

I'll die in here if I wait long enough, I thought, and in an instant, I jolted upward, scrabbling for the door.

The lever gave under my pressure and I gulped oxygen like I'd only just learned how to breathe. Wobbly-legged and short of breath, I got out of the car and leaned against it. "You're not thinking straight," I said out loud, each inhale a reminder.

You're alive.

You're alive.

You're alive.

It knocked me sideways, how welcome a thought that was. How for a split second I craved the relief of letting go, of falling into nothing.

It was just a thought.

Trembling, I made my way across the grass toward the hill. I took the long way down through the pines—I wasn't ready to see my friends, and not just because Rosie and I had fought or I'd have to see Nathan. What if they saw it on my face? That I'd wanted to die, that I'd stayed up there, alone, in a car with sealed windows and doors. For a split second, I wanted to die. For a split second, I could have. But also—

They didn't come to check on me.

It hit me so hard I stumbled, the sun blinding as I emerged from the trees. I'd been in that car a while, and not a single one of them climbed back up the hill. Logically, I knew they might have gone for a swim. But a low current buzzed through my veins, and when I saw them ten yards upstream, five feet deep in conversation, not a single drop of water on their skin, the buzz burned high and bright, and I clenched my fists in my hands and stalked through the mud to the trestle until the structure loomed over my head.

I'd beaten the darkness. I'd beaten the darkness *myself*. I didn't need anyone, and I'd be fine on my own, I'd be more than fine, I knew. The ladder's rust flaked beneath my fingers and hand over hand, I climbed to the top. The trestle only rose ten feet. But I owned the world when I reached the top, nothing but trees and sky, iron and wood, sunlight and wind and wonder. I lay back on the ties, wood at my shoulders, sun warm and lovely on my face.

Water splashed beneath me. I rolled on my stomach. A fish? But something caught my eye—I pressed my face against the wood, one eye closed, the other shielded against the glare, and peered down at a ragged daisy.

Somehow, beyond reason, a flower grew in a rotten joint.

I *needed* to see it. Just to paint it, not to take. It shouldn't have been too hard to do; after all, I was pretty acrobatic. All I needed was something to—

My dress caught the breeze. *I'm brilliant.* I pulled it over my head. In just my swimsuit now, I knotted the hem around the closest tie and the straps around another. A solid four feet of fabric hung loose in the center—a dress hammock. A swing.

Blood roared through my veins as I scooted backward on my stomach, the wood's edge biting the flesh of my hips. My legs cycled the air and I propped my arms against the ties like I was leaning against a pool deck.

One — I hooked my left arm through the fabric.

Two — I let go with my right.

Three—a shirtless Nathan peered over the side, face inches from mine, mouth contorted

I reared back. "Get away."

"Don't move." He grabbed me. "I'm going to pull you up."

"Stop it!" My shoulder socket ached, and he still had my arm, and he was so dang hot with his muscles all ripped and his board shorts hung low, my irritation skyrocketed. *"I am not a damsel in distress!"*

He held tighter. "You're a damn *something*, alright." Our scowls met over the edge and time stood still until a violent *rip* cracked the air and gravity gripped me by the ankle, pulling Nathan with me as we fell.

Our bodies smacked the creek surface in a tangle of contorted limbs. But the force of our fall must have knocked something loose, because as we plunged into the murky green, I wasn't angry. Instead, I fought a ridiculous urge to laugh. With my arms looped around Nathan's shoulders and my legs locked around his waist, I giggled as we went down. We touched the bottom with a soft sort of *ploof, and* I relished the tightness in my lungs, savored the press of Nathan's skin, treasured the sweet caress of the water. I mumbled into his neck, my last air escaping. *We can stay here in the water, if we want.*

He didn't answer, at least not with words. Nathan's fingers found my hair and pulled my head back in a gentle but assertive tug. We floated face to face in the half-dark, bits of lightning, the flecks of green in his eyes. Bright pinpricks of olive green that I wanted to touch, tug out, and spread across a canvas.

I kissed him instead.

The soft press of our lips sent me reeling, but only for a moment or two. Then I went quiet, like the creek, no more racing thoughts, no grand ideas rushing through me. Just Nathan and Dewitt; water and silence. Wonder, potential, and sparks.

Until his shoulders went stiff beneath me and he jerked back and broke the kiss. He wouldn't look at me at all, his gaze averted to the creek floor, then we were rushing up, fast, toward the surface, my sinking feeling against the growing light.

"Are you out of your *mind,* Dewitt Griffin?" The silence popped, long and loud. We surfaced with a gasp; Rosie hooked me beneath the arms, rocks and creek grass abrading my skin as she dragged me up through the mud to the creek bed. "What has gotten into you?"

"Where's Nathan?" I pushed my hair out of my face and coughed. Rosie threw a towel at my head, and I breathed into it, distracted. *Why wouldn't he look at me?*

Rosie's grimace held my gaze. "He's fine. He's over there. Were you trying to kill yourself on purpose?"

The irony. "Not on the trestle, no."

"What the hell does that mean?"

You didn't come and get me, before. "I wasn't trying to kill myself, Ro."

"So you were just...swinging from the trestle. As something to do. For fun."

"There was a flower," I said. "I wanted to see it."

"You were *hanging* from a literal dress!"

I giggled, an awkward lightness frothing up in my head. "Well, when you say it like that—"

"You scared us out of our minds!" Her bottom lip shook, and I shivered.

"I'm...You're really upset."

"I saw you up there, and you and Nathan were under so long I thought—" She hiccuped around a sob, and a jab of guilt wedged into my shoulders. "You can't do stuff like that, you hear me? If I lost you, I'd freaking *die*."

That's when it hit me. I'd been looking from the inside out. I'd been so sure the dress would hold, that rigging it up that way was not only normal, it was useful. That I could live beneath the creek. A bitter sobbed worked its way out of the shallows, my soul mourning something I couldn't name.

Rosie cursed under her breath. "I shouldn't have yelled. Not in the car, and not just now. I—" She wiped at her eyes. "My mama says love can make you stupid, no matter what kind of love it is. You're my person, Dewitt. My sister. You make me so stupid it hurts."

I sniffled. "You're *my* sister. And I'm sorry, too."

Rosie pulled me into a hug, then shook her arms out and called Gil over my shoulder. "Sutton! I need you to drive me home!"

"I'll get my...stuff." There wasn't much to get, just my ruined dress and flip-flops. I spun around to see where they'd gone.

But Rosie said, "No," and I stopped mid-spin to stare at her.

"I mean, my dress is done for, but I'd at least like to get my shoes."

"That's not what I mean. Gil is taking me in my car. I need you to ride with Nathan."

"Are you *kidding?* I can't talk to Nathan right now."

She sized me up and down. "Your mouth's working. And you're talking to me."

"That's not-" I tangled the wet strands of my hair, tugging so hard I they nearly snapped."I kissed him, okay? When we were under the creak, I kissed him."

Rosie gaped at me, clearly gobsmacked. "Did he kiss you back?"

I paused. "Kind of?"

"Dewitt Griffin. He either didn't, or he did."

"He wouldn't look me in the eye." I twisted my hands. "And after everything you said about me leading him on..."

She pinched the bridge of her nose. "Just *talk to him.*"

"I *can't.*"

Her eyes drifted to the right and widened slightly.

"He's coming over here, isn't he?"

"Yes," she said through tight lips. "But you'll feel better once it's out."

"I feel fine," I lied, and Rosie made a face like, *you do not.* The set of her brow shifted hard into determination.

"I love you, and this is for your own good."

My lungs seized. The sound of footsteps made me break out in a sweat. "Rosie. *No.*"

"Yes," she hissed, pasting on a bright smile.

Nathan's heat burned at my side.

"I'll walk home," I said.

"You will not."

"It's not far."

"It's ten miles," she said. "On a highway."

"I'll stay on the shoulder. Walk fast."

"That's crazy."

"It fits. Isn't crazy my brand?"

Crimson burned Rosie's cheeks, and she muttered a bitter, "Whatever." I watched her walk up the hill, aware of Nathan now beside me.

"Let me take you home," he said.

Against my better judgment, I trudged up the hill and into Nathan's truck. I glued my arms around my waist and shoved my knees into the door panel, eyes fixed on our small town as it whizzed by. He glanced at me occasionally, the start of conversation on his lips. But I didn't want to talk. What was there to say beyond *I'm a mess?* and *You can't trust me?* I picked at the skin around my fingernails.

"You're shivering."

Nathan's voice burst through the AC's hum. I dropped my feet to the floor as he pulled onto the shoulder.

"You're stopping. Why are you stopping?"

"To give you my sweatshirt. You're cold."

There was only one in the cab as far as I could see, and that was the one he was wearing.

"I don't need it. I'm not." Except, my legs *were* a little blue, and I when I looked at my hands, they were trembling.

He jerked the parking brake and gripped the fabric behind his shoulders. "Dewey. Just put the thing on."

That nickname.

I grumbled. "Fine."

He tossed it in my lap, the still-warm jersey knit instantly comforting despite my best efforts to ignore how it felt. Nathan pulled back on the road and I clutched at the hoodie, bringing it close to my chest. I made a mistake—I inhaled. It smelled like pine and saltwater and something uniquely *him.* I shrugged the fabric over my head like a total goober. He didn't have to be so nice. I deserved the silent treatment for what I'd done, not a peace offering in an oversized sweatshirt.

Walking home would have been safer at this point.

Nathan silenced the stereo, jaw working beneath his cap. "Rosie says we need to talk."

"There's nothing to talk about." Nothing that was safe, anyway, and he was quiet for a minute while I listened to the road noise.

Nathan's voice broke through the quiet. "That was a really stupid stunt you pulled."

My shoulders tightened. "I don't think you have room to judge."

"I wasn't—" He pressed a fist to his lips. "It was scary, watching you. We haven't spoken in days. And then I look up at the tracks and you're, like, hanging from the edge and I was...*frantic-*"

"Which was stupid, because I was fine!"

"I know that now. Or I know you think you were."

"*I know you think you were?*" I scoffed. "Have you always been this insufferable? Or am I just picking up on it now?"

Nathan shifted into third gear and the truck shuddered, mimicking the tension in the cab. "*You thought you were fine.* I didn't know if you were, but then I got up there and we—" his hands left the wheel, miming an explosion. "We hit the water and we sank and you were—"

"I was what?"

"Half-naked, okay? You were half-naked." Heat crawled up his neck to his ears. My stomach fluttered in response, a millions wings taking flight despite my best efforts to ground them.

"I had on a swimsuit," I said.

Again, he went quiet, and in profile, I watched his jaw work. "You don't get it," he finally said.

"Clearly, I don't. It might not have been the brightest idea, fine, but you were the one who tried to save me. And if you have issues with girls in swimsuits—"

"I am *so* attracted to you."

The words hung in the air, an eruption. Fragments, drifting through space. I couldn't breathe. I couldn't speak. I tried in vain to swallow. He kept talking, and I just sat there, dumb.

"Happy? I'm attracted to you, and I have been for a very long time. I just—" He banged his fist against the wheel, then shook out his hand like maybe it hurt a little. "Holding you like that—kissing you? That was the second best moment of my life. But until I know you're okay, until I know, for sure, you really, really want this, I don't have the strength to go there. Not when our friendship means so much."

Out of everything he just unloaded, in that moment, only one thing stood out. "*Second* best moment?"

Nathan's face flushed a deep, beet red. "You don't get to know the first one."

"I mean, I thought the kiss was pretty good."

He scrubbed a hand down a face. "This isn't about the kiss. It's about trust, and, like, protecting myself. Because I don't trust you, Dewitt. And I want to."

A cavern opened inside my chest. He didn't trust me, and that was my fault. If I told him the truth, would he feel better? Would it fix things?

I gripped the door handle. "I think there's something you should know."

Nathan slowed the truck at an intersection. "You don't owe me anything."

"No, I...I really think I do."

"Whatever we are, Dewitt, it's not a business deal or a bargain. You mean way more to me than that." He took a hard right, bumping the truck into the lot at Daughtry's. After parking, he climbed down from the cab with my heart. "I'm making a pecan roll run for Lil," he said. "You want anything?" His gaze fell above my shoulder.

I swallowed. "No, thanks. I'll come with you, though?"

The air heightened. "I need a minute," he said. And I watched him walk away like Rosie had, for a breather, I knew, not forever. But in the quiet of the cab, I wondered—when did I get to exhale?

SIXTEEN

NATHAN

September 2002

"What's up with you and Dewitt, nimrod?" Gil speared his mystery meat with his fork. We sat in the senior cafe, the auxiliary space where they shoved all the seniors. Exclusivity was supposed to make it cool.

"What's up with you and Rosie?" I countered. I didn't want to talk about Dewitt. Things were...fine. Same as they were over the summer. We hadn't kissed again, not that I didn't want to. But I stayed true to my word—we weren't getting involved until I knew she was okay and I was in a place where I could trust her. Hadn't been much progress on either front.

Gil set his fork down and pulled a small velvet box from his bag. "Square-cut solitaire on white gold, half a carat."

"Holy hell, you did it."

"Told you I would."

He opened the box and turned it toward me. The stone sparkled multi-colored in the light. "You talk to her parents yet?" It wasn't that unusual in the country—getting married young. But Rosie was still sixteen, and a ring, well. It felt early.

Gil snapped the box closed and put it back in his book bag. "We both did. Rosie gave a talk. She had statistics and slides and a bunch of young marriage success stories." His eyes glazed over and his smile got all gooey. "Girl's magnificent, I tell you what."

That was that, then. "Better make me your best man." I held out the scar on my thumb and waited for Gil to press it.

He returned the motion, smirking. "Like I have any other choice."

I thought he'd forgotten about the whole Dewitt question until he tipped up his chin. "It's your girl."

My heart thumped. "Dewitt?"

"Don't turn around."

"I know how to behave around women."

"News to me," he said, forcing his lips shut. He murmured. "Stop talking. Act cool."

"What are we, twelve?"

"You're the one who can't find his way out of a paper bag with Griffin." He shouldered his bag and pushed up from the table. "Why don't you tell me?"

Gil walked away, all cocky, just as Dewitt plopped down on the bench. "Tell him what?" she asked. She looked like the ocean, her tide tugging at me in a light blue dress. Those dang tiny straps messed with my head, and I watched her dark hair dance in waves around them. Her skirt curved along her thighs and poured down to her ankles.

I flexed the pen in my hand.

"Gil's being Gil." I tapped the pen on the table. "Were you in the art room before lunch?" A smidge of purple marred her thumb, but today was a core day. No electives.

"I had to meet with Mr. Hamer." She grimaced. "My portfolio needs a little work."

I'd never talked that much to Hamer, but right then, I kind of hated the guy. "He didn't like your art?"

"It's not that," she said, fiddling with a loose strap on her book bag. "It's more that I don't have enough."

That was...unusual. Dewitt was prolific. She churned out art. "You've done at least five, right? Since school started?" She'd definitely shown me a few. I tried to count them all up—one was of the shore. Two of them were portraits—the same woman, someone I didn't know. "How many do you need?" I asked, still counting up what I remembered. She'd painted Pinecliff, I knew, and wasn't there a shrimp boat?

She fiddled some more. If Gil were still here, I would've bet him ten bucks she was about to change the subject in four, three, two—

"Your senior survey," she said.

One.

A packet sat on the table, six stapled pages next to me. A rite of passage for seniors. Your goals. Your dreams. Your intended colleges.

In five years, I'd like to...

Still be in Minnesott, building boats.

Dewitt slid the pages toward her. "You left the college part blank."

"Because I'm not applying anywhere."

"What about Broward?"

I groaned inwardly. "That's not happening."

The Broward School of Maritime Engineering was one of the nation's top schools in that field. They'd been hounding me about their vessel craftsman track since a rep saw my work at the Oriental Boat Show.

Dewitt stared at me, dumbstruck. "You don't want to go?"

I didn't. The school was six hours down the coast. And I'd coped with my dyslexia, sure, but the idea of four more years of classes didn't appeal to me. Reading books, writing papers, and traveling six hours away from everything I loved, present company included? "No, not really. I don't."

Her eyes narrowed. "I don't get it. Why? I mean, I like Minnesott—"

I laughed, and she scrunched up her lips and swatted at me. "Goober. I'm serious. Growing up here, it's beautiful. But, like, don't you want to stretch yourself? That's why I'm applying to VCU—"

I smirked. "Because Ms. Schulz went to Paris…"

She swatted me again, this time holding back laughter. "You're impossible, you know that?"

Staring at the way her skin glowed, I could have kissed her right then and there. But I twiddled the pen back and forth and teased her. "Ms. Schulz lives in Minnesott, you know."

She dropped her head in her hands, groaning. "Yes, she lives here now. But she came back on her own terms. It's inspiring."

"Then it sounds like she got to live her dream."

Dewitt's hands dropped down to the table, and she breathed out a vindicated, "*Yes.* What if Broward could be that for you? Catapulting your career in ways you never could have imagined? Helping you inspire someone else?"

Her eyes searched my face for an answer, gaze piercing me down to the bone. A tight sensation I couldn't name—and didn't like—wound up my spine and held. For the first time in years, I wasn't her *friend*. I was the kid she found abandoned in East Acres. The one who got placed in a foster home with Lil.

"College doesn't make you an inspiration," I said, thinking of strawberry jam and kind eyes. "You learn stuff, yeah, but it's who you are deep down, not where you to go school or what degree you get or whatever. I've learned a lot, done a lot, just working and living here."

Her dark waves scraped the table as she shifted. "Is it really that bad to *want*?"

I wanted. Not Broward, but her. Only I wanted her to want me, too, the real me who wasn't perfect. Whose dreams were on a local scale.

"I don't think so. I think it's okay to want different things." I paused and exhaled, working to breathe out the tension. "You want to go to VCU. I have no doubt you'll get there. With Broward, I don't want or even need what they have. Your dad pays me well. I get to work on builds over the weekend. The last boat I sold made me enough to pay for Judy."

Her lips quirked. "You named your jeep."

She was a 1978 CJ-7 with a *second row*, so of course, I had to. She'd been rotting in Daughtry's vacant lot. I'd gotten the engine running good, and the plan was to take her across the river that weekend.

Dewitt's hand brushed mine, pulling me to the moment. "Are you refusing Broward because of me?"

My breath caught. I didn't want to lie. But I also didn't want to tell the truth, so I settled for something in the middle. "My family's here. Gil's staying to run Sutton Seafood. You and Ro have another year. Lil's not going anywhere, and she's not getting any younger either. Why should I be the only one who leaves?"

"Because Broward is the Harvard of boat building."

"I don't get why you're pushing this."

"You have a chance to get out. You can leave, and grow, and you're not even going to consider it?"

Thick tension filled the air, so taut I could have reached out and plucked it.

Dewitt sat back, frustrated. "Don't you want to be something more?"

Ink seeped out of the pen cartridge, the shattered plastic hitting the table with a clatter. "Because I'm from East Acres, right?" I started to stand, and Dewitt grabbed hold of my arm, eyes frantic.

"I didn't—"

I jerked away. "Not now."

I hated fighting with her like this, hated leaving our conversation unsettled. But as I walked through the halls on my way to English, mostly, I hated myself.

"EITHER YOU HAD a bad day on the farm or a good day in the pigpen. You look like you've been rolling in mud." Lil barred the kitchen door with her arm and pointed toward the outdoor shower. "Don't come in here looking like that."

Like that was pit-stained and muddy, the result of an afternoon's hard work. I stayed out in the yard, as far away from the house as my tasks would let me. Didn't see a single sign of Dewitt.

Lil handed me supplies and a towel along with a fresh t-shirt and shorts. She was waiting for me on the back porch rocker when I emerged, a plate of cookies set out on the small wrought-iron table. I grabbed a bottle of water from the mini-fridge she kept near the doorway and sat down in the rocker next to hers.

Lil's backyard that evening was cool and inviting, the last of the fireflies flitting through the air. I stared out at the boxwood hedge, the one Lil planted against the mouth of the trail to Minnesott Acres. *"To mark our yard as private property,"* she told me. Pretty sure it was to protect me from the past.

"You're grumpy," Lil said, like a comment on the weather. *Cloudy with a chance of Nathan's rain.* "Should I assume it's thanks to Miss Dewitt?" she asked, and I shoved a snickerdoodle in my mouth, my posture overly guarded. Lil nodded, watching me. "I thought so. It's Dewitt."

My jaw ached. "It's nothing."

"Looks like something to me." Lil stood, then rummaged in the pocket of her floral cotton housecoat. She dropped my crumpled senior survey in my lap.

"You went through my bag?" I sat forward.

"I moved it, and this fell out."

"You sure it didn't have a little help?" I said, my tone decidedly skeptical.

"That's neither here nor there."

Lil sat back in her chair and crossed her legs, hands folded. I knew what that look on her face meant. That she wasn't letting it go, and the only way out of this was to tell her. "I haven't filled it out or turned it in, and Dewitt got on my case about it."

My mouth twisted. *Happy now?*

She read my face like a novel. "No, Nathan. I'm not."

I squirmed in my chair. "Dewitt thinks I should apply to Broward," I told her. "I'm not interested."

The gentle creak of Lil's rocker filled the early-evening quiet as I waited for her to speak. "It's an excellent school," she finally said, like I hadn't heard the same thing from Dewitt.

"I've learned enough on my own."

"You've developed quite the skill. You're like...what's his name? Sculpted that naked man with all the muscles. Sistine Chapel, and all that."

"Michelangelo," I deadpanned. She knew exactly who she was talking about. But she kept up the ruse, slapping her thigh in recognition.

"That guy. Michelangelo, yes. I seem to recall he never cared much for school." She gave a pause, then heightened her gaze with the lift of an eyebrow. "Guess that makes you the Michelangelo of boats."

I exhaled. She was teasing me. "I take classes at the Beaufort Watercraft Center." No reading; not six hours away.

"There are scholarships and grants. You have options."

"It's not the money, Mama Lil." Broward's tuition did clock in at twenty thousand a year, but I had other qualms. "I don't like the idea of you being alone during storm season. And I owe you. So dang much."

"You don't owe me anything." Lil squeezed my fingers in the deepening dusk. "*Nothing* but a life well-lived, because you may not be my blood, but you're my son in every other way that matters. You going away to school isn't shirking your end of the bargain. That's me, Nathan, doing my job."

My throat went tight, my eyes watery. I sniffed and looked at the ground. Lil pressed on, not one to let tears slow her progress. "If you don't want to go to Broward, fine. But if you have even the *slightest* inclination, I think you should apply. Get in and go. Rub elbows with the best of them. Whatever you decide, I support your ultimate decision—but that decision is up to you."

Lil stood and ruffled my hair a little before heading inside the house. I kept my eyes fixed on the floor and listened to the cicadas, hot tears sliding down my cheeks. In my old life, I was a transaction to Mike and Sue. But I *was* the deal for Lil—the boy she took in, *wanted*, and loved.

Night fell, stars shone, and distant waves crashed on the shoreline. And there in the backyard of an old, white farmhouse, I learned the definition of *enough*.

SEVENTEEN

DEWITT

Someone — probably Nathan — leaned on the horn as I fumbled down the steps. The clock in Daddy's office chimed once, then twice, then seven more times as I tripped into the foyer, cursing. I glanced out the window toward the Neuse, my stomach jolting at the sight of the ferry in the channel. *Probably Nathan* leaned on the horn again.

"I'm coming!" I shouted through the screen door. We'd missed the ferry because of me. I woke up face down on the floor with paint stains on my fingers and drool cementing my cheek to the floor. But I had three finished canvases propped against the wall and Mr. Hamer would be happy as a clam at high tide. My friends, though—I had a feeling they'd want to drown me. Nathan and I hadn't spoken since our argument over Broward. We were supposed to head to Last Gasp, the last official concert of the summer. It was an hour away across the river and all three of them had wanted an early start.

Through the screen door, I watched Nathan climb down from his new jeep. New to him, anyway—the thing was thirty years old and two miles short of the junk heap. It shut behind him with a metallic *thunk*.

"Hold on!" I yelped, desperate, fighting for my life against my shower-damp, sticky skin. The denim cut-offs snagged at my thighs, the rough fabric cutting my circulation. My shirt was sticking to me, too, and I'd already worked up a sweat trying to put on my dang two-piece. *This will be how I die.*

I told myself to get a grip and get moving, then wrenched the rough material up my legs. I straightened my shirt and pushed through the door straight into a late September sauna. In coastal North Carolina, fall always sent the memo late.

Nathan leaned against the Jeep in cargos and leather Havanas, a gauzy blue button down competing with his scowl. "What part of *ready by eight forty-five* did you have a problem with?" He asked, and I tipped my chin up in defiance.

"I slept through my alarm."

I walked toward him, throat burning around the lie. His gaze dropped to the raw skin on my hands and I flinched; I'd scrubbed them too long under a too-hot tap. Calloused fingers gripped my wrists and he turned them, inspecting my palms with angry hazel eyes. Excuses raced through my head—all of them lies and equally ridiculous. But he just said, "We're late," before he let me go, then turned to wrench the driver's side door open. "Are you coming or not?"

I climbed into the jeep on autopilot, our argument about Broward in my head. I was already off when I sat down: *It's not the number of pieces,* Mr. Hamer had said. *It's more the subject.* He'd gestured to my spot on the drying rack, to the two paintings I'd done of Effa. *I'd like to see you branch out.* I'd walked down the crowded hallway toward the senior cafeteria and all I could think about was getting out of *here.* And so we fought, and I said things I didn't mean, and while a tiny voice whispered that of course I could trust Nathan to make his own decisions, I fixated, somehow, on my father getting his claws in, especially if Nathan stayed.

A jolt pulled me out of my navel-gazing. We'd boarded the ferry with seconds to spare. The jeep nearly hung off the back, the last of three dozen cars packed bumper to bumper on the wide-bottom, three-hundred ton boat.

Once settled, Nathan slid from the jeep without a word. I watched him snake the through the tight lines of cars, watched him climb up the stairs to the observation deck.

Gil climbed out after him and leaned against the doorframe. "Ro, can you..."

He motioned at me.

"I'm sitting right here," I said, sulky, and he squinted, tongue pressed inside his cheek.

Rosie climbed into the front and sat behind the wheel, pressing a kiss to Gil's cheek and shoving him fondly. "Get out of here. Go do bro things."

He glanced from me to Rosie, taking a hesitant step back. "You got this?" he asked Ro, and she shooed him away. "I've got this."

Gil made his way through the maze of vehicles, following Nathan up the steps.

Cruising out of the channel, the ferry shuddered and increased its speed. A salty breeze pushed the air, but the unease in my heart held steady. I fixed my gaze on the truck in front of us and pretended to study the NC Fisheries stickers plastered to the back.

"I don't need a chaperone, Rosie."

"I know that," she said. "I'm sorry about Gil. We, um...we have some news, and I think he was asking if I could tell you."

She paused, the silence stretching so long I shifted in my seat to look at her. Same rosy cheeks. Same dark curls blowing into her face and dragging across her freckles. But there was something new—a light in her eyes. And that color in her cheeks—was she *glowing?*

My brain jumped from one to one hundred. "Are you *pregnant?*" I blurted out.

Rosie's jaw dropped. "I say we have news, and your mind goes to *pregnant?*"

Indignation warred with embarrassment. "What was I supposed to think?"

"That it's crazy. Gil and I haven't...*you know...*"

They were firmly in the *wait 'till marriage* camp, and I owed it to her to remember. "Okay. I overreacted. But you're, like, all happy and glowing, and—"

"Because we're getting married," she said.

The world stopped, except for Rosie, who bounced in her seat. "Gil proposed," she squealed, and grabbed my hand, still bouncing.

A salty burn climbed my esophagus.

"You're joking."

She held still. "No, I'm not."

I should be happy for her. I should be happy for her. I'm not happy.

"I...I have the ring, if you want to see it. I, uh, wanted to tell you before I put it on." Rosie reached over the console, tentative, her muscles tightening mid way. "It's in my bag."

"In your bag," I said, heaving. *Am I going to be sick?*

"Are you about to puke?" Rosie asked me, disbelief lodged in her voice. Irrational rage festered below my skin. Anger at being pushed aside for Gil. Frustration that my best friend and I now had goals that were so very different. Anxiety—intense worry—about what would happen to us next.

"You were my best friend before you fell for Gil Sutton." I dragged a hand across the sweat on my face. *"You can't marry*

Gil," I said, believing every word, knowing this wasn't my decision.

"The hell I can't," she said.

A lone seagull squawked above us and I flinched, hypersensitive, at the sound. "You're sixteen," I said. "That's crazy young."

"I'll be seventeen in three weeks. You know that."

"But your parents—"

"Are *ecstatic*."

"*His* parents—"

"Are over the moon."

"Does Nathan know?"

At least here, she had the decency to look embarrassed. "He helped Gil pick out the ring."

I sank down into my seat, bones aching, a second wave of nausea tipping back my head. "How long?"

"How long what?"

"How long have you been planning?"

Rosie shifted in her seat beside me. "July."

"You never said a word."

"Because you were dealing with so much, and I didn't—I didn't know how to tell you."

I scoffed. "And now you do?"

Rosie tossed her hands in frustration. "I swear, Dewitt. I can't win."

"You always win." *The boy, the perfect life, the brain that wasn't burning.* "What happened to not keeping secrets, Ro?"

Rosie snatched my hand and pressed my fingers open, inspecting the raw spots on my palm. "Why don't you tell me?"

"This isn't about me." I jerked away.

"I think it is. You've always had this *plan* to get out, but the minute anybody else has dreams or a plan, or even suggests for a second they might want to stay here, you act like we're destroying our lives."

Betrayal, thick and salty, filled the inside of my mouth. "Nathan told you about our fight."

"He did, and I defended you! I said you wanted what was best for him, right? But after this—" She opened the door and slipped down from the jeep, more angry than I'd ever seen her. "I'm seriously regretting it. Ten minutes ago, you were the first person I wanted to stand with me when I married Gil Sutton. But you know what, Dewitt? I don't need you. And I'll be more than okay if you won't."

NORTH CAROLINA'S barrier islands curve like a bow along the coast. Atlantic Beach sits at the southern tip, its half-mile spit of land the very last of the islands, separated from the mainland by the Bogue Sound. I leaned out the side of Nathan's jeep as we crossed over it, watching the Bogue's sandbars pop beneath us like white hills. Traffic slowed to a crawl as we came off the bridge, two long lines of cars in search of limited public parking. "Head to Oceanana," Gil said.

I'd been thinking the same, honestly, that the fishing pier twelve blocks from the main stage would be the best place to park. I kept my mouth shut, though, aching.

Nobody wanted to hear from me.

My head bumped against the roll bar as we bounced into the lot, its one remaining space wedged beside the dumpster in a fog of rotten fish. I held my breath as I got out, pulling my t-shirt off and stuffing it in the glove compartment.

"You need sunscreen," Rosie said.

"We're speaking now?" I wasn't giving in to false hope. This was Rosie being Rosie, butting into everybody's space.

Nathan rolled his eyes, then reached into the jeep and grabbed the spray can. He wouldn't look at me as he held it out.

"I'm *fine*," I snapped. I wasn't a child. "Why don't y'all put sunscreen on?"

"We did." Gil tugged at his cap. "While we were waiting for you this morning."

"Because obviously I'm self-absorbed."

I could have kicked myself—they didn't deserve to be treated this way. But I was so mad, and so hurt, and so confused about what I thought was true and who I was and what I thought was right and perfect, that I couldn't keep the barbs from flying out of me like arrows.

You're just proving everybody right.

"Dewitt, the dumpster smells awful." Rosie's exhaustion bled through her voice. "Can you please just put it on?"

"You don't have to wait for me again," I said, and finally, Nathan's gaze turned my way.

"Just...turn around," he groused.

Angst and apprehension bled from him in waves. Nathan was hurt; I could see that now, thanks to Rosie's thrashing. Maybe I *was* being unfair. Or maybe *they* needed to stretch themselves beyond our tiny border.

Usually I would have held to the latter. Now, I wasn't so sure.

A cold mist coated my back and brought me back to the moment, body shivering from the change in temperature. "Sorry," Nathan breathed, his breath on my neck caressing the goosebumps.

"Whatever. Just hurry up."

I'd missed him, his proximity dredging longing from my core. I leaned back into his space and he inhaled. His chest grazed my back. "Dewitt," he whispered low, and I thought to myself, *Apologize.*

Gil's voice pushed space between us. "Y'all coming? Or do we need to get you a room?"

***

Last Gasp's main stage sat at the center of the boardwalk. From Oceanana, it was a ten-minute walk. Faint strains of music filled the air, and the closer in we got, the more concentrated the crowds grew. Vendors packed the boardwalk on both sides, hocking their wares and creating out in the open while the scent of spun sugar filled the air. Last Gasp wasn't just a concert. It was an artist's daydream, a study in the old, the alternative, the young. The kind of character-fueled spectacle that should have had me bouncing from booth to booth, shoving fried Twinkies in my face and making friends with other creatives. But I lagged behind instead, picking at the raw flesh on my hands, not entirely sure where I was going or how badly I'd damaged things.

"Nathan Cartwright!"

A grizzled voice called from a nearby booth. A shiny wooden pram stood to the side, its smooth lines and varnished hull practically screaming for the water. A banner—*Win this boat! Support the Beaufort Watercraft Center!*—hung proudly from the port.

"Mr. Eddie," Nathan said. "Good to see you." Our group slowed to a stop at the booth.

"Son, what'd I tell you? *Mister* makes me feel old." He motioned to the woman at his side. "I don't think you've met my wife, Verna."

Nathan reached out and shook her hand.

Mr. Eddie and Mrs. Verna were in their late seventies, if I'd had to guess. Tufts of white, unruly hair jutted out from the mesh of Mr. Eddie's ball cap, *I'd rather be sailing* on the front. Mrs. Verna's pedal pushers reached just below her knees, and the deep blue of her sleeveless blouse played off her bright pink visor. Together, they smiled at Nathan. He looked back at them and beamed.

"Nice to meet you, Mrs. Verna," Nathan said.

"Are you the prodigy I keep hearing about?" The back of Nathan's neck burned red as Verna looked to Eddie for confirmation.

"This is, indeed, the master boatbuilder." Eddie nodded at his wife. "Built this pram and donated it for the raffle, all before completing his senior year."

Nathan built that. I blinked, having a hard time trusting my eyes. I knew he was good. I didn't know he was *that* good. The closer I got, the more I could see he hadn't used a single piece of hardware. He'd put the whole thing together with dovetail joints.

"This is amazing." I flushed at the awe in my voice. His gaze burned the side of my face, and I could feel it when he breathed a quiet, "Thank you."

"You've been holding out on us, man," Gil said.

Eddie let out a full laugh. "You been sneaking out here, to this side of the river?"

"Lil knows," Nathan swore.

"It was just the rest of us in the dark," Rosie said, elbowing Nathan in the side and stepping forward. "Nice to meet you, Mr. Eddie. Mrs. Verna. I'm one of Nathan's friends, Rosie Bennett."

While the group made small talk, I studied Nathan's craftsmanship. It wasn't like I hadn't seen his work before. I guess I just hadn't...gotten close to it?

The acid in my stomach curdled. I'd been such a jerk.

I wandered back toward the table, Eddie and Verna deep in conversation with my friends. "That's quite a ring," Verna said, nodding at the diamond on Rosie's finger. I hadn't realized she'd put it on.

Rosie blushed. "Thank you. This guy did a pretty good job." She smiled at Gil, but it morphed into a frown a second later. "*Some* people think we're too young and stupid to get married."

Everybody turned and looked at me.

Verna broke the tension with a well-placed clearing of her throat. She stared at the diamond on her hand, the light catching in the facets. "I got this lovely piece when I was seventeen. Granted, times were different then, but I'd known Eddie my whole life. Grew up next door; used to pester me something crazy." She eyed Rosie and Gil. "When a girl knows, she knows. Y'all have spoken to your parents?"

"Yes ma'am," Gil said.

Rosie's side-eye screamed at me. "They trust us."

Verna's laugh rang clear, and when she turned to me, her eyes smiled at the corners. "The lone dissenter. I don't think anyone's introduced us yet."

"Sorry," Nathan said. "This is Dewitt."

"Dewitt, huh?" Eddie said. "I've heard a lot about you."

Next to me, Nathan sputtered. "That you're a friend of mine, that's all."

"Right," Eddie said, drawing out the word while the tips of Nathan's ears glowed pink.

I stood off to the side as the conversation finished, my recent choices warring with what I knew now. Verna winked at me as we said goodbye. Rosie wanted a slushy, but my stomach already burned sickly-sweet. Seeing the pram Nathan built; listening to Eddie and Verna...

I had apologies to make.

Rosie gave me an opening as we watched the boys throw darts at a booth. "*Verna* thinks I know what I'm doing."

I breathed out a rough, "She's right. I wasn't—I didn't see the ring coming, and what you said, about how I have a plan?"

My throat closed up, but I pushed myself to say it. "I do expect everyone else to follow it. You were right."

"Really." Her delivery was as deadpan as her face.

A thousand nerves sped through my blood. "Really," I said. "You have the right to your dreams. Gil loves you so much, and it's not my place to referee your future. I'm...I'm happy for you."

Or at least, I'm trying to be.

Ro's left eyebrow went up. "You're happy."

I grimaced at my omission. "Yeah?"

"Happy enough to go dress shopping in New Bern?"

Rosie's arm went through mine and squeezed. I barked a disbelieving laugh in response, because she'd forgiven me far faster than I expected.

"Of course," I said. "I'm forgiven?"

"I don't think either of us handled it well. If Gil and I are in it for the long haul, you and I are, too, you dummy. I shouldn't have reacted the way I did."

"I deserved it." Even so, I felt a heady flush of relief.

"You did. But we all do, sometimes. We're only human." Her gaze lifted over my shoulder. "You need to figure out what to do about him, though."

Nathan—the *him* in question—stood with his back to us, muscles flexing through the fabric of his shirt as he aimed. He wore his cap backwards, too, wavy brownish-gold strands poking out from the bottom. "I should talk to him," I said, more to myself than Rosie.

She gave me a side-hug. "Yep."

We followed the boys as they wandered, staying a few feet back at each stop. They looked like they were deep in conversation themselves, and if I'd had to guess, I would have wagered it was the same topic: the mess that was Nathan and me.

"Nothing's changed, you know," Rosie said. "He's still stubborn and crazy about you."

"That first part might break the deal."

Rosie hummed. "Not for Nathan."

"What do you mean?" I asked.

Rosie shook her slushy, the icy red liquid nearly down to the dregs. "I mean you've got to bend, too, or it's not going to work, no matter how much you might want it."

The truth smacked me in the chest and nearly knocked me over. I needed to meet him halfway. "Why are you so smart?"

"It's my mama," she said, tossing her cup into a nearby trash can. "She's irritating, but she makes a lot of sense."

The boys had moved on, to the Coastal History Foundation booth. "And right now," Rosie said, "Mama would tell me to grab Gil and let you and Nathan fix things. So that's exactly what I'm going to do."

Feeling unmoored without her, I watched her swoop straight into Gil's side. She whispered something in his ear, and he nodded, walking off to a nearby stall.

Nathan's hands stayed in his pockets as he studied the displayed artifacts. Each step forward stoked the nerves in my gut, and I drew in a steadying breath when I reached him. I touched his hand; he startled. "Nathan?" I said. He turned to face me then, the look on his face impassive. I swallowed the lump in my throat.

"Nathan, I owe you an apology."

He stiffened. "We keep having conversations like this."

"Because I keep messing up. And one of these days, you're going to get tired of it. So I figure I gotta make things right."

If I hadn't been watching closely, I would have missed the slight shift in his jaw. I would have missed the way his shoulders dipped, too, the way his lip tugged at the corner like he'd bit it, the only sign he'd been affected by what I said.

"Lil agrees with you about Broward," he said. "You sure you still want to apologize?"

I nodded, throat thick. "You didn't need that pressure."

He picked an antique sextant off the display and spun the gears with his fingers. "It wasn't the pressure. It was the implication. That I'm not enough for you. That I'll never be enough unless I go to Broward."

Quiet tears rolled down my cheeks. I didn't hide them this time, not from the boy who stood across from me right then, the same boy who bandaged my hand when he was fourteen and I was prideful. Who carved a sailboat for me out of birch. Who jumped from a trestle to save my life. Who absorbed my half-starts and half-truths at face value. "You are so much more than enough, Nathan. You're loyal and you're brave. I'm such an idiot for making it seem I ever thought otherwise. I love you," I said, the feeling swelling up inside me. "I know that's a weird thing for me to say. I'm totally fine if you don't say it back or even feel the same way but—"

I didn't get to finish.

Nathan's lips on mine cut me off.

The crowd pulled thick around us, but I couldn't have cared at all. Nathan's hand cradled the back of my neck, his fingers in my hair and his calloused thumb dragging sweetly across my cheekbone, his lips wet and salty from my tears.

I was gone for this boy, completely. I had been for a long time. And as he kissed me in the middle of that crowd, dizzy with forgiveness and hope and the promise of new beginnings, I wasn't sure what sort of future I was facing.

I only knew I would face it with him.

EIGHTEEN

DEWITT

June 2003

"This is a wedding reception, not a funeral. Would it kill you to spare a smile?"

I studied my mother in the soft light of Griffin Barn and wondered if I'd been that transparent. "How's this?" I asked, and stretched my lips upward.

Mama squinted. "You look constipated. Maybe just..."

She waved her hand in my face like the motion could rearrange it before tossing u her hands. "Whatever." She breathed out through her nose, a magnolia-mannered dragon. "Just look happy for Rosie and Gil."

I'd been trying. And deep down, I *was*. But I was also scared, the practical side of letting go a lot harder than I anticipated months ago. I changed the subject to the weather. "It's hot as a stray dog's balls."

Mama gasped. "Dewitt Griffin!"

"What?" I asked. "It's true."

"It's vulgar, is what it is. Lou would have a coronary if he heard you."

"Mama. Look at the company I keep."

I didn't have to point, really, not with the commotion in the center of the floor, but I *did* have to keep a straight face at the display. The deejay had put on Marvin Gaye, and while the soul singer crooned about getting it on, an incandescent Gil shimmied toward Rosie, twirling his tux jacket and gyrating his hips. Rosie's hands covered her face as she doubled over with laughter, and I was glad I insisted she do the garter toss tradition from a chair. A chorus of catcalls and *whoops* rose from the crowd—Gil slid to his knees and under Rosie's skirts. She yelped and blushed *hard*, kicking playfully at her new husband when he emerged with a blue lace garter dangling between his teeth.

"For heaven's sake," Mama muttered.

I stifled my first laugh of the night.

Mama gave me a playful swat and swallowed her own giggles. "And to think Gil's parents spent all that money on cotillion."

Nathan's appeared at my side and floated an arm around my waist, his thumb trailing goosebumps over the exposed skin on my back. "I hate to break it to you, Mrs. Deebie, but Gil never actually went."

"He didn't go?" Mama gaped and I shifted, electricity from Nathan's touch lighting me from the inside. Nathan's grin turned coy, like he was letting Mama in on a secret.

"He sneaked out and went fishing instead."

"Y'all are the worst bunch of hooligans," she said, grinning in affection. "But it just makes me love y'all more. Now you be good." She winked at us. "I'm off to get another glass of wine."

Mama moseyed away with a wave and a smile and I smoothed the chiffon of my skirt. I tugged the bodice down, too, scraping my fingers across the beading and inadvertently brushing Nathan away. He jerked back, and I could feel the heat on his face before I turned to see it. "Sorry," he said, mortified. "I didn't mean to make you uncomfortable."

He made me too comfortable, was the truth; every touch quelling the chaos that lived inside my head. Not that he knew —we'd been together eight months, and I still hadn't told him about my trips and surges. I knew I should have, I just didn't want it to be a *thing*. And since we were together all the time, and my brain settled when we were together, it was a moot point.

The night of the reception, though, was different. "I'm just fidgety. It's not you." But *fidgety* wasn't the right word, and I fiddled with my bodice again, pressing my skin into the beads and wincing.

Nathan's index finger tipped my chin to face him. "What's going on?" he asked.

I forced my smile wide. "Nothing. It's...I'm hot. Could you go to the bar and get me a glass of water? I'm gonna step outside."

Cheeks aching, I said a silent prayer he'd let me go. He swept the contours of my face and narrowed his eyes, but in the space of one held breath, he nodded. I wandered out into the courtyard while he headed for the bar.

String lights cast warm shadows and the buzz of early locusts filled the trees. If I tried hard enough, I heard the crash of a wave on a distant shore. Or maybe I imagined it. The barn looked so different in the half-light, a far cry from the worn structure it used to be when Daddy would shoo me away—*it's not safe. Don't play there.*

Curiosity may have killed the cat, like he warned me, but complacency was so much worse.

I'd been stupid for letting Nathan's presence convince me I

was fine. Clearly, I was wrong, and as the buzz spread to my toes and a slip in reality felt more likely, I wondered if the change had triggered it. The boys had graduated three weeks ago. A week later, Rosie and I took our exams. A few hours ago, Rosie and Gil had gotten *married*. I'd come to terms with that last one, mostly.

At least I thought I had.

"Something's bothering you."

The voice came out of nowhere, and I nearly toppled into a bush. "Shrimp on a biscuit," I said, pulse pounding as I searched for my assailant. "You gave me a heart attack, Lil."

Lil leaned against the stone wall along the edge of the courtyard, a slight breeze moving the hem of her dress. "I called your name, shug. Twice."

"I didn't hear you." Winded, I dropped my weight against the wall.

"A little lost in your thoughts?"

I laughed to myself. *That's an understatement.* Held hostage was a better term. "I'm…" *Confused. Scared. Probably jealous.* "Having a hard time tonight."

The soft warmth of Lil's arm pressed into my shoulder. "You're trying to make sense of a million things at once. I don't think you have to do that," she said, reading my soul like tea leaves.

I snorted, because didn't I? "My best friend got married today."

I'd barely hinted at the tip of my emotional iceberg, but as intended, it gave Lil something to grab.

"You know that doesn't change her."

"I know." But Rosie belonged to Gil now, not me, not really.

Lil bumped my knee with hers, perceptive as always. "We're not looking at Dewitt's best friend *or* Gil's wife. Her role can be both. The only major change is that she's going from her mama and daddy's house to a new double-wide in the same complex." Her lips quirked. "Instead of your typical three minutes, it'll take you four minutes when you sneak out."

I flushed so hard my toes curled. This woman was so observant it hurt. "I have no idea what you're talking about," I said, and she laughed, eyes crinkling.

"I may be old, Dewitt Griffin, but I'm not blind. I know y'all sneak out. Poor Nathan's about as smooth as an aggravated cat."

She paused. "Speaking of Nathan." I turned to see Nathan cross the yard. He'd lost his tux jacket in the Barn and rolled his sleeves up to his forearms. My heart fluttered in my chest.

Nathan nodded to us both in greeting and held out the Mason jar of water in his hand. "I got this for Dewitt," he told Lil, "but I can go back inside and get you something."

"Don't even think about it," she said. "Take this young lady for a spin on the dance floor, son."

Lil stood and stretched a little, leaning forward to whisper in my ear. "You can trust him, shug, I promise."

She walked in the barn without looking back.

"What was that about?"

I wiped my damp palms on my skirt. "You know Lil," I said.

"Passing along the wisdom of age?" he asked, taking my hand and curling me toward him.

My skin tingled. "Something like that."

We swayed together in the courtyard, and I buried my face in his shirt. I focused on the rough scrape of Nathan's calluses against my back instead of what Lil said, trying desperately not to bounce on my toes. Nathan's lips brushed against my temple, a quiet whisper passing the shell of my ear. I nearly jumped out of my skin, the ball of lightning in my core growing taut. Cracking. "Wh—What?"

His shoulders deflated underneath the weight of my arms. "It was stupid. The song..."

He trailed off bashfully, and I shook my head to clear the static between my ears. Eric Clapton's *Wonderful Tonight* drifted through the barn doors, the warmth of realization dawning, cutting my voltage by several amps.

"I said you looked wonderful tonight. I was trying to be smooth but I think it just turned out awkward."

"You were smooth," I promised. "As buttery as a baby's butt."

He chuckled, and his thumbs pressed the divot of my waist. I dropped my head into his shoulder and breathed him in, the steady thrum I'd been feeling growing. "Run away with me."

"Your father would kill me."

"My father loves you."

"And I love the use of my legs."

"They are pretty sexy," I said, and a gruff sound scared the back of his throat. I'd assumed he'd tighten his embrace, brush the shell of my ear as he whispered something swoony. But his shoulders tensed beneath my arms, and I leaned back, my face a question. "Guess it's my turn to ask if *you're* alright."

"I have...something to tell you." His head dipped, and he wouldn't look me in the eye. "I applied to Broward—"

"You did?"

I couldn't help the happy note in my voice, but it died away when Nathan grimaced.

"Yeah."

We stopped swaying in the dark, questions looming. "What happened? Did you not get in?"

"No, I got in." He chewed his lip. "I decided to defer."

"That's all?" I laughed. "You made it sound like something awful."

His mouth pulled tight in response and my thoughts clicked. "Wait a second. Are you deferring because of me?"

The words hung in the air, weightless, and I studied his inscrutable face.

"It's mostly tuition." His voice scraped raw.

"Mostly," I said, hoping he'd take the hint and expand a little. But he just watched me. "*Mostly*," he said again.

Mostly was what—eighty-five percent? Ninety?

I was probably the rest.

"You're quiet," Nathan murmured.

On the outside, I was. On the inside, my brain spun a blast of thoughts and images, colors and shapes and euphoria and rage over Nathan's future resting on me, over fire and sparks in my palms, in my fingers.

You can trust him.

You need to go.

"The truck." My voice exploded.

Nathan lurched back. "The truck?"

"Gil's," I burst out. "Before they leave, I need to decorate it."

"Isn't Brent supposed to do that?"

He was. He'd already started, probably. But it was carved on my bones, a visceral need so sharp I vibrated. "It should be me," I said. "I'm the artist. He's not going to do it right."

Nathan might have called my name as I sprinted, blood racing, for the barn. *Run to the house, run back. Get the brushes and the paint*—my feet tangled in my skirt and I hit the pine floor in the Barn entryway. Nothing hurt. My heart soared, actually, when I glanced to my right. *Chalk markers,* the ones I'd used to letter signs, sat in a box shoved to the side near the coat check. Box in my hands, I was weightless. Sprinting toward the parking lot.

"Brent!" I screamed it, guttural against the pounding in my ears.

Asphalt bit my hands and knees. Nathan cursed, then he was at my side murmuring he was sorry. "I didn't see you stop. Are you hurt? God, I'm so sorry."

I jerked away from him. "I'm fine!"

His face twisted. Shock. Sorrow. Pain.

"I don't have time for this," I wheezed, and he pulled me up, patted my arms with frantic fingers.

"Your skirt. Dewey, it's ripped."

"It doesn't matter. I need the markers. Let me go."

"You're bleeding," he said.

"Get off me." I cursed. Pushed him with sticky palms, then flailed to get away from him. My fist connected with something hard. And then I hit the ground, gasping for air, chest tight. Chest burning.

My vision faded.

The world went black.

Breathe in.

Quiet.

Breathe out.

Bright sun.

Breathe in.

Tongue coated in salt and copper.

No darkness. Tobacco fields.

I rolled and surveyed my surroundings. My eyes landed on the tobacco barn. Someone hummed inside. Someone I knew, the voice familiar.

Is that Lil?

It sounded like her. I crawled, bones aching, to the barn. Effa, I saw first, perched cross-legged across the wide, bare room on a table used for leaf tying. "You know what they say about humming?"

Lil's laugh answered from the loft. My pulse beat fast in my ears as a young woman leaned over the top of the ladder. "That it's the hallmark of a brilliant mind."

My breath caught. Gone were the lines on Lil's face. Gone were the gray streaks in her hair, the slight stiffness that slowed her movements. She wore smart navy twills and a button down, an old fashioned camera in her hands.

Sliding the camera strap around her neck with precision, Lil climbed down the ladder and landed with a graceful *thump*.

"Not hardly." Effa laughed. "Humming's the first sign of mental illness."

Lil's voice brimmed with mischief when she answered. "Well. You'd know all about that."

If Effa was offended, it certainly didn't show. She stuck out a playful tongue, and Lil held up her camera. "Stop moving. The light's perfect across your face."

Lil's subject went still. "Your camera habit's getting out of hand," she said.

"You're the perfect subject," Lil said. "The stunning, lovelorn poet."

Effa's lips twisted and she sighed. "I'm not lovelorn," she said. "Things are fine with me and Patrick. It's my father I'm worried about."

"Josiah." My whisper rippled in the not-there space. A grandfather I barely knew, a blurry face I couldn't conjure from memory.

"Josiah will understand, or he won't."

Lil had moved toward the table and leaned against it with a hip. Effa scooted to the table's edge and dangled her legs over the side, still elegant. "Easy for you to say."

"You're married." Lil took Effa's hand. A diamond ring caught the light, facets sparkling. "Your father can't change what's done, not the marriage or the baby."

The baby? I stumbled backward. Immediately, the room went dark.

No! I thought. *I'm not finished!*

"Dewey, you didn't start." Familiar hands gripped my arms. The summer night caressed my skin. My ears popped like I'd resurfaced from the depths of the river. "You're okay, Dewitt. I've got you."

"Nathan?"

He let go.

Voices. Sirens drifting through the air. I opened my eyes into the starlit sky, into the soft glow of the Griffin Barn event space.

Straight into the furious expression of Luther Griffin, my dad.

NINETEEN

NATHAN

I pulled Mr. Luther's golf cart into the marina just after seven forty-five. Dew clung to the grass, and the clear morning sun burned the mist off the river. The sting of diesel fuel burned my nose.

Duvall Harmon hunched in the dockhouse doorway, his wrinkled skin creased like a leather glove. He was ninety if he was a day, grumpy and persistent as an arthritic hound dog in suspenders and polyester pants.

"You're a mite bit early, I reckon," he said to me. "Not that I'm surprised."

"That a compliment, Mr. Duvall?"

I parked the cart in the grass next to the old man's Chevy and he scratched the whiskers on his chin. "Well, now," he said, voice straining. "How 'bout you take it however you want?"

"I'm just here to do my job," I said, tighter than normal. I wasn't in the mood to play. I wanted to cut and build and sand and polish. Wash last night off my hands.

Mr. Duvall cackled. "Woulda figured he'd give you the day off, what with last night's *festivities*."

"Just a wedding, Mr. D."

He gave a snort. "Not what I heard."

Duvall side-eyed my nod as I walked past him. "Sounds like you heard wrong."

Minnesott Marina perched by the water, a complex built of two parts. The dockhouse jutted off the front, a small, square-shaped building with a covered dock behind it. Farther inland, the spacious workshop loomed.

I signed out a radio and clipped it to my belt. Mr. Luther's Boston Whaler was first on my list, a fifteen footer called the *E. Marie*. She bobbed all the way at the dock's end, a gleaming white from engine to bow. Mr. Luther didn't use her much, but he loved her, so I came down once a week to check her out.

Duvall's voice split my radio, disrupting the rhythmic slap of river against hull. "I got the *E. Marie's* inspection papers," his voice said, sounding like sandpaper, forty grit.

I pressed the talk button. I'd get the papers on my way out. "You quit smoking yet?" I asked, then chuckled at the silence.

Thirty seconds passed, and then a crackle: "Mind your business, son."

I couldn't help it. "I ain't afraid to tell Mrs. June."

"You no-good son of a—" static burst right out, too loud for me to hear him until the last part: "—my wife anything. Luther Griffin's crazy to let his daughter spend time with you."

Instantly, my skin felt heavy, like I'd leaped into the river fully clothed. Maybe Duvall was right—I took all the blows. I'd tried to hold her in my arms and tell her I loved her. I did every-thing I could to pull her out of that fury.

Nothing I did worked.

I tightened bolts and flushed lines more aggressively than warranted, trying hard not to think about Dewitt. Once the *E. Marie* was done, I cleaned up my tools and headed to the work-shop, craving the quiet, satiny feel of teak. Music floated through the doorway and I checked the schedule posted on the outside wall. No one else had reserved the slot, and I yanked on the door. Stubble dotted Gil's face, and his shoulders drooped in a Pamlico County Middle School t-shirt.

"Shouldn't you be occupied, currently?" I asked him. "Like, I dunno. In bed with your wife?"

Gil smirked. "You shocked my stamina has limits?"

"Matches your intelligence, so, no." Gil was like a brother to me, but working in the shop the morning after his wedding? Dude was risking his life. "Rosie's gonna kill you, dipwad. What are you doing here?"

He leaned back against the workbench. "I'm worried about y'all."

"Me and Lil?"

"You and Dewitt."

"You should be on the road," I said, squeezing words out over emotion. "On the way to your honeymoon. Or in bed."

Cocky, Gil said, "Rosie's got no complaints. Except for Dewitt, so she's at Pinecliff throwing pebbles at her window." He glanced at his watch, then looked at me. "Until Luther runs her off."

"Look," I said, weary. "I appreciate your concern—"

"What's going on with Dewitt?" Gil asked, cutting me off. I flipped the workbench light to its brightest setting, desperate to occupy my hands.

Loving Dewitt was living through hurricane season, plotting points on a map. Guessing where the wind might lead; staring wide-eyed as it came ashore, at the mercy of its power. Hoping that when it's done ranting and raging, there'll be something of you left.

"You'd have to ask her," I told him. Gil leaned in and plucked the screwdriver from my hands. "Good way to get your nose bashed in," I said, and Gil said, "Try me."

I wanted to, so bad.

He stood too close to all of it, to the bench, to my arm, to the truth. But he wouldn't let up. "She hasn't told you anything."

She hadn't.

After all those conversations about trust.

Gil interpreted my silence the only way he could. "The irony," he said, deadpan, the delivery curling my hands into fists.

"Are you here to help?" I asked him. "Because if you got something to say—"

"Have you told her?"

"Have I told her what?"

"That she can trust you, man. Women—"

"You've been married sixteen hours and think you know everything."

"*Women* like to know how you feel."

My jaw ached, probably from clenching my teeth. "Thought it was obvious," I said.

"I'm gonna ask again—Have you *told* her?"

Dang it. "Yes, Gilbert." *Maybe?* "I have."

"You used words," he said. "Real ones."

Regret squeezed the back of my neck. "I told her last night." Dewitt had been beside herself in the lot, and the words fell out right before she punched me.

Gil seemed to read the truth on my face, pinching the bridge of his nose. "Before or after the meltdown, Nathan?"

I winced.

"During? I didn't say it was ideal! She was...we were dancing, it was fine, and the next thing I knew she was tearing across the lawn, screaming about your truck. And when I tried—" I took a breath. "When I tried to stop her, Gil, when I tried to hold in my arms, she..."

Gil set his elbows next to me on the workbench. "You tried to help her and she turned on you."

My cheek throbbed. Dewitt always did have a mean right hook. "I'm no good with words," I said, swallowing.

"Clearly. But you are good at showing how you feel. You been doing that since we were stupid and fourteen. But I think with women—"

I glared at him.

"With *Dewitt* specifically, she needs to *hear* the words. You need to say it, and then we need to get her help."

The last part was just as scary as the first. How did you get someone help when you weren't sure what they needed?

The radio squawked. "Can we turn that crap off?"

"You gonna tell her?"

"Is this coercion?"

"Motivation."

"Fine."

Gil cut it off. "Thank you," I breathed, and his new cell phone gave a low buzz as he pulled it from his pocket. He flipped it open, listening.

"Hey, baby...." More listening. "No...no...alright."

I tipped my chin toward the phone as he closed it. "Rosie?"

He nodded. "Luther told her to git. She sounded good on the phone, but..."

I saw the look in his eyes. "You're worried about her."

He didn't move to go, he just nodded. "Dewitt ain't gonna leave you, you know."

My lungs seized. "Where the hell did that come from?"

"Our conversation just now. All the years I've known you. You're afraid to say the words because if you do, it makes you vulnerable. You're worried she's gonna run."

"She is leaving." At least, that was her plan. "I don't know what's gonna happen after last night, but she wants to go to VCU. She's not staying."

Gil twirled his keychain on his finger. "Maybe, but you're her home."

Longing, thick and heavy, planted itself in my chest. I stared at Gil, not because I didn't know what to say, but because I didn't know how to say it.

Gil was right, and I knew it.

I had to get the words out of my mouth.

TWENTY

DEWITT

When I was little, Daddy hung a photo on his office wall. It was his family, his mom and dad, and a dark-haired, fat-rolled baby. They stood underneath the tallest magnolia at Pinecliff, only half its current size. "That's you, Daddy," I said and pointed at the baby, my tiny voice dwarfed by the leather furniture.

The next day, the photo was gone.

My father was not the baby in the photo. His sister, Effa, was. Daddy didn't admit that to me, of course: the confirmation came from my new psychiatrist, Dr. Adrian Lane. He went to school with my dad, and the day after I destroyed Gil and Rosie's wedding, Daddy had me in his office first thing. I talked about my trips; Dr. Lane wrote things down. And after what felt like hundreds of rating scales where I answered, *always, sometimes,* or *never,* we sat in his office three weeks later for my test results.

"Most likely, Dewitt," Dr. Lane said, caterpillar eyebrows turned down. "Your *trips,* as you call them, were hallucinations. Brought on by Bipolar Disorder I."

He checked his notes while my mother sniffled. "During testing, you reported visions. A woman. *Effa*, you said."

Daddy shifted in his chair. I nodded.

"Luther, Effa was your sister, correct?"

Daddy grunted his assent. Mama put a hand on his arm while Dr. Lane waited a beat, presumably for Daddy to say something. But when the room remained still, aside from Mama's quiet weeping, those bushy eyebrows turned back to me.

"Bipolar I has several characteristics." Dr. Lane paged through my report. "Manic episodes—what you called your *surges*, I believe—followed by inescapable fatigue and feelings of worthlessness."

"A depressive episode," I said, and he tipped his chin down.

"You fit the profile for Bipolar I quite well."

Dr. Lane folded his hands on the desktop, looking oddly pleased with himself. I was happy to have an answer, sure, but I could have done without the celebration. The smug look on his face ticked me off.

"Why Effa?" I asked the room. "Why was I hallucinating her, and not other stuff, like talking rabbits?"

Daddy burst, pacing, from his chair.

"Sit down, Luther," Mama murmured, but he kept circling the small room, fists clenched.

"We had an agreement, Adrian," he said, and my head snapped in Daddy's direction.

"What are you talking about?"

Dr. Lane studied my father as my mother stifled sobs to my right. "Somebody tell me what's going on," I demanded, and three sets of eyeballs blinked at me. "If my disorder makes me hallucinate, fine, whatever, okay. But why Effa? Why *her*? Was my brain just...inventing moments from her life at random?"

A marriage. A baby. A car accident. I was an artist with a

vivid imagination, but this seemed far beyond the scope of *dreamer,* even *dreamer who is mentally ill.*

Dr. Lane leaned forward. "You've studied your family history. You must have come across her somewhere." He looked at Daddy. "A photo?"

"In my office," he bit out.

Dr. Lane held out his hands—*there you go.* "Your brain must have held onto that, Dewitt."

There'd been the letter, too. If Dr. Lane was right, would treatment stop the hallucinations? My leg bounced as I tapped the desktop with a finger. "What's the treatment plan for Bipolar I?"

Mama's quiet sobs grew louder while Daddy ground his teeth down to nubs. "Treatments were primitive in the past," Dr. Lane said, "but we've made significant improvements over the last twenty years. We prefer a more life-affirming approach to what we had just fifty years ago. Medication, therapy, and family support.

"That seems easy," I said. "So this isn't going to ruin my life?"

"No. Most patients live full, healthy lives, assuming they continue treatment."

My lungs filled. "So I can go to college, right?"

"I'm not sure that's wise." Dr. Lane glanced at my dad, and all the air left the room unbidden.

"I mean next year," I said. "Once I've graduated."

Daddy's pacing lurched to a stop, the set of his shoulders angry. "Adrian. A word?"

I spun in my chair to face him. "You don't want him to talk to me about school. This is my brain," I said. "*My diagnosis.*"

"Quiet!" Daddy barked, and the windows shook with it.

Dr. Lane cleared his throat, his expression indecipherable. "We'll only be a moment, I'm sure."

"No, thank you," I said, and my mother sprang from her chair. She turned the glass knob on the door and ushered me into the hallway.

Liquid anger seared the back of my throat.

"I deserve a say in this."

Mama seethed. "We don't have a choice. "This is a *family issue*, Dewitt. And you're a minor."

"Not for long. Once I turn eighteen, I'm an adult, and I can handle this the way I want to."

Dr. Lane opened the door and squashed the tension. Mama smoothed the wrinkles from her pants. Daddy stalked through the door, jugular pulsing, and Dr. Lane reached out to shake my hand.

I crossed my arms against my chest. "Well then," he said, head tilting toward my parents. "My receptionist will follow up."

"With them? I'm the patient, Dr. Lane. I have a right to know what's happening."

Dr. Lane's gaze shot to Daddy.

"Fine," I snapped. "My shrink's a coward. At least I know what I'm dealing with."

Mama gasped. "*Dewitt Griffin.*"

"Young lady," Daddy said. "*The car.*"

"What are you afraid of?" I bit out, and my parents shared a glance I couldn't make sense of before they escorted my rage down the hall.

A DIAGNOSIS DIDN'T FIX things for my parents—I was the same embarrassment I'd always been. I hid under the covers when we got home, content inside my artificial darkness until Mama arrived in my doorway, silver tea tray in hand.

"I'm not hungry," I told her, voice muffled underneath the quilt.

"Good thing I didn't bring food." I heard the tray wobble in her hands, and I sat up just in time to see her set it on the nightstand. She'd brought tea and my favorite mug.

Sunlight shone through my window and caught an amber pill bottle on the tray. I had no clue what the label said, what the drug was, or how often I should take it. "Minnesott Pharmacy works fast."

It was snarky, but I couldn't help myself. "Is Daddy gonna let you clue me in?"

Mama let out a weary breath. "Your father loves you, Dewitt. So much."

The bed dipped as Mama slumped down next to me. "Luther looks and acts tough. But he carries a lot of guilt, more than he should, honestly."

"Over what?" I asked. "Effa?"

She nodded.

"Why won't he talk about her?"

It was a question I'd been pondering since I realized who Effa was. Lil clued me in a bit, that Daddy was a stuffer, but I wondered what my mother might say.

To my surprise, she answered. "Grief is personal. Your father's journey has been...difficult. I'm not his therapist, I'm his wife, and Lou's got to decide what help he wants, and when he's ready for it."

My mood soured even more, if that was possible. "So he can suffocate me while we wait."

Mama's head tipped back in irritation. "Dewitt—"

"Do you not see how unfair that is? This is my brain, my life, my hopes and dreams he's railroading. He gets to decide what path he'll take and when he'll take it, but I don't get the same choice?"

Mama took my hand and held it, rubbing a thumb across my scar. "I'll talk to him," she said. "I think it would help if we had a little buy-in." Her potent gaze found the pill bottle on the tray.

Give an inch, Daddy used to say; *gain a foothold.*

"How many do I take?"

TWENTY-ONE

NATHAN

July 2003

I showed up for work one sticky July morning to find Mrs. Deebie on the front porch swing. A thick book sat open in her lap, her favorite coffee mug on the table beside her. She closed the book and looked up, her right thumb playing bookmark. "Well. Aren't you a sight for sore eyes?"

"Pardon?" I glanced down at myself. Muddy boots. Stained shirt. I mean, I looked alright for working construction.

"You look fine," she said, dismissive. "I just mean I haven't seen you recently."

She hadn't since the wedding, and not because I'd taken time off. The opposite was true—I'd been at Pinecliff more over the past month than I had since I started working for Mr. Luther. Hard work cleared my head, and I told myself the more I worked, the better I'd be at telling Dewitt how I felt about her. Problem was, I had to see her first.

After the reception, Dewitt ghosted all three of us. I thought maybe she'd come around when Gil and Rosie got back from their honeymoon in Wilmington, but Ro tried calling and had no luck. Dewitt kept her bedroom shades drawn. I never saw her leave the house. Wouldn't answer phone calls or texts. It was a lame excuse, what I said: "Mr. Luther keeps me busy."

An eyebrow lifted. "Well now. Is that right."

It wasn't a question. She saw right through me, that much was clear. Deebie's fingers drummed the book in her hand in a solid, steady rhythm. "I'm assuming Luther told you about the porch."

"Yes, ma'am." I exhaled, relieved to talk carpentry. I pressed my foot into the bottom step. "This step here's nearly rotten, and it looks like other boards are wearing out, too. I can replace them right quick—if I get started today, should be done by tomorrow."

Deebie grated the air with a dry chuckle. "Lordy, can I sympathize with those boards."

I'd known Deebie for a while. She was a steel magnolia, through and through. A comment like that—and its implication —were out of the ordinary for her. I took a good look at her then, at the stain of coffee on her shirt and the wrinkles in her chinos, the way dark circles puffed beneath her eyes. Deep lines carved through her face, not the product of time, but exhaustion. "Mrs. Deebie, you alright?"

She snorted. "You can tell me I look a right mess."

"I didn't mean—"

"I'm not offended," she said, running a hand through her hair before she winced around a sip of coffee. "The way I see it, Nathan, it's high time we spoke the truth around here. You've been avoiding Dewitt."

I panicked. What would she say if I told her why? "My workload's been tough. And I got a new boat I'm working on, a commission. CEO-type in Raleigh, he's—"

Deebie chuckled. "You're an awful liar, son."

I wasn't lying. I was avoiding telling the whole truth. I supposed that from Deebie's point of view, it was the same thing in different outfits and she didn't much like either one. If I told her everything—that I'd caused Dewitt to shut us out—the nightmare would be real, and more than likely, I'd be unwelcome.

Sweat pooled under the brim of my hat.

Deebie eyed me like a vulture, and under her scrutiny, I caved. "I'm not good at words, Mrs. D. Your daughter's special to me and I never told her, not in the way I should. I mean I tried, but I picked the worst possible time, and by then..." I paused. "It was too late, honestly. Whatever we had, Dewitt and me...she's avoiding all of us."

The chains on the porch swing rattled as Deebie rose to her feet. "I think you're done for the day."

"What?"

"You're off the clock."

I glanced at my watch. "It's ten thirty."

Deebie dumped her coffee over the rail. "Your work ethic is something else. Dewitt's up at the Arts Building, and I think you ought to go see her. Right now."

Still unsure what was happening, I said the only thing that seemed relevant. "It's Tuesday. They're closed."

"They gave Dewitt a key," she said, pressing her lips down like she thought it was stupid. "Dewitt told me *y'all* quit coming around, not that she'd been the one doing the ghosting. Go up there, please, and find her. Don't leave until she tells you the truth."

ORIENTAL'S MAIN Street stood quiet in the late morning heat. Pamlico Arts looked locked up tight, shades pulled down against the sun and the *Come back later, we're out of paint!* sign in the window. I let the door slam shut on the jeep. Dewitt took to being cornered about as well as a feral cat, but Deebie had been a wreck and it didn't sit right with me not to follow orders. I'd have to figure things out as I went.

Bells bounced against the door as I opened it and Dewitt's voice swam through the dark. "We're closed," she called, the sound a little muffled.

"It's just me, Dewitt."

Just me. It echoed. A bit of rustling, then a curse. "Go away," she bit out, and I was back on the pier, convincing the prettiest, most frustrating girl I'd ever met to let me extricate a fishhook from her knuckles.

I hadn't backed down that day.

I wasn't gonna back down now.

I shuffled toward the back in the dusky darkness, bumping into tables left and right. A heap of fabric lay on the floor, the shape of it distinctly human. Dewitt lay facedown in a sea of canvas and paint. She'd called out—logically, I knew she was breathing. But I still dropped to my knees and pressed my fingers below her jawbone.

"Would you quit it?" Dewitt screeched.

She bolted upward, scattering art supplies across the floor. "I'm having a pity party, Nathan. I'm not dead." Her hair dragged across her face, and she huffed to try and move it. "What are you doing here?"

I startled at her question. Honestly, I wasn't sure. Had I come to take her home? Or had I come to get the truth, per Deebie? Or did I just miss her so much my entire body ached with it?

I answered with the only thing I knew for certain. "I was looking for you."

"You found me. Congratulations." She flung a paint rag at my chest. I caught it and held it up like a 4H fair ribbon.

"This mean I won first place?"

"In being annoying, maybe." A streak of yellow rippled across her nose. Dewitt's eyes dropped to the floor, and I followed her gaze to the sea of canvas.

"I didn't know you painted abstract."

Most of the pieces were ruined, their surfaces ripped and frames cracked wide. There weren't any landscapes or homes; not a single detailed portrait. Just muddled colors in circular shapes. One canvas caught my eye, though; intact, its swirls of dark blue and green coalesced in the center and met at a fluid yellow point. I held it to the sparse light, inspecting it. "It's like surfacing in the ocean. Cool."

Dewitt lurched into my space and ripped the canvas from my fingers, her mouth inches from mine. "Don't patronize me," she spit out, charged air crackling in the space between us, our lips close enough to touch. We were close enough, too, that she could shiv me if she wanted, and for a second, I worried she had a putty knife. I counted backward from ten, hoping by the time I reached one, I'd know if we were making up or sparring.

Ten. Nine. Eight. Seven—

On six, Dewitt burst into tears.

Dang it. I pulled her into my arms. Pressed her damp cheek against my shirt and rocked us both until her tears slowed and her breathing evened. She whispered an apology.

"It's my fault," I murmured. "I shouldn't have touched your stuff."

"It's not about the paintings," she said into my breastbone. "Well, maybe partially it is. But I'm sorry I ghosted you after the reception. I don't remember all that much, but I think..." She trailed off, then sat up to face me. "I hit you, didn't I?"

My cheek throbbed, a phantom memory of the faded

bruise. "I healed," I said, and Dewitt trailed her hand across the memory.

"I couldn't promise you'd be safe," she said.

Dewitt had me tied around her finger. "I've never been safe from you."

Her face flushed, two bright spots on the apples of her cheeks. "I don't—that's not what I meant. I could have hurt you, physically, and I didn't want to do that. Not again."

She could have. Dewitt held my heart in her hand. But I had a feeling that wasn't what this was about, that it had more to do with Deebie's insistence. "I saw your mama this morning. At work."

Muscles tightening, Dewitt sat back and turned away from me. "She tell you what's going on?"

"She told me where to find you. The rest of it was your story, she said."

Her laugh was rueful. "That's Mama's favorite thing to say. If you've got problems, it's your *story*. And it's your responsibility to tell."

"I don't disagree," I mused, "except maybe for the telling. Just cause something happened to you doesn't mean you have to share."

Dewitt hesitated. "What if I want you to know, so you can make your own decision?"

My chest burned. "My own decision about what?"

She scooted toward me, resting her back against my front. My legs circled hers, and my arms looped around her waistline. "About me," she murmured. "Whether or not I'm worth it."

"You're worth it. You can...you can talk to me, Dewitt."

"I have Bipolar Disorder, Type I."

Senior year, I took a psych class. Lil suggested it. It filled an elective and it was fun, and as I held Dewitt in my arms, I thought back to what we'd learned about mental health disorders. Pieces began to fall into place, the ups and down, the rapid speech, the rage, even the violence. I wasn't an expert, but it made sense.

We were quiet for a minute, until I asked her, "How do you feel now that you know?"

She huffed. "I don't care. Actually, I take that back. I know what's happening to me now, so I guess, in a way, I'm grateful. But my parents...Daddy's being difficult. I'm going to the therapist he chose. I'm not allowed to talk to the psychiatrist. I don't know the details of my meds aside from the name, and my art —" she motioned around her—"it's suffering. It's like everything I paint is wrong."

We shifted, and canvas splintered beneath my legs. "Do you think the art block is from the meds?"

"I don't know," she said, shrugging against me. "I can't even talk to the doctor to ask."

"I'm sorry." It ripped me from the inside out.

"This isn't your fault."

"Part of it is," I said. "I made trust such a big deal before we started dating and then...when it was my turn to open up...I should have tried harder, I think, to tell you...I love you. Maybe you would have trusted *me* more."

Dewitt turned in front of me, facing me this time, on her knees. I shifted up to mine, too, paint tubes squelching under foot and canvas popping. Hands trembling, I reached out and brushed her arms.

"I'm a mess, Nathan. Look at what we're kneeling on. This is me. It was me before, and it's me now. Different, yeah, but still a gigantic, unmitigated disaster."

"Dewitt." I lifted her chin. "I have loved you for a very long time. With paint on your face; with a fishhook in your hand; in a courtyard, punching bullies. And somehow, you love me, a kid from the wrong side of town. A kid who can't say the right things, who's an idiot when it comes to expressing his emotions. Every day I spend with you is like discovering a...a...new color. And I'm in love with every shade of you."

Her breath caught. My thumbed tugged the yellow across her nose. "I really want to kiss you right now," she said, and my hand froze, because absolutely, I wanted to kiss her. But she'd just been crying in my arms, and she'd just opened up her heart, and—

"I don't want to take advantage."

"Of me?" She made a face. "I may be crazy, but I promise I know what I want."

"You're not crazy." I watched my thumb drag its way up her cheek.

"Then what are we waiting for?" she asked, and Dewitt leaned in an kissed me. Nothing mattered beyond the soft smile against my lips. It was like the creek all over again, only sweeter somehow, more intimate. My hands found the swell of her hips. The fabric crinkled beneath my touch, the stickiness ripe and familiar.

Dang it. I pulled back, irritated. "I just got paint on your skirt."

Dewitt laughed and brought her fingers upward, skating three silky pads down to my jaw. Her mouth held millimeters from mine; "Now we're even."

I pressed my mouth below her ear. Trailed paint along her jaw, used my thumb to trace her neck toward her collarbone. Dewitt looked at me, heavy-lidded.

A curved arc of yellow caught me smack in my chest.

Dewitt scrambled to her feet, cackling. She'd unloaded an entire tube of paint on my shirt. "Oh, it is *on.*" I pushed up to my feet as her squeal hit the rafters and our feet slid across the floor. I circled her waist from behind, linen and lavender enveloping us both, her feet lifting off the ground as we spun in a dizzying circle, stumbling back to earth.

She turned in my arms and laid her palms on my chest, the heavy thud of my heart unmissable. "So it's not just me," she said.

I shook my head. "We should clean up," I rasped, and her chest heaved like mine, naked want in her eyes as she studied me.

"It can wait," she said, and I kissed her.

We fell back into each other.

Whole.

TWENTY-TWO
DEWITT

October 2003

Quitting my meds was the Expo's fault.

The North Carolina Art Foundation ran a weekend of exhibitions every fall. This year, the Eastern Art Expo would invade historic downtown New Bern, thirty minutes from my house.

Ms. Tabor, my AP art teacher, tacked the event poster to the art room wall. She pushed her glasses up her nose and leaned in like she had a secret. "The exhibit hall for young artists is a *huge* opportunity. Gallery owners come, art school reps..." She held up a brochure splashed with the poster's same colorful branding. "I see a bunch of top schools...Savannah College of Art and Design...Rhode Island School of Design... The Pratt Institute..."

Please don't say it.

"Carnegie Mellon, Parsons...and a little closer to home, UNC, NC State, VCU..."

Quiet panic spread like wildfire. All my recent work was

abstract. I swallowed hard and put my head down on the drafting table. Banged my forehead against it, once. The bell rang, and I stood up fast, the metal legs of my stool screeching against the linoleum.

"Dewitt—hold on a moment, please."

I could feel Ms. Tabor tracking me as I made my way to the door. "I need to get to Calculus," I said, and turned around to see Ms. Tabor pointing at her t-shirt. *Proud Pamlico Alumni!* it read.

"Old man Dorchester still passing out detentions?"

"Like a human Pez dispenser."

She laughed. "I'll make it quick. I know VCU is your top choice. I also know that while *I* love Dewitt Griffin's Abstract Period, *you* are not a fan."

That was an understatement. "Ms. Tabor—"

"Let me finish, please. I want you to submit. If not something new, why not dig into your backlist? Select a few pieces from your standing portfolio. Something you painted last year."

"Something from last year." The polar ice caps were warmer than my voice. Daddy may not have appreciated my *hobby*, but pride would bring him to the Expo just the same. If I chose something from last year, I'd be digging through piles of Effa. I needed something fresh. Realistic. Not my dead aunt, the proverbial lead balloon.

My current drug brought more than an end to Effa. It killed my talent, as well. So I started with one skipped dose, then two, and by the time I got to four, I'd painted a sunset in awkward strokes and dull colors. It wasn't good, but it wasn't a circle, either.

I flushed the rest of my pills.

By the opening day of the Art Expo, I'd submitted three finished pieces I loved. I was doing fine without the meds. My Bipolar didn't control me. At least, I thought so, standing in an alcove of the Convention Center's Craven Hall. The youth exhibit earned the natural light in Craven Hall's window-lined space, a definite perk that made the noise level worth it. Spectators meandered here and there, chatting with artists and taking photos. I soaked in the atmosphere, buzzing.

And then my parents showed up.

"Lou, you have to see this." Mama took Daddy by the arm. She'd worn a chic pantsuit today, red trousers and a navy blazer over a white pin dot shell. Daddy's lips held a grim line and he pulled on his bowtie while I tugged down on my dress. Pretty in a soft shell pink, the tailored lines weren't something I would typically have chosen. But Mama picked it out, and she was proud of me, so I wore it. Figured I owed her one.

They stopped in front of my first submission, a painting of Pinecliff at dusk. She'd already fawned over it once, at home, and the slight sheen in her eyes said the impact hadn't wavered. She looked at Daddy. "Luther, this is perfect. See how the shadows fall across the porch? It's just..." she shook her head. "Absolutely perfect."

I beamed.

Daddy's approval came grudgingly, communicated with a quiet grunt. He shifted to the right, his eyes drawn to my second painting. "This my barn?" he asked.

"Before the rebuild," I answered, like he couldn't tell. A shadow passed over his face, and all he said was, "Nice looking."

"It's beautiful." Mama bumped him with her hip. "And this —" she moved to piece number three. "Have Gil and Rosie seen this?"

They'd come through earlier, so yes. *"That's what you were sketching in my lap,"* Nathan said, *wrapping his arms around my waist and kissing my temple, his scent warming me from the inside out.*

"You sketched us at the bonfire." Rosie looked at me, mouth agape.

"I didn't even know," Gil said. His eyes were fixed on the focal point, his and Rosie's intertwined hands. I blurred the rest of out it in the last rays of sun. Rosie cried, and Nathan looked at me like I was precious. Gil sniffed and complained about allergies before excusing himself.

"Dewitt, are these your parents?" Ms. Tabor's eager voice cut through the hall.

"Ms. Tabor, hi," I said. My spine jolted ramrod straight at the dark-skinned woman behind her. Her name tag read *Serena Thompson, Virginia Commonwealth University School of the Arts.*

Ms. Tabor offered a hand to my mother, wearing a smile roughly three feet wide. "Jenna Tabor," she said. "So nice to meet you. I teach AP art up at Pamlico."

"Oh! You're Dewitt's teacher!" Mama took Ms. Tabor's hand in both of hers. "Tabor...I bet...are you Lyda Tabor's granddaughter?"

"Well yes, ma'am," Tabor said. "I sure am!" I wanted to shrivel on the exhibit hall floor, their conversation proof I lived in a podunk town where everybody knew everybody.

Right in front of VCU's rep.

Daddy made an irritated noise.

"Oh! Luther!" Mama turned toward him with a laugh. "Jenna, this is my husband, Luther Griffin."

He nodded. "Ms. Tabor. Hello. I believe we have another guest?" He asked, and Ms. Tabor turned to the VCU rep.

"Mr. And Mrs. Griffin, this is Serena Taylor from VCU."

Serena's stack of bracelets bounced on her arm as she held out a hand. "Nice to meet you," she said, then turned in my direction. "You must be Dewitt."

"Hi." It came out breathy. "Hi, yes. I'm Dewitt."

"Ms. Tabor tells me you've been interested in VCU since middle school."

My tongue felt fat and fuzzy in my mouth. I managed a few words, something about studying abroad and inspiration.

She nodded, then asked, "Is this your work?"

"Yes," I said. And offered zero explanation. Serena didn't seem bothered by it, though.

"I'm impressed with your talent," she said, and I died, right there, in the hallway.

"Thank you," I squeaked out.

Moses, I was ridiculous. But I had all these thoughts in my brain. I wanted to blurt them all out, tell her about my work and my dreams, but Daddy stood right there, murderous.

I looked at my mom. *Help me.*

"Oh! Would you look at the time!" Mama never wore a watch, but she sure acted like she did, hooking her arm through Daddy's elbow and apologizing profusely. "We were supposed to catch a speaker five minutes ago. The one on agriculture in art."

I watched the tic in Daddy's jaw throb as Mama dragged him toward Ballroom B. "Parents," I said.

Serena's smile was soft as she said, "Tell me what you love about your medium."

And for the next fifteen exhilarating minutes, I did.

———

I CAME HOME SPINNING.

Serena Taylor loved my work.

She gave me her card. Offered an exclusive campus visit. And she said that when I applied, I should send my portfolio directly to her. My heart sang with hope, with dreams of next year and visions of fresh, new artwork. I let the screen door drop and Daddy's voice curved from the office. A standard, run-of-the-mill, "Dewitt?"

I kicked off my shoes. "Yes, sir?"

"Office," was all he said.

Too giddy to find his tone offensive, I glided down the hall. "I was heading up to change." I rocked back on my heels outside the French doors, eyes drawn to the bulging vein in his neck.

"That can wait," he said gruffly. He straightened a stack of papers before he stood. He pointed at the armchair in front of his desk and said "Sit," like I was a hound dog.

I bristled. "What is this about?"

"Paperwork. You've been offered a job." Daddy's voice was tight, and his shoulders flexed to match it.

"I wasn't looking for one."

"'Course you weren't," he said. "You were too busy making nice with collegiate art departments. The charter school's art teacher put in for retirement. Come April, you'll be taking her place."

"April?" Weren't they going to want someone long-term? "I'm going to school in the fall. I—"

"You won't have to go to school. You'll start your career and get to dabble in your hobby."

"I don't want a teaching job!" The antique windows rattled, wavy in their wooden frames. It was like watching myself through a fog, knowing I needed to get out, go upstairs, and give myself a minute. "I'm sorry for yelling, Daddy. I—"

"If you're going to yell in my house, that's your choice. But shut the doors so your mother doesn't have to hear."

Chastened, I pulled the French doors shut and sat across from him in the armchair, the leather cool against my skin. Daddy's face remained eerily impassive as he steepled his fingers and leaned back.

"Speaking of your mother, we had a *conversation* on the way back to town. She made a few things clear, things I may have done without...realizing the ramifications. Specifically shielding you from my past."

Mama had talked to him like she promised. *Maybe she's on my side.* "Daddy, you lied to me."

"I didn't lie. My sister and I were close. Our mother..." Daddy's mask slipped for a fraction of a second, long enough for me to see the hurt. But then he inhaled, face hardening, and he continued with the truth. "Our mother was sick, and I don't want you to go through the same sort of struggles. I didn't tell you because I wanted to protect you. That's all I've ever wanted, in fact."

I blinked at him. "Protect me from what?"

There wasn't much I remembered about his mother, just her name—Annie—and the year of her birth. Clearly, there was more, and once again, he'd glossed straight over Effa. "Daddy. Protect me from *what*?"

Across the desk, he pushed a folder.

"What's this?" I asked. I slid a finger beneath the edge, flipping the front to reveal a stack of papers, my father's handwriting trailing down the page.

Painted all night—second occurrence

Destroyed the sunroom and lost track of time

Principal called—physical violence against Brent Summers

The list went on and on. "You kept a gossip file. *About me.*"

"I kept a record of safety concerns."

"That's not what this is!"

Daddy's gaze was stern enough to peel the wallpaper in the kitchen. "College is important to you. I know. But your treatment team is *here*, and—"

"And they have doctors in Virginia."

He swallowed and averted his eyes. "Orientation for new faculty is the first week in August—"

"Daddy—"

"Pay isn't much, but your mother and I won't charge rent until—"

"You're not *listening!*"

"Until you've built up a cushion," he said, voice rising. "Probably December. You'll—"

My fist slammed against the desk, the pain in my hand as satisfying as the sound of it. "Why don't you want me at VCU?"

A potent silence enveloped the office. Lungs bursting, I held my breath. "Because you're unstable, Dewitt," he said. "Your disorder requires monitoring. What if something happens while you're away? Home is where you belong, close to the people who love you."

"Home is what I make of it," I snapped. "I'm going to school."

"I won't pay for it."

"I have money saved in my account." Not enough, but there were grants. Loans. Scholarships.

My father opened his laptop and tapped a series of keys. When he turned the machine around, my bank account looked back, the current balance at a whopping zero. "What did you do to my account?"

"I moved the balance into a trust. It will stay there, safe, until you're stable enough for me to sign it over."

My strained emotions pulled taut. "Don't do this."

"We'll reevaluate after a year. I can't, in good conscience, let you leave Minnesott. Not if you're not alright."

The moment was like an icepick piercing the back of my skull. Like fire scorching my hands, like every twisted, unhinged thought I'd ever had took root in my brain and flowered.

Like every molecule of air glowed red.

I bellowed. Slammed the laptop shut. Curled my fingers around the edge and hurled it to the floor, keening like a wild banshee before knocking over the leather chair. Wood splintered at my back and glass shattered, the echo of it satisfying in their wake. On fire, I pulled books from the shelves, hefting the family Bible at my father. I welcomed the sharp pain in my palm and the warm, sticky wetness as I sliced my hand open on the French door's broken glass.

Eyesight hazy; blood pounding in my ears, I trailed scarlet handprints down the hall and into the kitchen, tripping over the back door's threshold into the spiky grass. Nausea welled up in my throat, hot-edged and brutal, and I dry-heaved, leaving snot in the dirt. Fury propelled me across the yard and down the hill, past the brambles that ripped my feet, onto the sand, past the waves, plunging my head into the water.

I screamed beneath the surface, spilling my rage into the endless deep.

TWENTY-THREE

NATHAN

For an artist, Dewitt sure was hell on her hands.

"We keep ending up here," I joked, clinging to my last shreds of humor, stomach churning at the red slash across her palm.

She winced as I drew her hand under the tap and, on reflex, I did the same. "Sorry," I breathed. "Sorry."

I hate hurting you.

"Not your fault," she whispered, eyes on the towel I wrapped around her hand. I set the first aid kit on the counter space, next to where Dewitt perched. It wasn't my fault. I knew that. Guilt still gnawed at me. I'd let Rosie bring her home, ignoring the twinge in my gut that I should stay with her. Instead, I left early to work an a dumb boat build.

"Mama shouldn't have called you," Dewitt said, pulling me out of my thoughts. "She would have found me if she'd walked down the hill."

Dewitt's gone. She trashed the house. Nathan, we can't find her.

I traced the cut on Dewitt's palm with an antibiotic ointment. "I never mind looking for you."

"You're sweet," she said.

"I'm serious."

Her eyes found mine. "So am I."

She took a shuddering breath, and I tucked a stray lock of hair behind her ear. "I'm sorry," she said. Sniffled.

"You got nothing to be sorry about."

I finished my first aid duties and lifted her from the counter into my arms. She wrapped her arms around my neck, her legs around my waist, and I carried her to the bed, unsteady, my heart way heavier than Dewitt.

"Do you want to talk about it?" I set her down on the bed. She still had on her Expo dress, and I turned all the way around as she unbuttoned the front and slipped out of it.

She snorted. "Not like you haven't seen this before."

Yes, I'd seen it. She still deserved respect. "You pulled the covers up yet?"

I felt the eye roll. "I'm covered."

She was snuggled beneath the blankets when I turned around.

I sat next to her. "You didn't answer. Do you want to talk about it at all?"

Her eyes drifted close, dark lashes fanning her cheeks like feathers. "The VCU rep thinks I'm amazing."

I hesitated. "Isn't that good?"

"It's great." She opened her eyes, a flash of regret passing through them before she blinked and focused on me. "Except Daddy got me a job, and he's been keeping a journal of my behavior. He said he wants to keep me safe—something about his mama and his sister, but...he made me so mad and he wouldn't...he wouldn't listen." She swallowed hard and looked away, her face turning toward the window. "Short story is, I went a little nuts."

I'd kept my focus on Dewitt when I carried her from the shoreline, but I remembered the broken glass beneath my feet. The sharp smell of copper burned my nose, a sense memory.

What was Luther playing at?

"I'm gonna get you some painkillers," I said. Dewitt answered with a soft snore. I cut off the bedside lamp, then left the room and shut the door behind me, ready to tend to different wounds.

I FOUND Deebie outside the office, alone and sweeping broken glass. I took the broom and finished up, pretending I hadn't seen her crying. She ran a knuckle under her eyes before she finally took a look at me. "Thank you," she said. "I should go find Luther. Could you—" She winced and surveyed the ground, right hand gesturing at the splintered wood and blood stains. "*Moses*, I hate to ask..."

"I'll take care of it," I said, and I meant it. I'd take care of it all. The floor. The French doors. The books discarded from the shelves in the office. The laptop. The bloodstains. *Dewitt.*

Repair work took a few days. I placed orders and made store runs. Dewitt stayed in her room, murmuring sleep words every time I checked on her. On Monday, she started a day program in New Bern, taking time off school for a week. I focused on the physical work of replacing glass panes and buffing out the bloodstains. By Thursday morning, I'd taped the French doors' fresh glass and had my trim brush ready when Mr. Luther came in through the front door.

"Nathan."

I set my paintbrush down.

"You got a minute?" he asked, and my fingers flexed with tension.

"Think I can spare a few."

An odd tightness hung between us, festering the better part of the week. Conversations were clipped, their focus on repairs and purchase orders with an undercurrent of Dewitt. He'd been strictly business; I'd been respectful but standoffish, at best. He seemed softer today, his navy pants unpressed and his dress shirt open at the collar. He hadn't straightened his windswept hair.

"Thanks, son," he said, pleasant. "Hoping we can chat about Dewitt. She's had a time of it lately, though, and I'd like to get your input on something."

I chewed the inside of my cheek. Luther paid me well. He treated me like an equal. I was grateful for that. But Dewitt was mine, and my loyalty lay on one side of the family. I was always gonna choose Dewitt.

My poker face must have surfaced, considering Mr Luther carried on without a hitch. "I see how much you care about my daughter—"

"I love her, Mr. Luther."

Well. I'd lost that hand. But Luther's exterior slipped, too, and for a moment, grief stalked across his face and squatted. "Dewitt doesn't talk to me about that sort of thing. I suspect she shares your affections, though," he said, and I offered him a peace offering.

"She's been focused on school," I said.

"Actually," he said. "About that..."

I knew I'd stepped in it. "Her decisions aren't my business, sir."

Luther pushed off the wall. "You're loyal. I've always

appreciated that about you. I'm only asking because I need your help, not because I'm betraying her trust or feeding you gossip." He ducked around me into the office and searched his desk with a muttered *where'd it go?* He made a little *aha* sound, then stepped carefully around the canvas tarps I'd spread out for painting, holding a paper in his hands.

"Dewitt is dead set on art school, but we've had a little...snafu."

My eye caught the letterhead at the top of the page: *Dr. Adrian Lane, Carolina Psychiatric.* "That's her doctor."

He nodded. "It is."

"Mr. Luther..." I shifted. Willed the hairs on my neck to stand down. "I don't think I should look at this," I said, my eyes catching on a highlighted portion.

He tapped it with a finger. "You have my permission. Just read that."

I read it:

The patient's diagnosis of Bipolar Disorder Type I, along with the severity of her symptoms, indicates the necessity for strong, well-formed support. Until Ms. Griffin is capable of improved decision-making, I recommend she avoid the distance and stressors associated with a four-year plan for secondary education.

"Her psychiatrist doesn't want her at school?"

"It's up to me and Dora Bell, ultimately, but we agree with Dr. Lane. Dewitt needs more time at home."

"To do what? Rot?" Hot coals stoked my voice box.

"To get treatment." Luther's voice remained cool.

"She's dreamed of VCU for years. If you don't let her go—" I faltered, brain catching on the memory of what she'd said. About how Luther got her a job, one she didn't want and wasn't looking for. At the damage that was done; at the cuts on her hand and the blood I'd buffed out of the floorboards.

My stomach clenched, lead-filled. "You told her, didn't you?"

Luther held my gaze. "Do your plans include my daughter?"

I stood up even straighter. "Yes."

"And yet you turned Broward down."

My chin went up, a challenge. "I deferred for a year."

"So you'll enroll for next fall?" he asked, the back of my neck pinched at his line of questioning.

"Maybe. Don't know."

His eyes danced like he found my answer amusing. "Well, then. I guess you're fired."

My stomach swooped. "I'm sorry. What?"

"Not right now," he said, crossing his arms in whole-body smugness. "I'm thinking mid-August, around the start of the school year. If you're fired, I can send you out the door. Free and clear, son, all the way to Broward. I'll pay your tuition *and* your room and board."

I wasn't even tempted. The whole conversation put a foul taste in my mouth. "I don't take handouts, sir."

"You will if you plan on marrying my daughter."

Phantom fire ants scaled my limbs and the foul taste in my mouth turned bitter. "Are you bribing me?"

He tensed. "I'm being practical. Dewitt's decision-making skills are poor. VCU's been tabled for now, and I need you to help me convince her."

"I won't break her dreams for mine."

"Dewitt needs someone to support her. I'd like that person to be you. You'll have a much better chance at success if you've gotten a degree, honing your skills at Broward."

Dread settled between my ribs. "You're underestimating Dewitt, Mr. Luther."

"Maybe." His tone grated. Moses, it was so nonchalant. "I

would love to be proved wrong. But dreams aren't reality, son. This—" he gestured to the tarp on the floor, the taped off glass inside the doorframe—"is our reality."

He turned and gave a parting shot as he headed for the kitchen. "One day, Nathan, it's gonna be yours."

TWENTY-FOUR

DEWITT

March 2004

Life on antipsychotics had its moments.

Specifically, children were not as loud.

It was a good thing, too, considering my meltdown in the fall landed me a new cocktail of drugs and sped up Daddy's plan for my future. If there was one thing Luther Griffin believed in aside from the importance of one's ancestry, it was squashing mental illness with effort and hard work.

I say that like it was awful, but honestly, it wasn't bad. Gap-toothed Marin was a case in point, my heart swelling each time she'd call out, "Ms. Griffin! I'm finished!" She was an absolute delight, bouncing in her seat while she created, wearing a grin way brighter than the sun. Her love for art knew no bounds; her enthusiasm for it endless. If I had to play the teacher game for Daddy, at least it was with kids I liked.

Because I hadn't yet graduated, I worked three days a week. My study hall became my teaching job, and I left school early to relieve the current art teacher. It was one of those days—a late March Friday—when I fished my phone from my pocket with slippery hands. My last class had just shuffled off, and I'd devoted myself to washing brushes and stowing paint. Rosie's one-word text stared up at me from the tiny rectangular screen. *Bonfire?* I grimaced and put the phone away.

Clean-up duties completed, I walked out the side entrance and tipped my face to the sun. I still *tried* to feel, to be whole and alive and a fully human person. It just didn't work all that well.

Nathan's presence was reassuring—at least with him, my body gave a response. He'd parked under a live oak that day, its spindly beaches barely budding, his legs crossed at the ankle as he leaned against the jeep. His work boots were still on, and the worn fabric of his jeans hung just right beneath a weathered Beaufort Water Craft t-shirt. He smiled as I approached, sweeping me into his arms and brushing his lips against my temple before boosting me up into the jeep.

"Got a text from Rosie." He put his arm behind my head-rest as he backed out.

"Bonfire?" I asked.

He nodded. "You good to shift?" He settled his right hand on my thigh, already confident in our routine. "I told her I'd check with you," he continued, "that we'd come if you were up for it."

"Thanks," I murmured, shifting into second gear. He knew me so well, anticipating my moods and my needs before I recognized or knew them, like my hesitance over going out. No matter the drugs they put me on, I still didn't feel like myself. Factor in Rosie and Gil and the torture of watching a love that steady... Nathan was my heart, my soul, my everything; bipolar, my variable.

Spring weather had waltzed into Minnesott seemingly overnight, sweeping in the sweet, freshly hewn air that lifts soft tops off vehicles and brushes the scent of wisteria through your hair. I leaned back in my seat and zoned out to the road noise and the feel of Nathan's hand on my leg. Until the jeep's tires rolled to a stop at my house and Nathan asked me a question. "You wanna check the mail?"

After Daddy *relocated* my money, Rosie and I scraped up an application fee. I sent that and my portfolio off; did a mild victory dance when I got the confirmation email and waited. Decisions were due any day. The *Pinecliff* sign on the mailbox creaked as it swayed in the wind, and I dropped from the jeep to tug the handle down, warm metal against my fingers.

A large, legal-sized envelope sat curved in the back.

Heart pounding, I tugged it toward me. Held it close as I climbed back into the jeep. Nathan studied my face. "You gonna open it?"

I traced the black and gold embossed logo with a shaking finger. "No, I don't think so. Not yet."

One of his eyebrows lifted. "Rejections aren't usually that big."

They weren't. But I'd waited so long, dreamed so big, and fought so hard the envelope in my hands felt sacred. I leaned across the console and kissed him, then said. "I think I need to do this on my own."

He understood immediately. I could see it in his eyes. Nathan tucked a loose strand of hair behind my ear, the brush of his fingertips achingly gentle. "I've got work to do," he said, quietly, "but I'll be here, out in the yard. If you need me"—a quick kiss—"come find me."

"I always need you," I said.

My parents' cars were absent as I sprinted for the porch steps, flying up the stairs to my room. I dropped my bags on the floor and slammed the door shut, then collapsed onto my bed. Stretching my arms out to the sky, I lay on my back and held the envelope aloft until my fingers went numb and my muscles seized in protest.

Outside, I heard the lawn tractor start.

Nathan. I sat up and tapped the envelope against my knee. What would the distance do to us? Would it hurt us?

What would it do to me?

Shaking my head to clear it, I slid my finger beneath the envelope's flap. I pulled everything out, holding my breath until I read the words, *Congratulations! Ms. Griffin, on behalf of the Virginia Commonwealth University Office of Admissions, we are pleased to inform you...*

I squealed, my insides sparking, a million dreams taking flight in my head. Down the stairs, out the back door, running for the one and only person I wanted to share this. Nathan cut the tractor engine when I'd made it halfway across the yard, grin shining like the sunrise on water. "Did you open it?"

"I got in," I burst out, unable to hold it, and I leaped into his arms.

"Never had a single doubt." He held me above the ground, salty tears damp on his t-shirt.

Except the tears weren't mine.

"Nathan?" I squirmed, his belt buckle scraping my stomach as he let me down. Red-rimmed, watery eyes studied my face; he gripped my fingers with one hand and scraped the tears away with the other. "I'm just really proud of you."

I believed him, but something else lurked behind the pride. Apprehension, maybe. Panic? Or maybe...was that dread?

He caught me staring, and it passed quickly, whatever it was. Like the end of a cloudburst on a summer afternoon, his eyes melted into something like contentment.

"We'll be fine," I said. "Long distance." It was a shot in the proverbial dark.

He cradled my face in his hands. "I know."

"It's six hours from Broward. Pretty drivable, but flights are cheap. We can take turns traveling to see each other every weekend."

"Hey. Hey..." He drew me in, wrapping me back in his arms so my cheek was at chest level. "Broward won't keep me from you."

"You sent in the deposit?" I asked, stomach dropping when I felt him flinch. I knew every inch of that boy, from his head to his toes to the soul in his body and the heart that beat in his chest. Yet there in the yard, fresh cut grass on the wind, he was a mystery I couldn't unravel. I pulled back just enough to look up at him. "Nathan, what's going on?"

"Like I said, I'm just proud of you." He let me go with a pat on my butt, and I took three steps back, still watching him. "I should finish this up," he said, motioning to the tractor. "Bonfire, yes or no?"

"No," I said, and he nodded.

"Then we'll stay home."

I watched Nathan climb back in the tractor, jeans flexing over the muscles of his thighs. He winked, the gesture awkward and forced. I squashed the impulse to chase him down—it wasn't safe to run after a tractor.

Not on a good day, when all was right with the world and the birds sang.

Not a bad day with an unsettled heart.

My phone rang in my pocket as I made my way back to the house. Rosie's name lit the display. Weary to my bones and wrung out like a washrag, I slid into the kitchen and shut the door.

"You didn't answer my text," Rosie said when I finally flipped the phone open.

"We're not going to make it tonight."

A brief pause cracked the line, a hard edge to Rosie's voice when she responded. "You're coming."

"Rosie. I'm tired."

"No, you're ridiculous. I need you to come tonight. Wilkinson's Point, nine PM," she said, ending the call with her final directive. The kitchen stood silent save for the faucet's rhythmic *drip*. I paced the kitchen once or twice, jammed the faucet handle down, and continued my little circuit.

Something was up with Rosie.

And Nathan.

I flipped my phone open.

Changed my mind.

SOMETHING *WAS* UP WITH ROSIE. Two Sutton babies were on the way.

"What are you going to do with *twins*?"

It sounded awful any way I asked. Nathan reached back and squeezed my hip. His head rested in my lap, and I'd been running my fingers through his hair before Rosie made her announcement. Pretty sure it was a warning shot.

Gil curled Rosie closer, hands settling on a slight bump I hadn't noticed before. "We'll save the kids from twice the trouble, right?"

Nathan gave a lazy thumbs up. I pushed it down—this was *not* a thumbs-up situation. "I'm excited for you, really. But—" My hands fisted. "What did your parents say?"

Rosie laughed. "Mama 'bout died and asked Daddy for a shot of whiskey, so you know it was a shock. Gil's parents didn't say much, but then what do you expect from a Sutton?" She leaned back on his shoulder and grinned up at him. "Though I did overhear his Mama on the phone with

Blanche Dorsey, talking about monogrammed baptismal gowns."

The four of us sat there, the only sounds the soft waves and crackling fire. Everything felt off. The gentle shushing too loud, the subtle roar too harsh, Nathan's hair through my fingers too rough. His eyes were closed, the tension he'd held earlier gone.

Rosie was freaking *pregnant*. How was everybody so relaxed?

Annoyed, I pulled my hand back. He opened one narrowed eye.

What? I asked with a wide-eyed look.

Be nice, his eyes said back, lips pursed in disapproval. He prodded me on the knee. "Keep going," he said, and I grumbled. But this was Nathan, so I obliged.

The love of my life was right, mostly: I wasn't being nice. "I guess I should have asked how *you're* doing, Rosie. How are you feeling about a baby? I mean, twins?"

She watched me, then looked up at her husband. "Wasn't what we planned on," Gil said. "Not this early, anyway."

"Figured we'd have a year or two before kids," she agreed, "but we got married young. Might as well be all in with it."

I swallowed. *Might as well.*

Typically, our bonfires were lively. We'd dance, maybe go for a dip. The boys would toss a ball. Rosie and I would lie in the sand and weave together pine needles. Every so often, Gil would score a six-pack from a customer and we'd split it, thinking we were so grown up. This bonfire, though, was different. A stilted sort of awkwardness hung in the air. Because as much as we thought we were grown up, two of the four of us hadn't graduated high school. In less than nine months, the Suttons would be thrust into adulthood.

Was I the only one who saw the issue? Or was I the one out of line?

Rosie got tired early, so she and Gil headed out about ten. Nathan and I stayed, making out in the sand, letting the fire die down to its embers. "It's late," he said into my ear, lips brushing my earlobe, weight pushing me into the ground. I shivered as he pulled away and sat back on his heels, brushing the sand from his t-shirt. "I've got an early morning," he said.

Nathan pulled me up with gentle fingers. "I'm gonna make sure the fire's out," he said. I wandered to the shore, the gentle lap of the waves a whisper, indecipherable in the static of the night.

"Gil's a good guy," said Nathan from behind me, and I startled, so in my head I hadn't heard him walk up.

"It's not that," I said. "He loves her. And he's goofy, so I know he'll love on those kids. It's just..." I turned around, planting my palms on Nathan's chest and feeling the muscles beneath his t-shirt. "Rosie had plans. She applied to four schools. Her first choice is UNC, outside Raleigh. Now she's talking community college and having twins."

"She can transfer, you know. Take distance courses. This is Rosie we're talking about."

"A force of nature," I said.

Nathan laughed, a short huff sound. "Second only to you."

Nathan's demeanor had flipped so markedly I wondered if I'd imagined his earlier angst. Or misread the whole thing, clocked his quiet tears as hurt when they were gentle celebration. A subtle joy I didn't know how to feel. My emotions stood in the shadows, a lurking presence I could sense but not see. I was so tired of being numb, tired of misreading cues and misidentifying faces. I leaned in for a kiss, desperate. Desperate to feel something. Feel him.

"You know..." Nathan said after a moment, breath hitched and fingers hot on my skin. "I hear June's a great month—"

"We are not getting married," I bit out, tone sharper than I intended. I inhaled and scaled it back. "Assuming I can find a way to pay for college, after graduation, I'm out of here. I've gotta figure Daddy out, too," I said, dropping my head against Nathan's shoulder. "The weight of all this...it makes me heavy."

He put a bit of space between us without letting go. "I would follow you literally anywhere. You know I love you, right?"

Of course I did. "Words won't fix this," I said, because they wouldn't, and I was being honest.

"What is there to fix?"

All of it. "Me," I said, "for one. That I live with Bipolar. That I'm leaving and you have your own plans."

A brief flash of worry lit his face. But then it was gone, and his eyes were soft and kind and looking at me with so much love I couldn't stand it. "I want to marry you, Dewitt, but I don't want to force it, alright? We don't have to do it now."

I hated the way my voice trembled. "Marriage is huge."

He held me so tenderly I thought I might break. "I know," he said. "But you're it for me. I trust you."

"I'm the town crazy, and you trust me."

"With every little piece of my heart."

I clung to his shirt like a shorebird in a storm, my heart scattered on the sand and waiting. Waiting for the next wave, the next break, the next peek of daylight.

Waiting for the wind to let up.

TWENTY-FIVE

DEWITT

May 2004

Bells jingled against the door of the arts building, the sound muffled by the storage room walls. "I'll be right out," I called, checking the day's schedule to see if I'd missed something—it was half an hour until we closed.

The movement sloshed the contents of my stomach, and I breathed through it, gripping a shelf. VCU's acceptance letter sat hidden in my bedside drawer, deposit deadline looming. The stress was getting to me. I had all the forms and the legal right at eighteen to enroll without my parents' permission. But securing financial aid and telling Daddy I was leaving had my insides torn to shreds.

"What in the ever-loving world are you doing back here? Organizing paint tubes by shade?" Lil stood at the storage room door, hand planted on her linen-clad hip. She wore a frown at odds with her sunflower-yellow tunic and a deep crease between the V of her brows. She'd twisted her hair in two braids, the streaks of grey hinting her age more readily than the smooth canvas of her still-perfect skin.

"Not sorting," I said. "Just stashing." I smiled against the acid in my throat.

Lil bent and grabbed a bin, groaning with exertion. "If getting old is death by a thousand aches, I'm halfway in the ground already."

"*You're not old,*" I said. "You're, like, fifty."

"Closer to sixty, but that's kind."

I rolled my eyes. "That's my job," I said, taking the bin from her hands and stowing it on the shelf next to me. I loved Lil, but she had this way of barging in and making everything hers until you had nothing left to do and felt guilty for it. I didn't need the additional sin.

With the last bins stowed on the shelving, Lil and I walked to the front desk. I made my way around the back and perched my butt on my favorite stool before resting my elbows on the counter. "You're not on the schedule. What are you doing here?"

Lil narrowed her eyes. "You don't look good."

My hands flexed. "Thanks for that."

"You look a little green around the gills."

"I'm *fine.*"

Lil scoured my face for the lie. But then her piercing gaze dropped, the tone of her voice when she spoke broaching no argument. "Dewitt, we need to talk."

I tapped my fingers against the front counter, the woozy feeling in my gut growing taut. "I'm closing up at three. You wanna talk here? Or should I come by the farmhouse?"

"Here's good. We can chat right now."

Lil marched around the desk and set a stool in front of me. She plopped down and pinned me with a look. "You're sleeping with Nathan, aren't you?"

My stool rocked ,and I tightened my grip on the counter so I wouldn't topple sideways to the ground. That was the last thing I expected from her mouth. Yes, I had been, but it wasn't...*like that.* The way she made it sound so cheap. I nodded quick, my heart in my throat and a lurch in my belly. My cheeks burned. "Yes, ma'am," I said.

Lil sighed. "I should have addressed this sooner."

"I have a mom," I said. "We had *the talk.*"

"And I know full well she told you to wait, just as I made that clear years ago to my Nathan. Your involvement with one another *at this level*"—she tapped the counter—"complicates matters quite a bit."

A gaping hole opened behind my sternum. "I won't hurt him, Lil."

"Oh, sugar. You will. I thought maybe if you figured it out for yourself, the rest of this would be easier. But as for as I can tell, that hasn't happened, and with the two of you standing on the edge of adulthood..."

"Could you just spit it out?"

Lil's propensity for riddles challenged my patience on a good day, but now stress hormones coursed through my blood. "I appreciate your concern about me and Nathan," I said, "but I promise you, it's not what you think. We're in love, and even if I go away to school, he is the one person I belong to. My mental health is being managed. I'm not leaving him. And we're—"

"Dewitt, Effa is real."

My brain screeched to a halt. "I know that."

Lil blinked twice. "I don't think you do."

I tugged my hair from its bun, raked my fingers through the strands, and then twisted it back up, away from me. "Daddy admitted to her existence. And even if he hadn't, you told me about her."

"Ah. That day in the garden."

"Exactly," I said.

"No."

I fought the urge to claw my eyes out of my head. "Would it kill you to be even the slightest bit straightforward?"

Her lips curved. "Bad habit," she said. "You went to see Dr. Lane."

Shock must have registered on my face, because she held up a hand. "I'm not psychic. Dr. Lane was a colleague of mine. Your mother called before they took you in. She wanted to get my impression."

That made no sense. "You're not a mental health professional."

"I was. Twenty years as a clinical psychologist in Greensboro, ten of those with Department of Child and Family Services." She paused, studying me with her trademark intensity. "How do you think I got approved as a foster parent so quick?"

I sat still while my brain recalculated, shifting pieces to make sense of things. The way she opened people up. The way she knew how you were feeling before you even told her. I didn't remember Nathan being away from Lil after she put him on that cart. I swallowed hard. Lil wasn't lying. "You know about my diagnosis," I said.

She paused. "I do. I also know that Dr. Lane was wrong when he said you hallucinated Effa."

"But he said Bipolar One—"

"Can present with false perceptions. What he didn't say is that it's rather rare. It's also not what Effa is, no is she a ghost or a figment of your imagination." Lil stood, gaze alert, movements sure as he watched me. "Effa is a memory."

Residual Hauntings. Rosie's voice echoed in my head. *The land remembers stuff,* she'd said. Lil spun my stool until we both faced the wall, a painted map of the local area across it. The river popped as I stared, the muted greens, browns, and blues looking more vibrant than usual. Lil traced her fingers along the line of the water. "How old do you think this river is?"

"I don't know," I scraped out. "Old?"

"Try two million years," she said, hand resting on the river's v-bend, the tip of her index finger on Wilkinson's Point. "The things she's seen..." Lil trailed off, her hand dropping from the wall the way her voice did. "The river and the earth remember, *especially* when people forget."

My father. The sister he ignored. Effa in the barn. In my room. On the shore. In that car accident. "Are you saying—"

"The river shares her memories with you."

The room swayed. I put my head down on the counter and breathed. My visions really had been *trips*, into the past, into specific, meaningful moments. "How do you know this?" I ground out. "Why me?"

Lil's hand fell against my shoulder. "Research. That, and growing up here, where the line between what we see and what we know is just as thin as the line between water and sand. You'd be surprised what you can learn when you slow down and pay attention." She shifted her hand to my chin, gently lifting it so I could see her. "As for the *why you*, well. It's the creatives, the ones whose brains are a little—*unique*. It's not witchcraft at all, or some sort of...spirituality. It's just plain old *sensitivity*."

"But my meds," I said. "The Olanzapine. I started them, and Effa disappeared."

"So did your ability to paint." Her expression was soft as she let go of my chin, settling back onto her stool. "Medication impacts brain chemistry. Your ability to see things. To paint."

I knew she wasn't wrong, logically. Emotionally...I thought of my last trip. Of the last thing Lil from the past had said, right before I went back to the real world...

Effa died in an accident. What happened to the baby she carried?

Before I could ask about the baby—before I decided if I wanted to ask—Lil took the reins again and continued the conversation. "I have a box of Effa's things, sugar. You can stop by the house and look through. It's been nearly forty years now. You'd think I could talk about it. But, well..." She lifted her hands, eyes misty. "I guess grief is the half-life of love."

I laid my head back down on the cool surface of the counter, salty spit pooling in my mouth.

"Dewitt, honey..."

Stop. I forced up a hand.

"You don't believe me," Lil said.

"It's not that," I choked out. It was the loss. The grief. The end of two lives, while so many others moved forward.

"Do you understand now why I wish I'd told you earlier?"

I swallowed acid. "No."

Lil's gentle touch returned to my forearm. "Where you are right now, facing school, wrestling your brain, trying to settle things with your parents, it's kicking up a beehive, adding sex."

"I love Nathan." I could barely breathe.

"And there's no question he returns it. But is that enough right now?"

Lil went quiet, the rustle of linen the only thing I heard. "Bottle's looking mighty full," she said, and I jerked up, finding her eyes on my bag and the medicine.

"That bottle is ruining my life."

"It's made life different, Dewitt."

"Same thing, *Lillian*."

Lil laughed. "Griffin women. I swear. *Things* don't ruin a life, sugar. Not pills. Not accidents. Not storms. Our choices do, the roads we travel in the face of challenge." She found my gaze. Held it. "Does anyone know how you feel about the meds?"

"Nathan," I said. "And now you."

"I'm assuming your doctor doesn't know."

I looked down at the floor, and she took that as my answer. "If anything ruins your life, Dewitt Griffin, it will be how you steer into the wind. You can hide, and blame it all on someone else, and destroy yourself in the process, or you can lean into it. Move with it. Do the hard things and learn from them."

"My life is full of hard things already," I told her. Every cell in my body burned. "Being with Nathan...before, it was the one time my brain just...stopped. Went quiet. Now, it's the one time I feel anything."

Lil surveyed me, the sweep of her eyes a look into my soul. "What's going to happen when you go?"

"I don't know," I said, sniffling through a sudden press of moisture.

"You deserve more," she said. "Both of you. Minnesott is Nathan's home. You know as well as I do his biggest fear is abandonment. When you go off to VCU and he goes off to Broward, is he taking your heart? Or his just his own?"

"Both," I said, vehement. "All that matters is that we're in love."

Lil patted my cheek and grabbed her purse from behind the counter, stretching the strap across her chest. "I've heard that before," she said, tugging at the exit, leaving me with choices to make.

TWENTY-SIX

NATHAN

Lil's note sat on the kitchen table, a yellow hazard against fresh biscuits and jam. *Eat,* it said first, then in bold letters across the bottom: *Come see me before you leave.*

The back of my neck went rigid. I tugged it, trying to pull the irritation out. Lil wasn't the note-writing kind; she preferred to hunt folk down and grab hold of them. After she cornered Dewitt in the Arts Building, I hadn't let myself get caught. The whole thing was humiliating, and believe me, I was *pissed.* Lil should have talked to *me,* not Dewitt, and I would have torn into her if Dewitt hadn't asked me not to. Dewitt swore their conversation was a personal thing, more about her than it was the two of us as a couple. She wrapped her arms around my neck and asked me to drop it, then shut me up with a kiss.

So Lil and I hadn't been talking, not like we used to, anyway. I wondered if that was behind the note, if her tidy scrawl was a quiet peace offering. I took a deep breath and padded to the front door, barefoot, unease jostling my ribs. Lil stood out front where I thought she'd be, elbow-deep in the hydrangea blooms. Floppy sunhat perched on her head; long gardening gloves that stretched all the way up her forearms. Pink pruning shears to cut back old growth.

The screen door thwacked behind me as I shuffled across the porch.

"You saw my note in the kitchen," Lil said. "You get a biscuit, son?"

"Yeah," I said, fingers tingling. I hadn't eaten a thing.

She looked up at me then from beneath her sunhat, heightened eyebrows wobbling the brim. "Have another," she said, which I knew meant *stop lying*. "And take the rest of them to the beach. Y'all don't eat enough, and I know Rosie's gonna be hungry."

This was Lil Rooney's factory setting: micromanage, then push food. We weren't going far; Memorial Day weekend on the coast meant crowds, and since Rosie was five months along with twins (*It's like dog years,* she explained. *I'm thirty five months pregnant*), we were sticking to Wilkinson Point.

Lil tugged the gloves from her fingers. "You're not surprised I know about your plans."

"No." I shrugged, because Lil always knew, and what was the point of fighting it? Like she could read my mind, the corner of her mouth lifted. "Alright then. Let's chat."

She set down her shears and turned toward me, one arm resting against the porch rail. "Based on the way you've been brooding around the farmhouse, I'm guessing Dewitt told you about our conversation. Is that why won't you talk to me?"

I bit down on my cheek and counted backward for a minute until I could say something without raising my voice. "I'm talking to you now," I said, and Lil gave me a look fit for burning down bridges. She shook her head, the motion louder and more potent than any words we'd said in conversation.

"You got in early this morning. Or should I say *late?*"

It was both, in fairness. I'd fallen asleep in Dewitt's bed after—well, *after*—and came home at four.

"I taught you better than that," Lil said. She had taught me better than that, how to be honorable and good, not to sneak in and out of my boss's house to be intimate with his daughter. But what I had with Dewitt wasn't a meaningless hook-up, and I needed Lil to understand.

"Being with Dewitt—"

"Don't sugarcoat it."

My hands flexed at my side. *"We're in love."*

Lil laughed, a sharp, bleating sound that set my nerves on fire. "It's not funny, Lil."

"Oh, son. It's hilarious. I've had this exact conversation many times. Three weeks ago when I talked to Dewitt. Forty years ago when—well, it doesn't matter. Sure, the faces change, but the feelings stay the same and in your case, seem to have gotten stronger. Makes me wonder why I'm even trying to keep y'all from destroying yourselves."

The porch creaked as I lurched backward. "You think—"

"I think it's irresponsible, and too soon."

"We're both adults," I ground out.

"That may be true, but I swear for the fog y'all can't see a mile." Lil pulled an envelope from her pocket, the Broward emblem loud and clear. "As far as I can tell," she carried on, "you haven't talked directions much, either. Who's gonna tell her you let the deadline pass for Broward? You gonna let her find out on accident? Maybe get a phone call, like I did?"

That stopped me. "Phone call?"

"From a Broward admissions rep. You let the deposit deadline pass, Nathan. Didn't tell them."

My leg bounced. "About that. I...forgot."

It was a flimsy excuse. Lil knew it, and she flattened her lips. "Is this about Dewitt?"

"Not the way you think."

"Explain it to me, then." She climbed the porch steps. Said, "Sit," and motioned to the swing. I sat, Mr. Luther's offer over my head, sliding lower every single day. Dewitt didn't know—I'd been researching aid, figuring if I could swing it by myself, I wouldn't have to tell her. But I couldn't, not unless I wanted to work like a dog while taking the first year academic classes.

All that reading.

My dyslexia.

"I haven't told anyone about this."

"Dewitt's pregnant, isn't she?"

The swing jerked to a stop; I choked on my spit so hard that snot ran from my nose from the coughing. "Why would you-" More coughing. "What are you talking about, Lil?"

Her shoulders lifted. "Dewitt was pretty sick the other week. And with y'all sneaking around, doing adult things you ain't got sense enough to be doing, it seemed a reasonable secret to me."

Suddenly, Mr. Luther's offer was the furthest from my mind. Dewitt would have told me, right? I wanted to have kids someday, but that was down the line. *Way* down. I put my head in my hands to keep it from spinning. "Dewitt's under a ton of stress."

"I realize. Her father is a difficult man."

I scrubbed my face with my hands and sat up, still sniffling. "He tried to bribe me, actually—"

"He did *what*?" Lil's eyes nearly popped out of her head.

"He offered to pay for school if I convinced Dewitt to stay here. Get her to give up on VCU. Luther thinks I can't take care of her without a degree, and—"

"Wait a moment," Lil said. "He said you'll need to *take care of* Dewitt?"

I gave a curt nod; the memory souring my stomach.

"Luther's been good to me, but he's a fool for believing Dewitt can't take care of herself."

"I'm inclined to agree." Lil clasped her hands in her lap, expression thoughtful. "Do you want to marry Dewitt?"

"I do. Not at the expense of her dreams," I said. "I tried to find a way to pay for Broward."

"I could—"

"*No*," I said, too sharp. "Sorry," I breathed. "It's not worth it with my dyslexia."

Lil sat back, quiet. Then said, "Does Dewitt know what you intend?"

"She knows."

Marriage is huge.

"Stay here." Lil stood and went inside the house. Long-closed drawers squeaked in the hall; the heavy lid thumped on the wooden hope chest. The ferry engine rumbled to life. Six watercraft anchored off Wilkinson. The world carrying on while I sat on the porch, waiting.

Idle.

Adrift.

An abrupt, rusty squeal from the screen door sent my pulse hammering hard in my throat. "Thought I'd put it in the side-board," Lil said, "then I remembered it was in the hope chest." She pulled a velvet box from the pocket of her skirt. "Hold out your hand," Lil said, and the box hinge creaked as she pried it open. "This belonged to Effa, a friend of mine."

Dozens of tiny, round diamonds sparkled back at me in the light. A square solitaire sat nestled inside, the tinier stones set around it in a delicate oval. More stones lined the white-gold band.

"Do you know Dewitt's ring size?"

I'd done research. "She's a five and a half."

"Tiny," Lil mused. "Effa passed, years ago, but I know my

friend, and she'd want you to have this. Tuck that away," she said, "until you need it."

My chest swelled. "You're sure?"

Lil took a sharp breath inward as though she had something more to say. But then she hugged me, hard, before whispering, "Sure as I've ever been."

She left me alone on the porch then. I watched four more boats jockey for space. My phone buzzed—probably Gil. A *where the hell are you?*

I didn't know where I was—not really—but I had a diamond ring, just in case.

TWENTY-SEVEN

NATHAN

The ring spent a week at a jewelry shop in New Bern while I lived in Minnesott with its ghost. In the yard, trimming trees; at the marina, tying a sail down; a heavy weight sat on my finger like a diamond-crusted phantom limb. On Tuesday, I picked the ring up. On Wednesday, it sat in my desk drawer. On Thursday, I moved it high on a shelf next to a box of Lil's photos in my closet. On Friday afternoon it came with me to the beach, a velvet anvil in my pocket, bumping my leg with every step.

A strong, briny wind tossed breakers at the shoreline, golden hour dropping gemstones on the waves. Gil's white cooler hung between us both, dragging my arm down and nearly out of its socket. "Why does this weigh ten thousand pounds?"

Gil grunted with exertion. "Rosie said she wanted to eat."

"Several bags of rocks?"

"Yogurt." A labored breath. "Two containers of dip plus three bags of cut vegetables. Lemonade. Cut watermelon. Two cartons of strawberries. Plus sweet tea in case the lemonade's too sour, and my mama's chicken wings."

My mouth watered. "I call the wings."

"Those are for Rosie," he said. "You can have *a* beer from the six-pack Mr. Duvall gave me."

"Is that what he paid you to fix his boat?" I would have clocked him if I had the strength, or if my arm weren't being ripped off at the shoulder.

"If Duvall wants to keep my fridge stocked, who am I to judge?"

"Idiot."

He side-eyed me. "What'd you say?"

"Brilliant! Great plan." It was a horrible plan, actually, accepting liquid currency for labor and parts. But I wouldn't have minded a beer, not with the week I'd had and the way the dang ring kept bouncing in my pocket.

Gil stumbled next to me. "Hot damn."

I followed Gil's gaze to the shoreline where Rosie waded in the water ankle-deep. Sunlight caught her silhouette and backlit the curve of her belly. Warmth filled my chest—I was gonna be an uncle to two babies, twins Rosie carried with grace.

Our slow and steady trek accelerated. I thought I might lose my arm for real. "Dude. Slow down."

"That's my wife."

"You've been whipped since you were thirteen, you goober."

Gil lifted his chin toward the jetty. "Like you haven't been."

"Not like—" *Dang it.* My eyes snagged on the girl I loved. She waded ankle-deep, same as Ro, but down in the tide pools formed by the jetty, ragged cut-offs hanging low on her hips. Golden light poured over her skin like honey and highlighted the swell of her curves. The red strings of her swim top tied at her neck, and the farther we walked, the more desperate I was to touch her.

I dropped the cooler and ran.

"Seriously?"

"You're manly. You'll be fine."

Grumbling followed me on the wind, but I didn't care. I had Dewitt in my arms the moment I reached her.

"Hey," she said, and I was home, counting the freckles on her nose and breathing lavender.

"Hey." I tugged her closer. "You smell good."

"New perfume." The tone of her voice didn't match the words. I knew she'd been shopping with Ro, but the raw scrape of her words stung angry and bitter. I stepped back and searched her face again, avoiding the freckle distraction. What I hadn't noticed earlier was the hurricane raging in her eyes.

Immediately, my mind went to Luther. "What happened? Did y'all have a fight?"

"She wouldn't shut up long enough, so no, we didn't argue."

Dewitt's gaze flickered, steely, to my left. I whirled around, expecting to see anyone other than Rosie. But the only people behind us were the Suttons, huddled together up the shore.

"Wait a second." I scratched the back of my neck. "I thought—this is about Ro?"

"Of course, it's about Ro. Baby this, baby that. I'm so tired of hearing about freaking babies."

My brows pulled tight. "You're tired of the babies?"

"She talks about them all the time. I spent the better part of the day listening to her ramble on about her birth plan. Literal nightmare fuel."

Sweat beaded her upper lip, and she dabbed at it. Dark circles pressed the hollows below her eyes. I'd been so caught up in holding her close I missed that she was struggling. "Are you...feeling okay?"

"What does it look like?" she burst out, arms wide. "My best friend is having two babies." She heaved a little. "Can we talk about anything else?"

I stepped backward. "Yeah. I, uh. Yes."

"Not you and me." She dripped disdain. "I meant *her*. Rosie. Like, not all of us want to hear about babies and birth on a loop while we're trying to go shopping."

My eyes bounced around her face (flushed red), her fists (clenched tightly). My ears caught the speed of her words. "Dewitt, do you—do you want to go sit down? Grab a beer, maybe? Some--"

"Are you *stupid*?"

The question stung. But she must have seen it on my face, because instantly, her face fell. "Shoot, Nathan. I—I'm sorry. I didn't...Of course you're not stupid. I'm just mad."

"At Rosie?" I swallowed. "I'm trying to understand here, Dewey. I swear."

Her face turned a little a green under the flush, and she took in a deep breath, puffing out slowly. "I'm mad at everything," she finally said.

I nodded, slowly. "There's only so much the heart can take."

"Yes," she breathed, relieved, like I was the only person in the world who understood her. She inhaled. "It's a lot."

My hand reached out and brushed hers, and she linked her pinky with mine. "I'll stay here," I said. "We can take a walk, or I can take you home, unless you'd rather not see your parents."

"They're in Greenville. They'll be back late."

"Alright." I gripped her hand. "Home, then?"

"You're perfect," she said, looking out over the river, her

profile stunning in the light. But her voice had wavered a bit, too, and I squeezed her hand.

"I'm just a good listener. You can talk to me."

"Not now," she said, turning back my way, eyes glistening a bit, but sharp. "I need a minute," she breathed. "Go eat."

I almost refused. But when I pressed once more, she rolled her eyes, and finally, I got a smile. A promise she'd join us, that she'd be alright. Shoulders tight and muscles weary, I walked up the shoreline to join Rosie and Gil. He handed me a long-neck, cracking the lid with the church key on his belt and lifting his chin toward Dewitt. "She okay?"

Dewitt was pretty much where I left her, settled on a jetty rock. I worried the label on my beer. "I'm not sure," I said.

"She was pissy all day today." Rosie lounged in a sling back chair, one hand resting on her belly. "We went to that perfume store she likes—Apothecary? I figured that would cheer her up. But she hardly talked to me at all, and I feel bad, because I just rambled on about the babies."

I scraped the beer label with a fingernail.

"Don't feel bad for that," Gil said.

"It was weird, though," Ro said. "Dewitt and I can sit for hours and just...be quiet. But it was different today. Made me nervous. When I'm anxious, I talk."

She took a swig of ice tea from her plastic tumbler. "Do you think she's sick? She hardly ate when we were out. A couple times, I thought she might throw up or something. If I didn't know better, I'd say she was pregnant."

The ground shifted. Gil reached out and grabbed my arm. "Dude. Is she..." His eyes burned the side of my face and my stomach flipped, queasy. "Have you guys..."

"Yeah, but..." Holy Moses. Was she?

I thought back to what Lil said a week ago, about how sure

I'd been in my denial. Dewitt wouldn't lie to me. *But you haven't asked her.* I swallowed the doubt. "She's not."

Gil and Rosie blinked at me.

"She's not pregnant, I swear." It wasn't an honest swear, though. The possibility grew tighter in my chest every second. "Look," I said, desperate to change the subject. "I'm not talking about our private business, alright? Gil packed five tons of food. I'm hungry."

I wasn't. A stone lodged itself in my gut.

THE SUN SET. Dewitt stayed in orbit, pocketing shark teeth and shells. A million questions swirled in my head, and I picked at my food instead of eating it. I built a fire. It felt good to work with my hands. It took to roaring pretty quick, and dusk had just about surrendered when Dewitt shouted, "Watch out!"

We turned in unison, Gil and I leaping to our feet. Dewitt stood about a dozen yards away, poised to run straight for us. "Get out of the way, y'all! I'm gonna jump!"

"Jump?" asked Rosie. "What is she talking abou—"

I cursed. Dewitt was sprinting across the sand, whooping into the air, heading for the flames and their heat.

"No," I breathed first. "Dewitt, no!" I yelled louder.

"She's not—"

I cut Gil off. "That's exactly what she's doing." Yards away, I could see it in her eyes. Fear gripped my limbs, freezing them solid for too many seconds.

"Nathan—"

"Ro, get up. Bro, we gotta—"

Stop her.

My brain kicked into gear and I ran for her, heart cracking

straight through my chest. I couldn't breathe—didn't want to breathe—it wasn't worth expending the energy. I had to get to her now, first, always.

I tackled her into the sand.

We rolled, over and under. Over and under until we landed near the surf. Dewitt had her eyes squeezed shut, her mouth screwed into a scowl, and I leaned over her, winded, on my elbows. "Dewitt," I breathed. "Talk to me. Dewitt—"

She opened one single eye. And then she laughed, long and hard and with the kind of joy I hadn't seen from her in ages.

I rolled over onto my back.

I felt sick.

"*That* was amazing," Dewitt said, laughter punctuating every word. "*You* were amazing," she said, flopping over on all fours. My body sang as she straddled my waist; my brain told it to go take a cold shower. She leaned down over my chest, close to my ear, and whispered, "Catch me if you can."

Like a shorebird lifting weightless from the sand, Dewitt was up and off, tearing across the beach and up the hill toward her house.

"What is—Dewitt! What are you doing?" Rosie's voice carried over the wind. I scrambled to my feet; didn't even bother with my flip-flops.

Something was very wrong with Dewitt.

"Y'all stay here," I told them, stumble-running past them toward the hill. Every step stoked the embers of my dread, and when I crested the hill, it took me ten seconds too long to find her, leaning seductively against a pine.

"I won," she said, lips curving. She pushed off the tree and grabbed me by the shirt. Then her mouth was on mine, all salty and sweet, and my heart split between fear and desire. Dewitt pulled away and left me dazed, her "Race you to the house!" an echo. I tracked her laughter through the trees, across the yard, around the back porch steps where I caught her, lips shining in the glow of the porch light.

That kiss—it rattled my brain. The feel of her weight on my lap—I craved it.

I wanted her, *badly*.

I *needed* to make sure she was okay.

"What's going on?" I asked her.

Dewitt lifted a shoulder. "I was ready to go."

I almost laughed, incredulous. "You tried to jump over the bonfire, Dewitt."

"It seemed like fun," she said. Then she pouted. "I'll never know now, will I?"

"That's not something we need to know. You've been all over the place today, up and down, and one minute you're about to puke, and the next, I—"

She's pregnant.

The thought rang clear in my head. "Are you..." I breathed against a cold, prickly sweat.

"Am I what?" she asked, leaning forward.

"Are you pregnant?"

"What?"

It was a whisper, barely breathed into the evening breeze. She opened her mouth, closed it again, fear ballooning in my chest as I watched her. Hope feathered up the sides, brilliant, and I couldn't tell which way was happily ever after, up, or down.

"You're pregnant."

She swallowed hard. Eyes averted she collapsed onto the steps, twisted her fingers in her lap, and I calculated in my head how much we'd need to buy a house, a crib, diapers.

"*Nathan,*" she said, and I startled. "I'm not pregnant. I quit my meds. I'm stabilizing right now. I'm acting weird because my body's adjusting."

I dropped, deadweight, to my knees. Relief, regret, and under it all, an ache of disappointment. She moved from the steps and knelt in front of me. "I should have told you."

"Does your doctor know?"

Everything hurt. I was thirsty. I flinched when she touched my face. "I need to be able to feel. I hate being numb, and this, this is the start of it. The plan is to start something new."

"You have to talk to me. You could have told me earlier on the shore."

Dewitt nodded, the earnest sweetness on her face ripping my heart to pieces. "I know," she said. "And I will."

She embraced me, and my arms threaded around her waist. It felt so good to hold her close, to breathe her in, to know she'd be okay even if the road would were bumpy.

"Let's go inside." she said, hooking my bones with the invitation because I was nineteen, stupid, and in love. I caught her biceps in my hands and brushed my nose against hers, asking permission. She opened her mouth to mine.

We were breathless in seconds, stumbling our way inside the house. Up the stairs; down the hall to her room, where we closed the door behind us. Moonlight danced across her shoulders, painting forever in my heart. I didn't just want her *right now*. I wanted her tomorrow. Next week. Next month. Next year. I went for the ring still in my pocket, hands trembling.

Dewitt's sob rent the night.

"I'm going to hurt you," she cried, sinking down to the edge of her bed. I forgot about the ring and slipped my arm around her. Remembered what she said about her meds.

"You won't," I said, and I meant it. I pulled her into my lap. Minutes passed—maybe hours, her shallow breathing slowing down. Her salty tears dried on my shirt. I shivered when she let me go, but liquid heat filled my veins when she looked at me. I watched her shift up the bed; watched her fiddle with the straps of her swimsuit. "Be with me," she said, gaze heavy with meaning.

I shut out the alarms, the glaring warnings.

I shut out everything and gave in.

I WOKE up before Dewitt the next morning, conscious of her cheek against my chest. Her face was relaxed, her skin soft and pale against my ever-present sunburn. Dark lashes danced across her cheeks like little fans.

I'd spent the night in Dewitt's bedroom, holding her close, skin to skin. In the watery light of dawn, I remembered the ring. I'd have to wait to ask her. I turned my head toward the clock on her bedside table. It was nearly six AM.

Slowly, carefully, against the longing in my chest, I slipped out from beneath Dewitt and toggled the switch on her alarm. As high as I felt, I was a coward. I'd sneaked in here under the cover of darkness and now I was sneaking out. Not without waking Dewitt, though. This wasn't an awkward one-night stand. I was going to make this woman my wife come hell or high water. I wanted to kiss her goodbye.

I slid into my jeans and searched for my T-shirt, finally finding it on the floor.

"Did the alarm go off?" Dewitt asked, her voice tired and smoky and what I wanted to hear the rest of my life. I perched on the edge of the bed; she sat up and pulled the sheets around her. Devotion bloomed in my core, the blood rushing through my veins a wild, raging river. "I'm, uh...gonna put on my shirt."

"Don't do that," Dewitt whined, pouty. I gripped the blanket to keep from touching that full lip. I couldn't help the boyish grin across my face, and Dewitt beamed at me, her smile knowing. She whispered to me. "Come here."

"You're killing me. I'm putting my shirt on. Right now." I pulled it down over my head. In a flash, Dewitt's lips were on mine and I was lost in her again, like always. Through the fog of it all, I heard voices down the hall and pulled away, the action painful. "Dewitt, I've got to go."

Dewitt gave a nod, her face clouded, the light gone from her eyes. She clutched at the sheet with one hand and rubbed the other across her forehead. Her teeth worried her bottom lip.

"Hey." I took her free hand and caressed her scar with my thumb. "Dewey, talk to me." I leaned in close, ducking my head to catch her eye line. Her mood swings were something, alright. She could always feel what she needed to feel, but it sure seemed like she was hiding something from me. "Are you worried about graduation? Your dad?"

Whatever weight pressed on her shoulders lifted like a river fog. "All of it. The ceremony. Telling Daddy about VCU."

"All you do is walk across the stage. And I'll be there. Front row. Wouldn't miss it."

She sighed and pressed her lips together. "Easy, yeah. Okay."

Tension filled the space between us. It took everything I had not to call her bluff. Face blank of the turmoil in my chest, I pulled her into my arms and kissed her temple. "I'll meet you at Lil's after graduation practice. Seven thirty, right?"

Her answering nod came so confidently I wondered if I'd imagined things. But doubt still gnawed at my gut as I climbed over the sill and pulled the window shut behind me, leaving my heart behind the wavy glass.

TWENTY-EIGHT

NATHAN

Dewitt didn't show after graduation practice.

When I knocked the next morning after breakfast, Deebie's strained smile opened the door. Dewitt was in the shower, and Deebie would have her call me. My phone stayed silent all day. Now it was early afternoon, and Lil and I idled in the jeep through a long line of traffic waiting to enter the high school parking lot. The skin on my knuckles flexed taut, and Lil patted my arm, clucking. "We've got forty minutes to find parking. Try to be patient, son."

I didn't want to be patient. I wanted to find Dewitt. The public library sat a block away from the school, and as I craned my neck around the line of cars, its lot looked mostly empty. I veered the jeep out of the queue, drove up the block, and parked the in front of the book deposit.

"Should have taken the golf cart," Lil said.

"That thing barely goes fifteen if I push it." I climbed out and walked around to her door.

"We could have driven right up to the event instead of walking the length of six football fields to get there."

"It's not that far," I snapped, then immediately backpedaled. "Sorry. I know it's hot."

Lil dropped from the jeep and slipped an arm through my elbow, offering a little squeeze. "We'll find her," she said.

It was muscle memory, the way swept the crowd for Dewitt. She wouldn't be there, I knew; she'd be in the gym with the rest of her class, probably talking to Rosie. My focus should have been on Lil, on getting her over the field and comfortably seated.

I loosened my tie and the ring of sweat beneath my collar. "Where do you want to sit?"

Like last year when Gil and I graduated, the ceremony was on the football field. Against the backdrop of a yellow goalpost, metal stairs flanked both sides of the stage. Two sections of chairs filed all the way back to the thirty-yard line. Lil surveyed the wide expanse.

"Not on the bleachers. And definitely *not* with the Griffin folk." She pointed to the front where Luther stood, holding court in a pin-stripe suit and navy blue bowtie. Mrs. Deebie stood next to him in a coordinating navy shirt dress, her face twisted into a scowl.

"Yeah," I said, gut churning. "Probably not a good idea." Maybe Dewitt fessed up about VCU, or maybe they'd seen me climbing out the window. Dread sank like a stone and I clutched my stomach.

"This ain't a funeral, folks."

Gil sidled up next to me, his presence the distraction I craved. One look at his khakis and crisp dress shirt and I got the urge to rib him. "Nice threads, Gilbert. Rosie pick that out?"

"Making fun of your friends for distraction purposes." He thumped me on the shoulder. "Nice."

Lil snorted a laugh and Gil turned her way, grinning. "How you doing, Miss Lil? Sure is hot today, ain't it?"

"Hotter than Satan's house cat." Lil set both hands on her hips. "Show me where y'all Sutton folk are sitting and I'll be better. Assuming it's five miles from Lumpy Head."

"Lumpy Head?" Gil asked.

Lil gestured to Deebie and Lou, and Gil's eyes bugged out as he swallowed his laughter. "I don't know about five miles. But I could get you ten rows behind and to the left a little," he offered.

"Five miles, ten rows...what's that they say about six of one, half dozen of the other?"

Gil swooped out an arm and dipped his head in invitation. "Then I'm happy to oblige."

"One season of Cotillion ten years ago," I muttered, "that you didn't even attend."

I earned a rude gesture for that one, and I laughed, the first bit of lightness I'd encountered all day. Gil pulled me aside once Lil was in her seat, voice lowered in a conspiratorial whisper. "What's bothering you? Use your words."

A sharp pain shot up my jaw from the clenching. "Still haven't heard from Dewitt."

His eyes darkened a bit, and he lifted his chin toward the Griffins. "There's that mess over there."

Luther and Deebie's argument had escalated into red-faced barbs. I scrubbed hard at the back of my neck, a motion Gil must have noticed.

"You worried?"

I nodded.

"Me, too."

Principal Healy tapped the mic, and the band rang out with the first notes of solemn music. The crowd quieted, and a rush of black and gold robes streamed down the center aisle. Flush-faced graduates walking two by two.

Rosie's pregnancy earned her the lead spot, so of course, we saw her first. Gil whistled as she passed; Rosie rolled her eyes, mouthing, *"Gilly..."* And because he was Gil Sutton, he bounced his eyebrows and blew his wife a kiss.

Dewitt appeared not long after, her eyes rimmed in scarlet and her gait painfully slow. She passed by without a glance. I pressed a fist to my chest and rubbed the ache behind my sternum.

Gil nudged me—*I got you.* Then he launched into color commentary.

"This is taking forever. Was our graduation this long?... I feel like ours was cloudy, right? It wasn't this sunny?...It is hotter than Satan's hen house out here."

That last one got me. "Satan's hen house?"

"Come on. You were thinking the same thing."

"Nope." I shook my head. "Not about poultry and the Prince of Darkness."

"It's way too hot out here for my Ro."

He'd made a good point. "Can you see her?"

"Not really." He sat up taller, craning his neck. "She's tough. She'll hold out."

And she did, gliding across the stage without a hint of discomfort. Dewitt's turn came quickly after that. She looked more at ease on the stage than she had in procession, strutting across in wedge heels with a smile. Despite the hollow in my heart, I gave a loud *whoop* as she took her diploma. She beamed at me from the stairs.

One by one, the graduates filtered; one by one we all wilted in our seats. By the time Malachi Zahn stepped off the stage, an audible gasp of relief went up from the audience, followed by a groan as Principal Healy approached the podium.

"Read the room, dude..." Gil muttered.

"He's not gonna read the room."

A finger tap against the mic, then, "Hurricanes, this day is momentous...."

He droned on. I tuned him out. Tuned the whole thing out, I guess, until harried whispers swept back from the stage. I nudged Gil in the side—he was staring straight ahead, eyes glazed over—and motioned toward the business up front. A collective gasp rent the crowd as Dewitt flew from her seat, crawling over classmates and chairs. She tossed her cap and gown at the end of the row, her urgent, *"Out of my way!"* caught on the stage mic. *"Rosie!"* She cursed. "Don't y'all just stand there with your mouths open—somebody call 911!"

The crowd erupted like a flock of seagulls, gawking and flapping their arms. Gil vaulted from his seat, and I leapt out of my chair to chase after him, sweat-slick and heart pounding in my ears. Sirens wailed in the distance, then closer, as the county's EMS rig bounced down the gravel service road. A ragged wail fell from Gil's mouth, and as I rounded the last row of seats, I saw it: Rosie draped pale and lifeless across Dewitt's lap.

Gil fell on them immediately, wrenching Rosie from Dewitt's arms. I dropped to my knees, Rosie's wrist in my hands, desperate for a sign of life. Her pulse beat steady under my fingers and I breathed a small sigh of relief. "Steady pulse," I told Gil. He growled at me.

Dewitt went after the paramedics.

"She is *pregnant!*" Dewitt's cry carried from my left. "What is taking you so long?" She looked magnificent in her rage, hair streaming out to the sides, the deep flush on her face like a warrior's. I crossed the space between us in three steps, the pride in my heart head to head with foreboding. Eric Kindle, the head medic, kept his focus on the equipment in his truck. "Dewitt..." I reached out and she flinched; pulled her into my arms and she thrashed against me. "It's okay," I soothed. "They're gonna help her."

Dewitt stopped fighting. She sobbed.

Tall and ash blonde with a sharp-looking crewcut, Eric knelt down next to Gil. "Hey, Gil," he said. "What's going on?"

Gil twisted Rosie away, the feral look in his eyes like nothing I'd ever seen from him.

Eric persisted. "Come on, bro. Let me do my job."

Gil just rocked Rosie back and forth, spouting nonsense words and refusing to let go of her.

"Nathan," Dewitt said. "Help."

The quiver in her voice broke me. Not that I had that much left to break. I pressed a kiss to her head and jogged the short distance between me and Eric. Back on my knees next to my friend, I touched his shoulder. "You gotta let Eric do his thing."

Gil keened.

"On three?" Eric asked, eyes catching mine, and I nodded in the affirmative. "Cartwright's gonna help you, Gil, so I can take care of Rosie."

One, two, three—

Gil fought me. He fought me so damn hard. "Get off me," he spat, twisting this way and that as I gripped tight around his arms and my throat burned.

"You need to let Eric help her, Gil."

"If I lose her..."

"We're not going to lose her, man." I held my best friend as he sobbed, letting his tears soak my shirt in the heat. The crowd of lurkers thinned out. Time stretched beyond eternity. Finally, from the spot where Rosie lay, I heard her quiet mumble.

"Hey," I said to Gil, nudging him. "I think she's coming around."

Fifteen minutes later, Rosie sat on a stretcher drinking juice. "We're gonna take her in," Eric said, "get her checked out at the hospital. She said she didn't eat before they left to come over here, and with the heat..."

"This is all my fault," Gil said, exhale so ragged it nearly split the air. He pushed Rosie's hair back from her face and incriminated himself soundly. "I was so focused on getting out the door—"

"Gil." Rosie said. "*I'm fine.*"

His face said he wasn't so sure as he turned back to Eric. "What about the babies?"

Eric nodded. "They look good. But we have limited equipment in the field, so I'm taking her in as a precaution."

"Y'all are making a mountain out of a whole lot of nothing." Rosie grimaced. "One of the twins just kicked me. Hard."

Unconvinced, we all stared at her.

"Seriously?" Rosie huffed. "Dewitt, back me up. We're all fine, and none of us needs the hospital."

Silence.

"Wait a second. Where's Dewitt?"

"She's—" I looked behind me, pretty sure what I would find. A blank space where she had stood; no sign of her dark, wavy hair in the stragglers.

Eric's rig mates stood by the truck, packing up equipment.

Gil and Rosie and I were here.

The Bennetts and the Suttons stood with Lil, the five of them peppering Eric with questions.

Dewitt's parents—Deebie and Luther—stood at the concession gate, apparent argument still going strong.

Sparks of concern lit my arms, my legs, my fingers.

Rosie tore at the strap across her waist. "Get me off of this thing," she demanded.

Eric jogged over. "What's up?"

"Dewitt's gone," she said, and Eric nodded.

"We'll check the hospital."

The stretcher lurched under Rosie's weight. "So help me God, Eric Kindle—"

"Hey—hey!"

The words scraped the back of my throat as I shouted. "I'll find her. She probably..."

I had no idea where she'd gone, but I sure as hell was gonna act like I had an inkling. "I'll check with Deebie and Luther. I'll text you when I find her, okay?"

I held my phone up before pocketing it and speed walked across the field. The Griffins startled at my approach, but Deebie's debutante mask went up so fast you would have sworn it was there to begin with.

"Nathan. Everything with Rosie alright?"

I took a deep breath. "She fainted. Empty stomach and the heat. Thought I'd let Dewitt know. Y'all, uh...she at the car already?"

Deebie's smile froze, the crinkles at the corners of her eyes flattening. "I thought she was with you."

"You lose my daughter?" Luther's voice was light. But his eyes held the truth, eagle-sharp and focused. "Not holding up your end of the bargain, it appears. I'm a bit surprised," he carried on. "And, well, so was Dewitt, when we talked this morning."

My stomach bottomed out. "You told her."

"You didn't do what I asked."

Acid squatted at the back of my throat. "You know what? I don't have time for this right now. Dewitt's important to me, and you're petty."

"Nathan—" Deebie's face fell, but I turned on my heel and headed back to Gil and Rosie. Luther and I would have it out. *Later.*

I had to find Dewitt.

TWENTY-NINE

DEWITT

I took Nathan's jeep.

He'd dropped his keys *right there* at my feet, and initially, my plan was just to hold them. Hang onto them until the crisis passed. I willed Rosie to come around, held my breath and the keys, sorting out the words I'd say to Nathan.

But then Daddy's seersucker suit approached Judge Norman.

Luther Griffin was a man of his word.

Daddy had used words like *court order* and *guardian* under the glow of the kitchen light. I'd been about to walk out the door, about to head to Lil's so I could come clean, finally to Nathan, when Daddy appeared out of thin air like a collegiate grim reaper, holding my VCU acceptance letter in my hand.

We'd argued. He said things I didn't believe. But my last shred of hope dissipated watching Daddy talk to the Judge. I knew then that I never stood a chance; that my father liked control; that he preferred to keep his world in a compartmental-ized box, stowing pieces in an orderly fashion. And because I was *mentally ill* with a *very short fuse* and *liable to erupt at any second*, Daddy announced he'd be filing for guardianship of my person.

I was not neat. I was not orderly.

I was the wildcard.

Halfway between pandemonium and panic, I slipped through the crowd toward the library lot. Pushed the jeep to an irresponsible rate of speed, hooking a left on 306 toward the trestle and flooring it when I hit the turn. Dust kicked up behind me and I slid the jeep into the grass. Popped the clutch and wrenched the brake into overwhelming silence.

I left Nathan's keys on the seat.

Maybe because it was a Thursday; maybe because the whole town was in graduation mode. Either way, not a single soul stood by the creek or climbed the hill or perched ready to jump from the trestle. Just the trees and the birds and the creek. I stripped off my dress and tossed it behind me, letting it fall like a leaf on the grass. In my underwear, I waded in, the water bracingly cold but invigorating, the shock welcome as I dove beneath. Kicking toward the deepest point, I closed my eyes and let the current carry me.

Two straight, pink lines—*Dewitt plus Nathan equals...*

Three lives that weren't our own, regardless. Not with Daddy filing for guardianship.

My hand found my stomach on instinct. I headed back to the surface with a kick. Limp and weightless, I floated, patchy sunlight barely warming my skin. I needed to tell him, and soon. He needed to know that I'd lied, that I'd peed on a stick three separate times before Ro and I went shopping. That I'd nearly choked on my tears. That I'd been glad I'd quit the meds; that for a split second, I wished I hadn't. That a dark, desperate thought besieged me: *maybe you can end this before it starts*.

Uncertainty fluttered.

What are we going to do?

I'd barely addressed the thought when static danced on my skin and I jolted with a splash to treading, a woman's laughter caught on the breeze. Effa, strolling the bank with a man, sunlight obscuring his face. Effa laughed at something he said, and he dropped a hand to the slight swell of her belly.

She is me, my brain screamed. *She is me, and I am her.*

I closed my eyes and sank, down, way down to where the mud caked my feet at the bottom.

I liked it there. It was quiet.

What am I going to do?

THIRTY

NATHAN

Gil's truck handled the roads like a wooly mammoth on steroids and I nearly blew my ears out on Garth Brooks, but my keys were gone and so was my jeep and Gil was refereeing Rosie's argument with Eric, so I took Gil's keys and drove off with his blessing to see if I could find Dewitt.

I knew she'd taken my vehicle the moment I couldn't find my keys. Only question was where she'd gone, and since she wouldn't answer her phone (again), I climbed in Gil's monstrosity of a truck and put in the road work, checking all the typical spots.

She wasn't at The Arts Center. She hadn't gone back to her house. I pulled up to the trestle around four, and when I tell you the sight of my jeep parked in the grass pulled out the greatest sigh I'd ever breathed into fruition—followed by a swift, deep-seated panic when I spotted my keys on the seat.

"Dewitt!" I hollered for her, tripping over branches and as I stumbled down the hill.

"Dewitt?" I hit the creek bed.

A soft rustling. "I'm over here."

I clocked her at the mouth of the Gut. My feet moved, and before my brain really caught on, I stood right in front of her, staring at the soaked fabric of her dress. Her tangled hair hung in ropes, water dripping like a rhythmic faucet. "What are you —why are you *wet*?"

"Went swimming," she said, like it was nothing. "Dress got wet when I put it back on."

"You stole my jeep to go swimming."

Her shoulders shifted. "I didn't think you would mind." She brushed her hands down her skirt, then twisted her hair up away from her neck. A single water droplet trailed down, sluicing its way toward the divot between her breasts. "Eyes up here," she said, and winked at me when I flushed at her. I needed to right this ship. I was confused. Turned on. Overwhelmingly worried and exceedingly irritated.

"You should have asked before you took the keys."

The playful spark in Dewitt's eyes went flint-like. "Of all the people in my life, I never thought you'd join the ranks of the Dewitt Griffin control board."

I winced. "I didn't take Luther's offer, Dewitt. I should have told you, I know, but—"

"What are you talking about?" Dewitt tilted her head to the side, and the wariness in her eyes made my gut twist.

My throat went dry and I wanted to vomit.

Luther had pulled a bait and switch.

"Okay. Wait a second. I—"

"Nathan. What did he offer you?"

"Broward tuition if I convinced you to stay."

"He tried to buy you off."

"I didn't take it. I'm not even going to Broward after all."

We were both breathing heavy, and I could feel the flush that marched up my face. Dewitt pulled her arms around her waist and studied me.

"Are you not going because of my dad?"

I tugged at my hair. "No, it's not...Luther. It's the course load. And the cost was already so much. When he offered that money with strings on it, I—" I scrubbed a hand over my face. *What am I doing?* "I thought he talked to you about this."

"Not about bribery." She looked away from me and picked at her nails. "This must have happened months ago."

"March." The admission stung. "You and Luther don't always get along, and I—"

"He's a master of manipulation! How can you not see that about him, Nathan? He can't stand not being in control."

I swallowed. Dewitt was right. But there was another side, too, a *both/and* I kind of hated. "Luther's been good to me. He gave me a solid job. He believed in me—a foster kid—when not many other people would. It killed me when he approached me about you—nearly ripped me apart. And I think, if I'd told you, at least, if I'd you then, the whole mess would have been true, and I didn't want to believe it. I didn't know what that would do to you or me or...or *us*, most importantly. The longer I pushed it down, the harder it got to just...open my mouth and say it."

Dewitt's eyes glistened in the light. Raw emotion filled her face, but then she blinked a few times, dismissing it. I'd never struggled so much to read her.

Are we over?

Is this done?

"I get it."

All the air rushed from my lungs. "You—what?"

"I get why you kept it close. But you could have told me—I knew something was wrong. Were you just going to wave and say *see you later* when I got in the car to go north?"

Her question landed like a gut punch. "I was going to tell

you. Soon." I shifted my leg and the dang ring box rattled in my pocket.

No more hiding the truth.

"One of the things your dad said when he made the offer was that I needed a degree to marry you. I was afraid that if I told him no, if I told you I wasn't going to Broward, I was afraid he wouldn't let me marry you. I was a coward, Dewitt. But I love you too much to let fear control me or my decisions."

Fingers buzzing, I pulled the box from my pocket.

Dropped on one knee to the ground.

"Nathan..."

A hinge creak. Sparkled dapples in the light. "My life was the definition of uncertainty until you found me that day, in the woods. I'm not a perfect man. I've made mistakes. I can't promise I won't make more of them. But loving you, being with you, that's not a mistake and it never will be. Dewitt Griffin," I said, voice trembling, "will you be my wife?"

"*Nathan...*"

The first use of my name was a warning. The second one, a benediction. A prayer. She dropped to her knees, buried her face in her hands and shook her head no, over and over.

A loud ringing sounded in my ears.

I closed the ring box. Slid it back into my pocket where it burned. And then I gathered her into my arms. Water seeped from her skin through my clothes, not just from the creek, but from the tears we both were crying.

No one knew where we were.

I nuzzled the top of her head with my nose. "Dewitt," I choked out, "we should probably get going."

She shifted and looked up at me, red-eyed. "I want you to give me the ring."

"I don't—you just said no."

Dewitt took a jagged breath in, her voice caught on a sob. Watery. "Nathan, I'm asking. Please put the ring on my finger."

Hope fluttered, a thousand sails lit with an eastern breeze. The ring glinted in the light. It was warm in my hand, my fingers trembling as they gripped the delicate metal, but it only took one attempt to slide the band onto her finger and ferry it up past the knuckle to the base. Dewitt's lithe arms clamped around my waist and we knelt there, tight potential.

It wasn't until much later I realized Dewitt never actually said *yes*.

THIRTY-ONE

DEWITT

Lil's farmhouse stood quiet in the last first rays of dawn. Nathan's ring hung from a chain around my neck, nestled against the notch of my throat. I'd biked up to Lil's early Friday morning after giving up on sleep. Daddy's bid for guardianship scraped like crumbs against my skin, and Nathan's proposal played on a loop so loud I couldn't breathe. I figured there was one thing left to do, one avenue I hadn't explored in my efforts to find our freedom. So I put the kickstand down, climb the steps to the farmhouse, and gave a light tap against the screen door.

Lil appeared almost instantly, mouth set in an inscrutable line. She held a dishrag in her hands and wore an apron over her housedress.

"Hi," I said, quiet.

"Morning. Nathan's still asleep."

"I'm not here to see Nathan." I twisted my fingers into a knot. "You said you had a box of Effa's things...."

I let the words trail off, waiting for Lil's reaction.

"Would you like to take a look?" She blinked.

I nodded. She held up a finger before disappearing inside the house. She hadn't asked questions, which was good, and I hoped the trend would continue. I didn't know how I would answer anything she asked. I was pregnant and confused, worried and in love, hurting and lost and grieving. Effa, I hoped, was the key. If I could prove to my father we were nothing alike, maybe he'd drop the bid for guardianship. Then Nathan and I could move to Richmond free and clear, away from my father.

The contents of this box had the potential to fix everything.

Or it could fix nothing at all.

Lil returned to the porch with a shoebox and set it on the small table next to the swing. "Here you go," she said. "Everything you want to know about Effa Griffin."

The drum beat in my chest sped up.

"You want to sit?"

I hesitated, then lowered myself into one of Lil's rocking chairs. Dust coated the lid of the box, motes catching the morning sun as I slid the away. Papers and photos nearly spilled over the side—mementos, certificates, notebooks.

"You can't hurt nothing, shug. Dig through it."

I dove in, grateful for steady hands. Mottled tickets from a dance. A dried boutonniere, the once-white rose now yellow and brittle. Sepia-toned photos of Effa and Lil, the girls I'd seen in my last trip after the wedding. Scribbled poems. More notebooks. Birth and death certificates.

"There's a lot in here." I kept digging. No lock of a baby's hair, no tiny shoes. No sign she'd been pregnant at all, actually, and my breath caught in my throat at the reason. "The baby..." I said.

Lil shifted. "The river showed you."

"Yeah. I thought it was a hallucination. Before. But then we talked that day, at the Arts Building. And—" I pulled my lips into a thin line. That conversation had changed so much, from how I viewed myself as a person to my nausea's potential cause. But I wasn't admitting as much to Lil, not until Nathan knew the truth and I'd found a way out of this mess with Daddy. I'd thought evidence of something good—a spark of hope, a new life, a reminder, maybe, of the niece that he'd forgotten—would shift the cards in my favor.

Except there was nothing of the sort.

Lil looked out over the water, focused on the opposite shore. "The baby died with Effa. She was in her first trimester, maybe eleven weeks along. Her father didn't know. Neither did Luther." Lil dropped her eyes to her lap and rubbed her thumb over a knuckle. "I don't think they ever did."

"That's awful," I said, an understatement.

Lil looked up at me. "That's life."

"I'm sorry," I said, and I was, devastated for Effa, for Lil, for my family.

"Thank you," was all Lil said.

We settled into silence. I peeled back the layers of my thoughts. Effa's death—the baby's death—was devastating. Tragic. Selfishly, though, I was panicked. Daddy didn't know about the baby, which meant I couldn't tell him to change his mind. It would only add to his distress, his fear that I would end up just like his sister. I needed another plan.

"Lil, can I ask you something?"

She gave a slight nod. "Sure."

"If Effa died in a car accident, why does Daddy blame it on her doing what she loved?"

"That's a good question," Lil said, settling into the front porch swing. "You know he was young when Effa died. The world looks mighty different when you're a kid, and trauma can change the whole course of a life for the worse *unless* that person is willing—or able—to work through it. Some people," she tilted her head, "like Luther, hold on a little too tight."

"To childhood?"

"To what they think they know." She pushed further back in the swing, a lazy hand pointing to the shoebox. "There's a drawing in there. Have you found it?"

Slowly, I shook my head. I rooted back through the box and found a rough sheet of paper folded into thirds. I flattened it out, revealing two stick figures in green crayon. One short, one tall; one with curly dark hair and the other topped with straight brown scribbles. They held hands—as much as that's true for stick figures—and a child's scrawl ran across the bottom.

TO EF. LOV LOUIE.

"Daddy made this." I had to speak around the lump in my throat.

"That little boy lost two women he loved. His mother first; she was so sick at the end...and then Effa, first to her writing. Then, the accident."

"What do you mean, *to her writing*?" This didn't bode well for me at all.

"Maybe I misspoke," Lil said. "It wasn't the writing so much as it was Luther's perception. Effa took care of Luther after their mama got sick, but she never let go of her dreams. She had so much talent. Effa couldn't wait to get out of her."

Soft tissue twisted in the center of my ribs. Effa really was like me, from her longing to get out to her talent and the baby.

I dropped the drawing in the box and stood, toying with the ring beneath my shirt. It felt cold, more like it was crusted in ice, not diamonds.

"You find what you need?" Lil asked me.

"I found enough."

DADDY WAS in the boathouse sifting through cans of paint. I stood just inside the door, the usually welcome sawdust smell turning my queasy stomach. Rosie would know how long this stage lasted, where even the slightest aroma made me sick. But I couldn't ask her yet, not until Nathan knew the truth and I'd convinced my dad to drop his bid for guardianship.

I owed Nathan an apology, and our little family deserved a chance.

"Hi, Daddy." My voice echoed inside the room.

"Dewitt," he said, brushing the dust off his shorts as he rose from a crouch to face me.

"Do you have a minute?"

"I'm not changing my mind."

Through the dim light of the boathouse, I watched my father cross his arms. "I'm not changing my mind." His eyes shifted just a bit, but in that split second, I saw a flash of the boy who adored his sister.

"I know about Effa," I told him.

"We've established that."

"I mean I know how she died, and I know you're worried you'll lose me, too, but Effa's death wasn't about art or being a creative. It was just an accident. Like, I could die today. I could walk outside and get whacked in the head by a tree branch. And it would have nothing to do with art."

It wasn't eloquent. It wasn't well-supported or thought out. But it was true, and as my father rose to his full height after leaning above the workbench, a rueful twitch caught the edge of his mouth.

"I've been unfair," he said to me, and hope surged through blood. I'd been expecting a fight, not an admission of wrongdoing.

I opened my mouth. "Oh."

He chuckled. "It's true. You don't know the reasons for

what I feel, and as your mama keeps pointing out, that's on me."
Daddy leaned against the bench, a grease-stained hand
scraping against his stubble. "My mama was an artist. A good
one, like you. But she'd get caught up in it, too. Work in this
boathouse all night. Disappear sometimes, and it'd be days
before we found her. Pop's friend..." Daddy grimaced hard, like
he'd just spit out something derogatory. "He suggested a place
for people. You know. Like that."

I stiffened. *"Like that?"* What he meant was *like me*, people
diagnosed with Bipolar Disorder.

"Not the best choice of words," he said, hands up in surren-
der. "It was the way we talked back then. But what I'm trying
to tell you is that Pop took her there for treatment. She was
gone a few weeks, maybe a month. And when she came back,
she, uh...she wasn't right. In the head." He blinked, and I saw
his Adam's apple moving. "She didn't engage with us at all. Just
stared into space most of the time, mumbling."

No wonder Daddy hurt so much. "I'm sorry," was all I said,
still mired in the processing.

A sad smile curved his lips.

"Thank you. But honestly, what can you do? I tried to pull
her out of her shell, try to talk to her, etcetera. Effa...I think she
knew it was hopeless. She started writing."

"Lil said she was really good."

"Lil Rooney says a lot of things," Daddy bit out, eyes hardening as he watched me. "She got ideas in Effa's head, ideas
Effa died trying to make happen."

"Ideas don't cause accidents."

"They can, and they do," Daddy said, lifting his chin at me
in a challenge. "Effa let her talent blind her to the world. To our
family. *To me.* To what it felt like to be left behind, abandoned
like none of us mattered."

"I'm not Effa," I said, gently.

"No, you're my mama *and* her."

His mother? Is that what this was all about? I didn't get a chance to ask, because Daddy carried on, and I had no other choice but to listen. "All three of you are beautiful and strong. Stubborn. Talented as the day is long. I loved them with all my heart, and I love you, too, Dewitt. To distraction. Problem is that love ain't enough—it never is. You need treatment, too. You leave home and you're arming an explosive. It's only a matter of time."

The room spun, the boathouse walls nearly caving in. "I'm a *person*, Daddy. *Not a bomb.*"

"A person who can't care for herself, not right now, and not in the immediate future. I have the paperwork right here. Soon as my lawyer takes a look, I'll turn it over to Judge Norman."

My blood boiled. "So you can destroy my life?"

"I'm saving it."

"I'm not a pawn in a game of chess!"

"You're my daughter," he ground out. "This family dissolves if something happens to you."

And there it was: he'd never cared about me. Not me, Dewitt. Just me, a Griffin.

I shoved him in the center of his chest.

Daddy stumbled backward, his curse barely audible above the ringing in my ears. "This is exactly what I mean," he said, righting himself, and I wasn't sure if he'd collapse on the ground or lunge for me.

He chose the second option, grabbing my arms.

"Don't you see it?" His spittle wet my face. "It's only a matter of time, Dewitt, before—"

I wrenched out of his grasp. "Before what? Before I leave? Before I die? Before I let the whole town know we're *broken*?"

Hot tears burned my eyes, and I stumbled for the threshold.

I couldn't leave the boathouse fast enough.

THIRTY-TWO

NATHAN

Three quick knocks sounded against my doorframe.

"Nathan, honey, can I come in?"

Watery light listed through the heavy navy curtains. I reckoned I'd been awake since four, pacing between failed attempts at sketching boat plans and staring, bleary-eyed, at the wall. Over-analyzing every word, every move, every bit of my proposal.

What Dewitt *didn't* say.

Lil's muted footsteps crossed the threshold and the bed's edge dipped under her weight. "You gave her the ring," she said, and I bolted up, rubbing my face out of its stupor.

"When did you—what?"

Luther and Deebie had come looking for us yesterday, just like I thought they would. I leaned against the truck, arms crossed, copper tinging my mouth as I glared at Luther. The man wouldn't look me in the eye. Dewitt and her mother conversed in hushed tones, and when they were done, Dewitt got in their car. That was the last time I'd talked to Dewitt—or seen her—since yesterday. My heart spent the night on the floor.

"Dewitt came by the house this morning."

Lil's voice brought me back. I fumbled for my phone; found it silent on the bedside table. No messages, no calls, no sign she'd asked for me when she got here. "She was wearing the ring?"

"You should talk to her," Lil said, my second non-answer in twenty-four hours. Was she wearing the dang thing or not? Lil had that look on her face, the locked-up one where I knew if I pressed I'd get a riddle.

"I didn't know she was here."

"It was family business." Lil laid a hand on my arm. "Dewitt wasn't here all that long, and not asking for you doesn't equal rejection."

Maybe. It still left a bitter taste in my mouth.

"Not everyone leaves, Nathan."

I twisted away, exposed. Lil was right—she had stayed, Gil had stayed, even Rosie stuck around and put up with me. Dewitt wanted to stay, I hoped, close to my heart, if not in Minnesott. But part of me would always be that abandoned boy, the bargaining chip discarded. My shoulders dropped, and my head followed. "Mike and Sue messed me up."

"But you've healed," Lil said. "I see it in your face, in how open you are, how willing you are to be vulnerable. Scar tissue grows tight. Sometimes, it tugs. Pulls you back to where you don't want to be."

I swallowed. "I don't know how to get rid of it."

"Time."

"It's been years."

"Healing takes as long as it takes. Growth is pain, son, and sometimes, the ache makes more noise than the progress. You have to learn how to shut it out, otherwise you'll stop moving forward."

Is that what I'd done? Let the ache take over?

I ran a hand through my air.

"Tonight is the girls' graduation dinner," Lil said, an unspoken question thick in the air.

"Yep. Far as I know." Gil said Rosie got the all-clear with her doctor, and as far as Dewitt was concerned, I hoped.

"You know I don't like to meddle..." Lil said, and I laughed, the sound too loud and foreign.

I fell back on the bed, an arm over my face and a tight knot in my shoulders. "You meddle all the time."

"I *prompt*, Nathan. That is the word I prefer. Look at me," she said, patting my foot, and a long ago adage resurfaced.

Eye contact's a sign of respect.

My arm fell to the side and I peeled one lid open, then the second when I saw her lips were pursed.

"I don't meddle. I prompt. And because I believe your relationships are important, even if you don't approach them the way I would hope...You asked if she was wearing the ring. The two of you need to sit down and have an honest conversation."

"About?"

"The elephant in the room."

"There's no elephant," I said, despite the weight on my chest and the doubt in my sternum, pressing me into the bed.

"The two of you," Lil said. "My word. You excel in leaving heavy topics hanging."

She stood. Lil walked to the door, reaching out with one hand to tap once at the doorjamb. "The truth is, Nathan, I'd really hate to see this crush you both."

I PARKED the jeep in front of Pinecliff, nerves buzzing like cicadas in the trees. Raised voices bled from inside the house, and Gil greeted me on the porch with his shoulders tightened. "Deebie knows we're here. She came out and said hello, asked me to call the restaurant and verify the reservation. Then she went back in and we've been standing here, waiting. Been about twenty minutes."

Inside, Luther bellowed. Dewitt sassed something back. "What's going on?" I asked, pretty sure I knew the answer.

"Fighting over school, I think."

Rosie pulled her phone from her purse and pressed a couple buttons. "At least that's what she texted this morning. She sent this." Rosie held out the tiny screen, a diamond ring pixelated on Dewitt's finger. "It's beautiful."

"Congratulations, bro," Gil said, and I nodded. I couldn't get my mouth to work. We all jolted as Deebie swept onto the porch, a cloud of perfume and chiffon announcing her arrival.

Strain tugged the corners of her eyes, and the smile on her face held plastic. "So sorry to keep y'all waiting. Lou and Dewitt will be right down."

Gil nudged me. "Go get Dewitt."

I should have walked right through that door. But I couldn't shake what Lil had said, and my feet stuck to the porch, and the scar tissue bent and tightened. "I don't know if I should."

"Of course you should. She's your fiancé."

"Lay off, Gil," I snapped, and he clamped his jaw shut. "Things are complicated, alright?"

Dewitt pushed through the door at that moment, thick hair twined in a braid down her back. My lungs squeezed in a breath—even livid she was stunning, the cobalt blue of her sundress catching the grey of her eyes. The dress puddled on the floor around her, and a slim gold chain graced the curves of her neck. As she took my hand, the ring glinted on her finger, melting the bands of worry in bones.

Dewitt tugged me off the porch. "Don't worry about them."

I had to jog to keep up with her. "Don't worry about who?"

"My parents," she said. She opened the door to the jeep, then slid across the center console to the passenger side. "Why are you just standing there?" she asked me. "Can we go?"

STORM CLOUDS PILED against the horizon like the tension squatting in the jeep. Dewitt kept her left hand on mine as I shifted gears, the only sound the wind and the road noise. Five thousand pounds of land mammal stampeded through my head.

"What happened, Dewitt? With Luther? What were y'all fighting about?"

She squeezed my hand.

"Dewitt—"

"After dinner, alright?"

I drummed my fingers against the wheel and took a breath, not sure how Dewitt would take this. "I think we should talk. Right now."

She pulled her hand from mine and massaged her temples, a motion I watched through the corner of my eye. "You can think whatever you want. But I've had a *hard*, miserable forty-eight hours. My head hurts. Can we just drop it? Please?"

I heard her. I promise, I really did. This was the pattern, though, and it took one of Lil's metaphors for me to see it. "Lil said—"

"Don't." Her voice cracked, and I felt like a tool, the air between us sharp and vicious. But then her head snapped toward mine and she stiffened. "Wait. What about Lil?"

"Nothing, really. She just…"

"*Spit it out.*"

"She said we don't communicate, alright? She said we don't talk about stuff until it blows up in our faces."

Dewitt muttered under her breath. "I *hate* bomb metaphors."

"Sorry," I said. "I didn't know."

Dewitt turned toward me, her expression unreadable. "I just…"

I just want out.

I just want you.

I just want you to take this ring back.

"I need you to stop acting like I'm trying to break us." She leaned back in the seat, deflated. "We always get it right eventually…"

I exhaled, my frantic worries puffing out into the air. Dewitt had a point. We did work things out. We'd fumbled through enough times to get here.

But honestly, was *here* enough?

"I hear you. I promise, I really do. But what's going to happen when we don't get it right? I didn't get a solid *yes* when I proposed. You won't tell me what happened this morning. We can't start a life together if we're not communicating. I don't want to marry you like that."

Dewitt went quiet, and I shivered in the silence left behind. "You don't want to marry me," she said, and I cursed at the way I'd slipped up.

"No, that's—" I tugged at my face. "That's not what I meant. I want to marry you, Dewitt. I want that more than I've ever wanted anything, you know that. But I want forever with you. Not a few months, or a few years, or until we've….grown apart or, like, hate each other. I've had a lot of time to think about what Lil said, and she's right. If we're going to last, we can't ignore things or...or hide them."

Arms crossed, she bent away from me. "I get it."

Damn it. "I don't think you do." I'd screwed this whole thing up, and the storm clouds in the jeep rivaled the dark streaks just above us. "Dewitt, I—"

She cut my apology. "Take me to Lou Mac Park."

Lou Mac Park sat ten blocks from downtown, a wide green lawn above the river, behind a bulkhead. I blurted a bewildered, "Why?"

"I need time," she breathed. "Just a minute to get my thoughts together."

We drove up and over the bridge. The jeep lurched when we got back on the road, and the tight bands of worry had returned, squeezing harder. I hesitated at the turn. Weighed my options.

"If you don't want to drive me," she said, "I'll get out here."

Dewitt gripped the door handle and I jerked to a stop. "But the storm," I said. "And our reservations."

"Aren't for another ten minutes. The storm will hold."

We *had* left the house first. And maybe she would change her mind at the park, and we could sit in the truck and talk things over. But Dewitt didn't change her mind, not on the way there, and not when I pulled along the curb for parking.

"You can let me out here."

"You want me to leave you with a storm coming?"

She nodded at me. "This won't take long."

Unease swelled under my tongue. I started to say something more, but Dewitt placed two fingers against my lips and held there.

"I love you," she said. "You said on the way here that we don't talk, but I'm talking now, telling you I need to do this."

If only I'd just said no. If I'd turned the jeep around and

driven back to the restaurant, Dewitt fuming at me in her seat. They say you do the best you can with the what you know, and as Dewitt walked away, I didn't realize I knew so little.

"I love you, too," I called, and she looked back at me, her reply lost to the growing wind.

THIRTY-THREE

DEWITT

Nobody knows what the river remembers; what the land holds and what it lets go. Some of us get a glimpse, but the process is so deeply painful that, given a choice in the matter, I think the vast majority would decline.

I didn't get a choice in the matter, and I suspected, for Effa, it was the same. For Effa's mother, too, a generational curse tied up in the land, the sea, the conduits of our brains and a web of fear and silence.

One the spark inside me didn't deserve.

Nathan didn't deserve it, either. I was an anchor around his neck. Daddy's bid for guardianship only tightened the knots, and once news got out about the baby...

No. I wouldn't think about that.

Instead, I would think about endings, about squashing the lies, the secrets, the fears. Breaking the cycle. Making a choice. Doing what needed to be done without doubt or hesitation.

I let the river swirl around my waist.

The sky let the storm clouds let go.

The water let my dress drag me down, filling my mouth and my nose until my eyes were at the surface.

And I let myself say goodbye, knowing an end was better than never getting a chance to start.

THIRTY-FOUR

NATHAN

Every storm evacuation comes with a point of regret. You get an hour down the road, the weather's still clear, and you think about what you left behind or, if you'd stayed, the extra prep you could be doing. You might fixate on the way you protected the house, regretting less plywood here or fewer sandbags there, and you just have to pray what you've done is enough. It's a quiet sort of fear, one that gnaws at your bones until you collapse inward.

I had the same dang feeling when I got back to the restaurant without Dewitt.

"What'd you do with her?" Gil stood on the restaurant's porch. Rosie had lowered herself into a chair, and as I walked up the steps, she craned her neck to look behind me. Guilt snaked up my spine and held.

"She needed a minute." By that point, she'd had five. I hadn't found the line between respecting her space and listening to my gut, given how the last one was screaming.

I rocked on my heels.

Shoved my hands in my pockets.

Pulled my keys out and made a choice.

"I'm going to get her. Can you hold off Deebie and Luther?"

"No, thank you," Rosie said. "One, you're acting weird. Two, Dewitt's *been* weird for weeks now." She stared at the fingers she held up, then shrugged, standing up with Gil's assistance. "I don't have any more points, but whatever. I'm still coming with you."

Gil nodded. "So am I."

He helped Rosie down the steps and into the vehicle before climbing into the back. "You drop her at Pamlico Arts?"

"Lou Mac." I winced.

"With that storm coming?"

I bit the flesh of my cheek.

Fat raindrops hit the ground as I turned onto Front Street and drove along Lou Mac Park. When I left, Dewitt was headed toward the bulkhead. Now there was no sign of her against the storm-heightened green of the lawn. I tossed the jeep in park and we tumbled out of it, Rosie holding her skirt against the wind. "I'm going down," I yelled over the surf, running across the grass as the sky opened, rain pounding in cold, sharp points. I kicked off my shoes and leaped down to the sand. Peered through sheets of rain; cupped my hands around my mouth—"Dewitt Griffin!"

And that's when I heard it. A mournful, muffled wail.

I pushed forward against the heavy blows of the wind. A blurred shape moved up ahead and I picked up my pace, knowing what it was before I got there. Dewitt lay crumpled in the surf, soaked to the bone, breakers tugging the beach beneath her.

"Gill!" I screamed, hoping he could hear me. "Gil! Call 911!"

Rain pelted my face and my body and stung my skin as I

ran. My knees buckled at her side, heart pounding in my ears, the salty scent of rain and seagrass turning my stomach. "Dewitt," I begged. Prayed it. With shaking fingers, I brushed her hair back from her neck. I nearly collapsed when her pulse jumped under my hand, and I pulled her into my lap and patted her down, checking for injuries. She was so, so pale, the ice-cold skin of her cheeks turning bluish. I lodged one arm under her upper back. The other I shoved beneath her knees, and the sand shifted as I stood.

Dewitt's ear-splitting sob cut through the rain, her nails biting me like pitons. "I couldn't...I'm such a coward."

"No," I breathed. Rocked her. "I've got you. You're alright."

Her head lolled against my chest. Red and blue lights danced in the corner of my eye and Gil's footfalls shook the ground, cursing as he knelt next to me, wet hair plastered to his face.

"Eric's here. What can I do to help?"

I looked Gil square in the face. My gut wanted the truth, but my heart begged for a different answer. "Tell me she didn't do this to herself."

Gil exhaled. Wiped his forearm across his mouth. "You found her," he finally said. "You found her, and that's what matters."

I'd found her, but what had we just lost?

THIRTY-FIVE

DEWITT

I moved my pencil across the sketchpad, trying to master Ophelia's face. The parted lips, the half-closed eyes, the way the water cradled her head as she floated...I'd been working to recreate Millais's masterpiece for hours, but I couldn't capture it.

Not with an IV in my hand.

A door slammed out in the hallway. Someone—a nurse or patient—called out. Shouting was a common occurrence on the psych floor, and I knew when I woke up in the back of Eric's rig this was exactly where they'd take me.

It's one thing to know, conceptually.

It's another thing entirely to *be*.

I looked back at my sketch, at the needle in my hand, at the tape over my skin, at Ophelia.

Floating there.

Drowning.

Mad.

"Knock, knock."

My door opened. Dr. Sawyer slid the curtain back.

Warmer and more personable than Dr. Lane, Dr. Sawyer, was also infinitely more casual. She wore jewel-toned scrubs instead of suits; held her frizzy salt-and-pepper hair out of her face with pens or colored pencils. Her scrubs were claret today, a deep wine red flanking her olive skin.

My brain made brush strokes with the tones across an internal canvas.

Dr. Sawyer smiled. "How are you feeling about visitors?"

I set my sketchpad down on the bed. Nathan was the first person I wanted to see; the only person I wanted to see; the person I was most afraid to talk to. "I don't think I'm ready for that."

She nodded. "I'll keep that in your chart."

That was another thing I liked about her: even though I was eighteen, Dr. Lane would have given in to my father, who had tried to muscle his way up here every day. Dr. Sawyer, on the other hand, took one look at my birthdate and told my parents to take a hike, nicely.

Autonomy was such a relief.

"Your medication..."

*About that...*I looked up at Dr. Sawyer. "Yeah."

"You stopped taking what you'd been subscribed; was that because of the pregnancy?"

I told her the truth. "I didn't like the way it made me feel. Numb, like my emotions were turned down."

"That's not unusual," Dr. Sawyer said. "But it is avoidable if we pinpoint the right combination of medications, the right dosage. But your pregnancy adds a layer of complication to what is already a delicate dance."

Her eyes dropped down to my midsection, covered by a hospital gown."You plan to keep it?" she asked, and I wasn't sure if she meant now, later, or forever.

It didn't matter either way: I decided in the water. "I'm keeping it, yes."

She nodded, noting something in my chart. "We can work with that, I think, but we'll need to discuss changes in your treatment. This floor at Craven General is more triage—stabilize and move you out. I'd like to transfer you to Havenwood, an inpatient program near Raleigh. We can fine-tune your treatment there."

Near Raleigh? "I'm supposed to go to school. In the fall."

Lips pursed, Dr. Sawyer weighed her head back and forth before she settled on an answer. "I have a colleague in Richmond. Dr. Suni. She's very good. We can transfer your care to her, post-inpatient. But the baby..." Thoughtful, she tapped her pen against my chart. "This is me butting in, more as a woman and a mom than as your psychiatrist. You can have a child and go to school. Your success will depend, in part, on what sort of supports they have in place on your campus. Daycare and housing options, things like that. If you have additional support, family, friends, the baby's father, that will certainly help. Based on your visitor requests, it looks like you've got quite the support system." She flipped a page in my medical records, scanning down with her pen. "The Suttons," she said. "Gil and Rosie?"

Everything inside me lurched. "They're having twins. I can't ask them to uproot and come with me to Richmond."

"Your parents?"

I pulled a face, and she laughed.

"I think you'd be surprised," she said, propping an ankle on her knee. "I've talked with them at length. Confidentiality kept, of course, but I think, perhaps, you'll find them more willing to help than you realize."

By taking away my rights? "They don't know I'm pregnant," I said, hoping that was enough for her to drop it. It seemed to work, because she went back to the list and perused it.

"What about...Nathan Cartwright?"

Heat bloomed on my cheeks.

"Is he—"

"He's a friend."

Doc Sawyer's eyes dropped to my ring, glinting on my left hand, fourth finger.

I slid my hand beneath the blankets and raised a defiant gaze to hers.

She set her pen down. "Is he a good enough *friend* to help?"

He was perfect. Absolutely perfect, I knew. I loved him so much, my body ached with it. But no matter how much he might protest, how much he'd swear this was forever, the past few weeks had proved two things: I was a mess, and my family was a cancer.

Nathan didn't deserve all of that.

"Dewitt." Dr. Sawyer pulled me from my thoughts. "I want to be completely clear," she said. "You are eighteen, single, and pregnant with a baby you want to keep. You also live with Bipolar Disorder I, and you are coming off the heels of a depressive episode in which you tried to end your life."

She dropped her foot to the floor and sat back, observant. "The descent was very swift."

I nodded. It was. Doctor Sawyer carried on, and I kept my face blank as I listened.

"My goal is to keep you and the baby safe. It will be challenging, but not impossible. However, I want you to know that no matter what sort of treatment we establish with my colleague, or what sort of pregnancy resources, if any, the school has, I will not be comfortable releasing you from Havenwood—or even this facility, for that matter—if you don't have a responsible person to help."

I looked down at my sketchbook. At Ophelia, floating away. Of all the people I had left, there was one I knew could keep a secret.

"There is someone. Her name's Lil."

THIRTY-SIX

NATHAN

A lot happened in three weeks.

Minnesott's weather forecast changed from cloudy to sunny to rainy and back again. Daughtry's printed a new line of shirts, and Benji from the Post Office got skunked, something about his dog and a hole in the ground and deja vu, or whatever. I took a week off work. And I made the drive into New Bern every day, standing in the hall outside Dewitt's room at Craven County General, counting the ceiling tile dots to pass the time.

Dewitt didn't want to see me. She didn't want to see anybody, actually. I didn't find much comfort in that, though, so every day when visitor hours closed, I buzzed back to Minnesott and the marina. Took my emotions out on building boats.

Poor Mr. Duvall didn't know what to do with me.

"You're better than this, son," he said. It was a stormy afternoon; the clouds hadn't quite opened up, but you could feel it in the air, that energy.

Definitely matched my mood.

"Better than what, Mr. Duvall?" I tossed my handheld into the cubby on the desk.

"I've known you a long time, boy, and not once have I seen you back down from a challenge. That girl don't want to see you? Fine. But I suspect it's less you than it is a matter of pride on her end. Those Griffins..." He scratched his chin. "Let's just say I been around long enough to know they're all the same. The walls they put up, most folk think they're stuffy. Truth is, Griffins are as soft as they come. If that young woman won't let you in, you gotta fight, and fight harder. Ain't no use moping around here like a sad sack of excrement."

"You're right, Mr. Duvall." Because I'd been thinking about how I let the guilt drag me down. I knew none of it was my fault—not her attempt; not her hospitalization. Dewitt wasn't rejecting me. She was acting out of fear, worrying what people might say if they found out what had happened.

"You agree with me," Duvall said, like he didn't quite believe it.

I kept my eyes straight ahead as I waved over my shoulder. "Broken clock's right twice a day."

Eventually, Dewitt opened up a short visitor list (just Ro.) I camped out on the floor by Dewitt's room. The first day they kicked me out at five; I slept on a loveseat in the lobby. Day two was pretty much the same. By day three, I'd earned the nurses' pity: they left me a pencil, a notebook, and a chair.

My first note to Dewitt was simple: *I love you. I'm not giving up.*

Days passed. I wrote more notes; she didn't answer. Until one day, I came back to a note after lunch. Didn't have words. Didn't have her signature, either. Just a pencil sketch of two entwined hands.

We carried on like that for a while, my words and Dewitt's

art. On Friday, a nurse met me in the hall. "Miss Griffin's not ready to *see* you, but she does want to talk to you, if that's okay."

I nodded, then shoved my hands in my pockets so I didn't grab the nurse. She cracked open Dewitt's door and a hand reached out, the diamond filigree ring still on it. It hovered about three feet off the floor, an indicator Dewitt was sitting.

Out of breath and out of cool, I leaned against the wall, heaving. Sank like an anchor to my butt.

"Hey," I said, a little shaky. On instinct, my fingers reached for hers. She took my hand without complaint, the soft warmth of her skin a blessing. My pulse spiked, and I racked my brain for something to say.

"How you doing?" I cringed.

The tinkling sound of Dewitt's laugh drained my embarrassment. "I'm doing okay."

"Yeah?"

I could hear her smile from the other side of the door. I rubbed a free hand down my face and ignored the tingling sensation in the other. "I've missed you."

"I've missed you, too."

We sat there, not speaking, on opposite sides of the door. My arm continued to go numb; my butt was already gone but I didn't dare try to move or leave her. I could turn blue for all I cared. I traced the lines on her hand by memory; she flexed her palm open like a cat. Desire sped through my veins and I squashed it. She needed my heart, not my body, right now.

"I'm being discharged tonight, Nathan. That's why I wanted to talk to you."

It takes talent to trip when you're on the floor, but that's what I did, my brain spinning like a top, the words *discharged tonight* coalescing, rushing to meet me as I hurtled down. "You're coming home?" I asked her.

"Yeah," she said. "But not to stay."

Ringing phones and call bells ground to a halt. "Another inpatient?" My stomach sank. I'd heard the nurses talk about a facility farther out. And while I wanted her to get well, I also wanted her to come home. I longed for her. The thought of another separation made every cell in my body burn.

Forced cheer lifted my voice when I answered. "I'll come up and visit you."

"I don't think that's a good idea."

I opened my mouth. Closed it. "Dewitt, I—"

"It won't be good for you."

"I can make that decision myself."

"Well then it won't be good for *me*."

"Are you...Are we breaking up?"

"No," she said, the sting leaving her tone and tripping my pulse down to even. "There are just...*things* I have to do. I'll make more progress without distractions."

I huffed out a breath. "I'm a distraction."

A light chuckle. "In the best possible way."

I dropped my head against the wall. *I hate this.* "How long before you go?"

Fabric rustled on the other side of the door. "A week. Could be ten days. And when I'm done, I'll head to Richmond."

I smiled. "You worked out school."

Dewitt squeezed my hand twice. She let it drop, and I rose up on my knees at the soft sob behind the door. "Did I say something wrong? Dewey?"

"No," she said, watery. "It's me. I'm a little emotional right now. I need a break, I think, before discharge. Could you—" She paused, and I leaned forward. "Can you come by the house tonight?"

I soared. "I'll be there. When?"

"Discharge is at three," the charge nurse said, and I whirled around to see her watching from the desk. "Six would be good, probably." She grinned at me.

Dewitt laughed. "Those nurses are your biggest fans."

"And I'm yours, Dewitt. Forever." An ache shot up my leg as I stood. Silence held me in the hall, and I thought I heard another sniffle right before Dewitt shut the door.

THIRTY-SEVEN

NATHAN

Counting backward should have worked.

Five—a screen door slam.

Four—a shout on the breeze.

Three—a text message from Ro: *We're coming 2 u. 2 mins.*

Two—gut wrenching silence

"Her room's empty."

One.

I'd waited. The night before, on the porch. First it was, "She'll be right down," then, "fifteen minutes?"

At seven, Dewitt was tired, and could I come back in the morning after she's had rest?

I came back in the morning. Same porch. Same house. Same me. Except nothing was the same, because Dewitt was gone and my ears were buzzing.

Luther cleared his throat.

"Son, her room's empty."

I shook my head to clear the noise. "She took everything?" I just—I had to be sure.

Luther's eyes were red, more bloodshot that I'd ever seen them. "Mostly. Clothing. Art supplies. Keepsakes."

"Call the Sheriff."

"Son, I—"

"Call the Sheriff, or I will."

Fire coursed through my veins; fear and regret and blistering, white-hot anger. A mottled sob slipped through Luther's mask.

"She's eighteen," he said. "And she's not missing. I know where she went."

I could barely look at him, could barely keep from punching his jaw. The hollow ache behind my ribs split anew. "You know where she is and you're not going after her."

"She made her choice as an adult."

"She never *had* a choice. You consistently backed her into a corner—"

"Nathan, I suggest you know your place."

"I suggest you tell me where she's gone!" I didn't care a wit about my job, or showing respect, or letting my voice carry. The only thing that mattered was Dewitt.

Luther's shoulders caved inward. "If I tell you and you find her, she won't come home with you."

"You're lying. *We're in love.* Is she at Havenwood? Did she leave early?"

Luther didn't answer. He pulled an envelope from his pocket instead. "This is one of five," he said. "One each for Deebie and me; one each for you, Gil, and Rosie."

A letter.

From Dewitt.

I slid a finger beneath the flap; opened it up to find a sketchbook page, ripped out. I knew what it was, the deeps shades of mossy yellow and emerald green, the water beneath the Gut glowing yellow-white around two figures.

One woman.

One man.

One embrace, vaguely heart shaped.

One message, scrawled out to me.

Counting would never work, not this time, not ever.

Nathan, I will always love you. This is for the best.

THIRTY-EIGHT

If there was one thing Lil Rooney knew for certain, it was, undoubtedly, this:

The more you tested love before it was ready, the more likely it was to break.

Of course she'd have been the first to tell you she didn't know when *ready* was. She just knew she'd seen love move too fast, fall too hard, shoot up out of the ground with rocks beneath it, crushing good souls in its wake.

Not that it was all bad. Good things came, too, from testing love. More lessons, more growth, more life, and, well, that was another thing Lil Rooney knew for certain.

Eventually, love made all things new.

The summer passed in Minnesott, same as it always did. July was *hard*—it was hot, and a hurricane clipped the coast and took a few of the pines down with it. Nathan fell on those things like a man deranged. A feral look haunted his eyes, but he got up and went to work and built boats. And for reasons Lil could not comprehend, Nathan kept Pinecliff straight for Luther.

"Aren't you angry?" she asked one evening after dinner, fireflies zig-zagging through the yard. "Why are you still working for him, son?"

"Don't have to talk to Luther much to work for him. And I'm gonna be here when she comes back."

She wasn't coming back, and Lil knew it. Nathan had to learn that on his own. It was a life lesson, yes, but Lil hated it more than getting stuck on a screened-in porch with five mosquitos.

Thank God he had Rosie and Gil.

When the twins were born, it changed him. She'd never seen a young man change diapers so fast. He'd cart those babies around, Evangeline in one arm with that full head of hair sticking up in all directions; Ezra in the other, looking dour, like an old man. Lil teased their parents: they'd be locking windows to keep one in at night and locking doors to make sure the other one made friends.

Truth was, she didn't mean it.

Well. She didn't mean it that much.

Summer turned to winter. Winter turned to spring. Trips up north became both more secretive and more frequent, same with phone calls to old colleagues and friends. Lil disagreed with Dewitt's decision on just about every front. But the girl had begged and begged, and so she said alright. With the caveat that one day, Dewitt had to reach out to Nathan. "The boy needs to know he has a child."

Whether Dewitt kept up her end of the bargain remained, indefinitely, to be seen. Lil didn't believe in regrets, but she did feel a twinge every time she looked at Nathan, even though he was doing well for himself. He bought a trailer on the west side near the Suttons; built a workshop of his own in the backyard. Kept it stocked with his tools and decorated it with artwork. Shadowy lovers beneath a creek in pride of place above his workbench. On the far wall, concentric circles closing in. Those were the moments she longed to spill it, when he was working late with a ghost. But he needed to move on, and spilling everything wouldn't help him. At least, that's what she told herself. And so Lil watched the years pass in silence, watched him as he healed again. Watched him become a fine young man, even reconciling with Luther, something Lil was too angry to do herself. She watched Dewitt, too, from a distance—sometimes celebrating, often shaking her head. She watched the Lima Bean with strawberry blonde hair, watched her grow up brave and strong and precocious.

And then one day the phone rang—

"Is this Lillian Rooney?"

"Yes. Who's this?"

"My name's Ana. I own Rhodes Gallery."

Ten-year-old girl.

Artists' retreat.

"You're in the file as Dewitt's emergency contact."

Lil grabbed the cart keys by the door and rubbed her finger across the keychain. Nathan made it for her—an circle of polished birch.

He'd engraved it, at Lil's request.

Initials to Lil; to Nathan, an acronym.

She'd lied through her teeth when she told him what it stood for.

"LMG, son. *Love mends grief.*"

EPILOGUE
MAE

Ten Years Later

Every school office I've been in has the same Elmer's Glue smell. Like they've got crates of it in the back, and somebody knocked one down, and the sticky scent mixed itself with whatever school lunch leftovers the cafeteria ladies brought over. Parklane Elementary has it, too, like Creekside last year and Ben Franklin two years before that. I tug the straps on my backpack tighter and wrinkle my nose against the stench.

"Lila Mae Griffin. Your mom is running late again?"

I force a smile at Ms. Stanley and try hard to stifle my sigh. Because first of all, I go by Mae, and I don't know how many times I have to remind the whole front office. Second, my mom is never on time, and acting like it's a surprise doesn't make me feel better. My mother, Dewitt Griffin, is amazing.

Really.

She just loses track of time.

Like, every day.

This fake smile is making my cheeks hurt. I plop down in a chair by the front door. "I think so, yeah," I say, kicking my feet for extra cute factor. I need them to think I'm just a normal kid.

Ms. Stanley must buy it, because her face looks sympathetic as she taps red-painted nails against her desk. Her rolling chair pushes back, and she swivels to face the other office lady. "I'm working on the schedule for next week's assembly, Ms. Jonas. Can you give Mom a call?"

"Sure thing, Ms. Stanley." Ms. Jonas's lanyard swings from her neck. I kind of feel bad for her, actually. Her afternoon's just been derailed because it's never just a moment with my mom, not for getting in touch with her and not for waiting.

I breathe in and get a nose full of Lunch Leftovers a la Elmer's Glue.

For a distraction, I study the decorations on the wall. Construction paper flowers. Motivational posters.

Mom would have done a better job with the flowers, and Mr. Elephant wants me to reach for the stars.

"Hi, Ms. Griffin." *Voicemail.* "This is Layla Jonas from Parklane Elementary School. We dismissed about twenty minutes ago and Lila Mae's here in the office...."

"We'll get in touch with her," Ms. Stanley says, fingers clacking against her keyboard.

I should tell them to give up, honestly. They'll be calling her all afternoon.

I stare out the front office window and watch the last of the school buses depart. "I just remembered I was supposed to walk home," I say in mock surprise, crossing my fingers behind my back and my toes for extra backup.

"Your mother didn't call to let us know."

Come on, Ms. Stanley. "She gets distracted. Hashtag *artist life*."

Ms. Jonas sets the phone down. "There's a note in Lila Mae's file. She has permission to walk home."

"*If* Mom calls to tell us." Ms. Stanley hums. "Let me check with the principal first."

"She went home early today," Ms. Jonas says on a wince, and I chime in with a bit of reassurance.

"I've walked home before, and it's not far. I pass two separate police stations on the way." And a bakery and an ice cream shop, but I don't think the office ladies need to know that. At home, I sort the bills. I prep the meals. I keep the house clean and the laundry washed and folded. I've been doing all that since kindergarten, basically. I think I can take care of myself.

Ms. Stanley gives in finally. "Alright. But we'll keep trying your mom."

Ha! Good luck with that. "Thanks, Ms. Stanley, Ms. Jonas. See you tomorrow!"

I'm out.

I burst through the front doors and squint at the sunshine, grateful today's ten-block walk is on a perfect D.C. spring day. Bright blue sky, cotton-candy clouds, and a delicate pink rain of cherry blossom petals slow my stride and lift my mood. I make the quick walk not-so-quick, looping around the city trees and bouncing through a neighborhood hopscotch. No eye contact, though, with the kids who made it. Life is easier if I don't make friends.

Twenty minutes after leaving the school building, I stand outside the doors of Mom's gallery, Rhodes. Well, it's not her gallery. It belongs to Ana, her boss. But Mom's the current artist-in-residence and she's been there about eight months.

I stare in through the big glass window, leaning against the building's red brick. Sure enough, Mom's there, straddling a stool in front of an easel. Her back is to me, but I can tell by her posture — legs wide, back straight and head tilted — that she's deep inside her work.

The door's heavy when I tug on it and I have to lean back to get it to budge. Cool air caresses my face, the scent of turpentine and oil paints filling my nostrils. Soft music floats from above—something from Ana's playlist, probably. Mom says Ana grew up in the eighties and has a thing for bands I've never heard of, like Mazzy Star and The Cure.

Speaking of Ana, she comes out from the back. "Dewitt. It's four thirty-five. Weren't you supposed to get your kid, like, an hour ago?"

"It's okay!" I pipe up from the front, letting the door shut behind me. Mom nearly falls off her stool. She staggers up, then whips around, eyes wide and features twisted.

"Fudge nuggets."

"It's a nice walk." I shrug. "I'm fine."

Ana throws her hands in the air, fussing at my mom in rapid Spanish. I catch a few words here and there, and I have to agree with her. Artists are too artsy for their own good.

Mom rushes to me, pulling me into her arms. "I'm so sorry, Lima Bean. I got carried away. Too focused."

"I said it's okay," I mumble, face pressed against her overalls bib. Mom's ring bops me on the head—the heavy diamonds hang from the chain around her neck, as usual. I squeeze her waist tight, then step back to get a little space between us. The ring glitters as it falls back against her chest.

Ana appears beside us, a disapproving look on her face. "Dewitt. Go home. Rest your hands so you can make more magic tomorrow."

Mom's fingers flex. "Actually, I feel pretty good. I just have this detail work I—"

"No. Go home. Get dinner. I've got a date tonight. Early close!"

"Well then," Mom says, rubbing paint from her fingers and patting the canvas with the palm of her hand. "Guess I'll get back to you tomorrow, buddy."

It's a landscape. "Is this where you grew up?" I study the foreground's bright field of green, the first hint of blue—water maybe?—along the horizon.

She doesn't talk about life before me.

"It's just a place, Mae," she says, and I square off, mostly teasing.

"Nope. This is where you grew up, I know it. You just don't want to tell me the truth."

"Lila Mae..." She sighs. She'll tell me someday, I hope. Until then it's just her and me, and if she didn't have me, I don't know how she'd function. She's funny during the good times, super creative, forgetful, and loud. During the bad times when she gets super sad and sleeps it away, I always call in sick for her. And on days like today, a happy medium, I drag her away from work. We clean up brushes and paint and I pull her to the door, away from her canvas. From Ana. I skip down the sidewalk, tugging on my mother's hand.

"Hang on a minute," she pants behind me. "Really, Lima Bean. Slow down!"

"I'm hungry," I say, but I'm not really. It's more Mom I'm worried about. She probably hasn't eaten all day—painting takes up so much space in her brain that she forgets to feed it.

"Now that you mention it," she says, and I smirk a little, "I'm kinda hungry too."

Home is a stone front townhouse a few blocks north of the gallery. I open the door and Mom follows me inside, blinking at the foyer. Several canvases lay spread across the floor.

"Whoops," Mom says, apologetic. "Forgot to put this away before work."

I hang my bag by the door and turn to look at her. "It can wait. We should eat."

She pauses, and I see the brushes pulling colors in her brain. But finally she turns to me and asks if I want Chinese for dinner.

"Sure," I say.

And because I know she'll never find them, I hand her the takeout menu and her phone.

———

FULL OF WONTONS, I'm sorting laundry on my bed. "You don't have to do that, you know," Mom says, eyeing me from the doorway.

"I'm gaining life experience."

Mom smiles, but it's one of the sad, sleepy ones she gets. They don't happen that much if she stays on her meds, and I make a mental note to check her pill bottles in the bathroom. I watch Mom wander to my chest of drawers. She picks up a carved wooden boat that I've always just *had*, honey-blonde and shiny. Dust motes fill the air, and a pang of frustration hits me. "I haven't dusted in a while."

"I've never dusted a single day in my life," she says. She turns the boat over in her hands, running her finger over the back. An engraving.

D-E-W-I-T-T.

Mom sits down on my bed. "I need to ask you something."

Her tone makes me nervous. I nod.

"There's an artist's retreat this weekend at a farm out in Charlottesville. The gallery's footing the bill. I'd like to go, and Ana said you could stay with her and Winston."

"Winston?" I love that fluffy, grumpy cat.

"Winston." Mom smiles. "The King of Floof himself."

An old worry pushes away my excitement. She must read it on my face. "I won't forget to come home," she says, and I blink, processing.

Has she finally figured it out?

Mom pulls me into a hug and I lean against her chest, listening to her heart go *thump-thump*. "I'll be back on Sunday evening," she says. "Promise. When my reservations end, they'll kick me out."

SUNDAY COMES — no mother.

Monday and Tuesday, no mother, too.

By Wednesday Ana's growing concerned, even though I explained this is normal.

"This is not normal. Your mother is supposed to be home!"

We know she's fine and safe and healthy because Monday morning, Ana called the facility. Dewitt Griffin was still in residence, yes; she paid for four additional days, through the following Saturday. Facility policy is not to disturb artists and Mom won't answer her cell.

Ana's just short of livid. "I mean, you're great and all, kid. But I'm not equipped for this," she says, staring at me over the dining room table on Wednesday evening.

"I can just go home." I'll be fine on my own for a few days, though I don't get to say that before Ana's choking.

She clears her throat. "Are you kidding? That's illegal, kid. No way."

Ana pulls Mom's employment file. "Do you know this person? Her name's Lillian."

I peer at the form. Mom's written the name in a gentle,

curving script, right next to a phone number. "I've never heard of her," I say.

On Thursday after school I walk to the gallery and let myself inside. Ana's there, of course, but she's meeting with two customers. An older couple, in their sixties maybe? Well-dressed, like most of the gallery clients.

"Oh! Mae! You're back," shouts Ana, a little too loud for the space. She jogs to my side, puts her arm around my shoulders, and propels me toward the customers. "Mae, these are your grandparents. Luther and Dora Bell Griffin."

"I don't have grandparents," I say, and Ana blinks, and the older couple goes a little pink so I figure I better explain what I mean in a hurry. "My mom's an orphan, and I don't have a dad."

The old man—"My name's Luther."—leans down carefully. His eyes shine just a bit, like water droplets on a window. "Your mother's not an orphan. We're her parents. Your grandparents, Lila Mae."

All the air rushes out of me. I sit, right there, on the floor. "Where's my mom?" I ask. *I don't have grandparents.*

Luther's wife—he called her *Doobie?*—looks at me, similarly sad-eyed. "Your mother is in the hospital."

Mom would have called me if that were true. Unless she was sick or hurt—

"Don't worry." The lines on Doobie's face go deep. "Your mama's not hurt. She's at a special hospital called Havenwood. A mental health facility a few hours from our house."

Something wiggles in my ribs. "Your house?" It's all I can think to say that isn't *no* or *go away* or *I want my mother.*

The lady nods, her blonde bob swinging. "Our house in Minnesott."

I wrinkle my nose. "Minnesota? I don't like the cold.'

"Minnesott," she says again. "A little beach town in North Carolina. You're going to come and stay with us while your mother gets well."

I put my head between my knees as the room twists. Mom needs me. She needs my help.

"Are you worried about school?" Luther asks, and I want to shout no, that I'm worried about my mother.

"Why would I be worried about school?"

The adults laugh, uncomfortable. Like that was the last thing they thought I would say. "We've made arrangements with Parklane," the man says, and for the first time, I hear an accent. "They'll send assignments so you can finish out the year."

"I don't want to go."

My voice is small. It's small and not at all like me, and I really, really hate it.

The air shifts and Doobie (what a weird name!) drops to her knees. She tucks a strand of hair behind my ear and I look up at her, looking a lot like my mother. "I know," she says. "But I'm so glad to meet you. We–" She stops, eyes glistening. "Luther, Mr. Nathan, and I, we're all pleased as punch to have you."

"Mr. Nathan?"

Luther speaks. "Nathan Cartwright. He works for us on the property."

"I think you'll like him," Doobie says. And I don't know what to say, not then.

Not the week after, when I stand on the upstairs porch of a nineteenth-century farmhouse.

Not when I'm watching waves churn on the river below.

Not when I see three kids about my age—two boys and a girl—screaming by on their bikes and throwing glances at me.

Not when here in this small town, the awkward new kid, desperately missing her mom.

———

Haven't read Mae's story?
Want to read it again?
Head to www.ginnykochis.com/books for links to book one and bonus scenes!

AUTHOR'S NOTE

If you've come fresh from reading *Blink and We'll Miss It*, you may have noticed differences in the finer details between the two. Originally, my intention was to have Nathan and Dewitt's story match everything you know about them from *Blink*, keeping conversations the same; making sure their ages matched exactly...

It didn't work.

As I wrote and revised (over and over), I discovered their *story* was more important than the details. To tell you about Nathan and Dewitt's love before everything fell apart, to do them justice as a couple, I needed to focus less on keeping everything the same and more on who they were as people.

And it was a beautiful story to tell.

I hope you've enjoyed getting to know them as much as I enjoyed the privilege of writing them, and for my detail-oriented readers, I apologize. Thank you for sticking with me (and with them!) even when it raised your hackles. I appreciate it more than you know.

If you are struggling and need help, reach out to your loved ones or the following organizations:

- IASP worldwide at https://findahelpline.com/i/iasp
- National Suicide Prevention Hotline at https://988lifeline.org/

ACKNOWLEDGMENTS

Thank you to my family, as always. Having a writer as a wife, mom, daughter, or sister isn't easy, as I am frequently hyper-focused and broke.

Thank you to my friends, both writers and readers, for reading over icky first drafts and reminding me to just keep going.

Thank you to my grandmother and her sisters. Without you, I wouldn't know Minnesott Beach.

Thank you to Nathalia Mondragon, my cover artist. You are always so patient with me.

And lastly, thank you, reader, for passing your eyes over the worlds I've created. It's such an honor to be allowed into your space.

ABOUT THE AUTHOR

Ginny Kochis writes books for the unique and unrepeatable, for teens and adults who don't quite fit the mold. She tells stories about love, friendship, faith, and family starring differently-wired characters. While Ginny lives in Northern Virginia with her husband and three children, she's happiest on the shores of the Neuse River, hunting for shark teeth with a good book in her bag.

Looking for more teen and adult books featuring neurodivergent characters? Visit Ginny on Instagram or at www.ginnykochis.com.

ALSO BY GINNY KOCHIS

Blink And We'll Miss It (Minnesott Beach Book One)